THE CANTOR'S SON

DAVID M. MANNES

Cover Art:
Michelle Crocker

http://mlcdesigns4you.weebly.com/

Publisher's Note:

This is a work of fiction. All names, characters, places, and
events are the work of the author's imagination.

Any resemblance to real persons, places, or events is
coincidental.

Solstice Publishing - www.solsticepublishing.com

Copyright 2016 David M. Mannes

The Cantor's Son

a novel

David M. Mannes

Dedication & Acknowledgements

This book is dedicated to the memories of my father, Cantor Fred S. Mannes (1929-1986), and my former teacher, Rabbi Phil Silverstein (1931-2015).
My Mom, my family and to my childhood partners in crime:
Audrey, Dave, David-aka'Mainard', Tate, and John
And to my fellow Musketeers who are no longer here: Lester Sadoff, Mark Shapiro, Craig Case and Bob Whiting. *Z'l-May their memories be for a blessing.*

I'd like to thank my wife Sandy, my good friend Caroline Simonson, and my coffee buddy and fellow bookaholic, Michael Alkalay, for reading the drafts and finding its flaws and inconsistencies. I'd also like to thank Solstice Publishing for deeming this manuscript worthy of publication, and especially thank my editor-in-chief K.C. Sprayberry, and editor Martha Spurlock for their hard work and diligence. I truly appreciate it.

Prologue
July 2012: Monday

The houses were worn but neat, like an old pair of slippers—comfortable. The trees still canopied the streets casting a natural tent of shade leading to the park at the top of the hill. It'd been several years since I'd been here, but I always came back to visit the old neighborhood that stirred many longings and memories of my youth. The sun burned into my back, sweat beaded on my brow and stung my eyes, and I knew I should've had a hat on to cover my thinning crown, but such is the price of vanity.

In 1960, my father got his first cantorial pulpit here in River City at Beth Zion Congregation. On a hot August day we moved from Chicago and drove five hundred miles to the northwest corner of Iowa. The city of ninety thousand sat on the banks of the Missouri River. It was quite a culture shock. I remember driving into town and seeing a farmer standing on a street corner, thick thumbs through the straps of his denim overalls. My mom laughed. We were certainly out in the country.

Our old house looks smaller now, and a washed-out gray has replaced the light-blue exterior. The white shutters are gone. Only one hedge lines the west side of the house. The big, old elm tree, the one whose branches had swayed over the screened back porch, the one from which our basketball net had hung, the one my younger brother Morrie climbed down when he was sneaking out or playing Tarzan, was gone.

Today kids amuse themselves online, playing video and computer games. They sit and watch downloaded movies or rent DVDs. Sports are more organized, with teams for soccer, T-ball, Little League baseball, football and so on. Parents are paranoid today about children exploring or doing something that might cause them to get hurt. They worry about depraved predators stalking their innocent offspring. But unfortunately, parents today forget—or might not even know—what it was like to be children, to explore and invent and create and live in a world of endless possibilities. Perhaps it's because often today both parents work. Or maybe it's because there is this obsessive need to have their children's lives organized through every waking hour. But when I was young, the world was ours.

Memories flooded my mind like a breaking dam, washing away forty-eight years… once again it was a hot summer day, and instead of being sixty, I was twelve and a half.

Part One: 1964-1965
The Bar Mitzvah Year Begins

Chapter One

August 1964

Life is about choices. Good choices. Bad choices. Stupid choices. Especially stupid choices. Some people don't want to make choices; they just drift along from circumstance to circumstance. Some people actually thrive on the knowledge that they have to make a choice. Others are afraid of choosing, afraid of the consequences of making a bad choice. And therein lies the problem. The old adage, hindsight is a wonderful teacher, is very true. If we knew then what we know now, we'd probably make a lot less stupid choices—maybe. But given that we are human, and to err is human as a great writer said, we seem to keep on making stupid choices. That's the good thing about being a kid. You're allowed, even expected, to make stupid choices. But being Jewish and coming towards the age of thirteen, when you become responsible for your choices and the consequences of them, is hard. The fact is that you tend to make choices before considering all the consequences. It's all part of growing up, I know, but there are just so many other things on your mind at that age. And there were a lot of things on my mind as the summer of 1964 was drawing to a close. In the real world, three civil rights workers—Michael Schwerner Andrew Goodman and James Chaney—were murdered. In Vietnam the Tonkin affair was blazing headlines across the news, and the Democratic convention took place in Atlantic City. These events, despite their significance, were not really on my radar.

They call it the Dog Days of Summer, because all you feel like doing is lazing around like a contented, tired old hound dog. And in that respect Paul Andersen and I were certainly content. The humid heat of August hung heavy like a saturated sponge under the darkening clouds that blanketed the Iowa town like a giant lead weight waiting to drop on the unsuspecting coyote of a Warner Brothers cartoon. On the weathered covered wooden veranda we nestled into a couple of green and yellow webbed lawn chairs, our hands clutching the latest issue of Superman and Batman comic books that we'd just bought at Klages Drugstore five blocks away. We enjoyed reading them and sometimes would draw and make our own, usually adapting our favorite characters with original names. I thought perhaps that someday, I'd like to be a comic book artist; so did Paul. On the porch lying between us was my two-year-old black lab-setter Shadow, utterly content to watch a butterfly flutter around his head.

"It's gonna be different without you at school," said Paul. He put down the twenty-five cent eighty-page giant comic of Superman reprints and looked at me, his friend of the past four years. Paul was eleven and going into sixth grade in the fall. He was slim with a white-blonde crew cut and clear, honest blue eyes.

"Well Junior high is going to be a lot different than elementary school. I guess I should start acting like a teenager now," I replied. "And of course I have my Bar Mitzvah next spring. You'll be invited of course."

"Of course," grinned Paul. "So how does a teenager act Jeff? I mean, you won't be thirteen until next April."

"Well I guess it's time I put all the kid games behind me. I don't know."

But I did know. I looked across Paul's yard and saw my brother Morrie and Paul's younger brother Robin playing cowboys. Morrie, skinny, wavy black hair and four years younger, was wearing my leather holster with the

Mattel Shoot n' Shell pistol. I knew that never again would I tie a towel around my neck and pretend to be Batman or Superman and play superheroes. I was growing up whether I liked it or not. It was time to put the pretend games behind, and listen to rock n' roll music; I did like the Beatles, whom I'd seen on Ed Sullivan back in February— my parent's only comment to their performance was, "Look at that hair!" The Beach Boys blared down the street courtesy of Rob Cramer's older, really cute sister Janice. She was a shapely sophomore at Central High School. She and her friends used to gather on summer nights in her backyard or sat along the retaining wall of their yards listening to records.

A rumble of thunder rolled across the sky. Morrie and Robin crouching behind a huge elm tree on the front lawn, were shooting at imaginary bad guys. I looked at Paul. "But I don't have to grow up just yet." I grinned.

Paul ducked into the house and came out with two Daisy air rifles. Aiming, we fired at the younger boys, who realized that they were being ambushed, ducked around the tree and returned fire. The sound of air blasts and caps echoed down the street.

The battle of Grandview Park took place the following Saturday afternoon and it was almost the last juvenile playing I did. Myself, Paul, Morrie and Robin, having nothing to do, walked up to Grandview Park at the top of the hill. Morrie and I were banned from riding our bikes on Shabbat. Not that my parents were overly concerned, but the congregants were. The Rabbi and Cantor and their families were supposed to set an example for the congregation. A couple of years prior I tried riding my bike in the alley that separated our house from the Belleview Apartments. Several old ladies, members of our congregation, just happened to look out their windows and saw me. They also saw Mom and Dad sitting out in our back yard once. The following week at services one of the ladies came up and told my Dad he had nice legs. That was the last time Dad sat out in back wearing shorts. Dad got a call from Mr. Shaeffer, father of my best friend Larry, and the President of the congregation. Unlike the congregants, we were obligated to set an example, to be Shomer Shabbat (Guardian of the Sabbath), which condemned us to following all the work and creative prohibitions as laid down in the Torah and the Talmud. I guess it felt good for them to know that someone was.

We hiked up Grandview Blvd. to the top of the hill where, across 24th Street, the park spread before us. I could smell the sweetness of freshly cut grass from some of the lawns. We followed the paved road, past the statue of Lincoln standing in the middle of a rose garden and through the rolling hills of the park. To our left was the white concrete band shell and behind it the flower gardens. Nestled in a small valley next to Sunset Blvd. entrance was the playground. In a small clearing on bare, hard ground surrounded tall elm and ash trees were two sets of swings attached to tarnished steel posts. One had worn wooden seats for toddlers. The other set used wide black strips of rubber attached to metal chains. A tall dull silvery slide stretched up fifteen feet; a few feet away was a merry-go-round. The merry-go-round consisted of a large patterned metal plate with bent metal handles spaced around the edges and going back towards the center of the plate. It was balanced on a metal turntable. We'd grab on one of the holding bars and start pushing and running, going as fast as we could, then we leaped aboard and felt our stomachs leave us. Afterwards we'd get off, wobble around until we regained our balance, only to do it again.

We were on our third run with the merry-go-round when three girls came up.

"How about letting us on?" asked this gangly red-haired, freckled face girl around ten. She wore a green t-shirt and plaid shorts. Her green eyes followed the rotation of the merry-go-round.

"Maybe next time around," said Paul. He waved to her.

"There's room for all of us," said the second girl. She had long black hair and wore a red and green striped shirt and jean shorts. On her dirty feet were sandals. Her dark eyes challenged us.

"We don't want any booger faced girls on here," yelled Morrie. He chortled loudly and stuck his tongue out at them.

"Yeah, you heard him," piped up Robin. Besieged by both older and younger sisters, Robin had no sympathy for females.

"Asshole!" said the red-haired girl, and kicked Paul in the knee as he ran by.

Paul hopped onto the metal plate and massaged his leg. "Fuck you."

Morrie and Robin gasped. Swearing was not allowed. I'd gotten my mouth washed out with soap one time because my Dad heard me swear when talking to some of my friends. I suspect Paul was letting out his frustration as well, outnumbered by the female species in his home.

The third girl, a short mousy brown-haired thing with glasses bent over and picked up a clod of dirt. She flung it at us. It grazed my head as I rode by.

"Sonofabitch!" I growled. I brushed the dirt from my hair and straightened my glasses.

"WAR!" yelled Robin, jumping off the merry-go-round. He immediately tripped and fell on his face. Not daunted, he jumped up and chased the girls, roaring at them like a ferocious lion. They laughed, screamed, then ran like the devil himself was after them. We followed Robin yelling war-hoops. We gave chase, growling like uncivilized savages.

The girls ran to the supply shed, gathering up small clods of dirt along the way.

The redhead used a garbage can and clambered up on top of the shed roof faster than a chimpanzee. Her aerial advantage took toll on us below as she launched dirt missiles. Narrowly avoiding the barrage, we abandoned the merry-go-round and ducked for cover under the slide.

Paul gathered up a couple of dirt clods. He handed me one. I jumped out, took hasty aim and threw. It fell short, breaking apart as it hit the ground.

"You throw like a girl!" cried the bespectacled mouse pointing her finger and laughing like a wounded banshee.

That's when Paul fired his dirt clod and hit her in the stomach. She staggered back. Her lip quivered, but she didn't scream or cry. Realizing her vulnerability, she ducked around the shed for cover. Paul usually pitched when we played baseball in the back. There was a good reason for it.

There was lots of ammo, and the battle raged on for a bit, both sides getting pelted, our clothes bearing the brunt of the dirt barrages. I had to admit, the girls were pretty good. Finally, though, we routed them. They'd run out of ammunition. The girls screamed and ran to the Ladies' Washroom. They'd outsmarted us . . . or so they thought.

While living in Chicago when I was seven, I'd gone to the Fullerton Beach Day camp. The camp straddled the beach and the heavily wooded park area along Lake Shore Drive. One of the tricks the older guys taught us was to gather toilet paper and paper towels, wet them down and clump them into a ball. Then you'd wait until some unsuspecting soul entered and was settled in a stall. A barrage of wet paper balls would pelt the user while in his most vulnerable position. A hearty laugh and we'd quickly disappear into the woods. I decided that a change of ammunition was needed, one that should settle the battle once and for all.

The washrooms were housed in a low white concrete building with a flat roof. Women's was on the left, Men's on the right. A water fountain was mounted on a metal stand between them. The doors were wood, painted turquoise. I gathered the guys and we promptly went into the Men's room.

A few minutes later we emerged—armed with soggy, soaking balls of bathroom tissue. I had Morrie go ahead and open the door on the Ladies side. I figured if they had any dirt clods, then Morrie would be collateral damage. No big deal.

A voice cried out, "You can't come in here—shut the door!"

We fired. The sounds of splats and screams echoed off the cinderblock walls. Morrie shut the door. We retreated a bit and hefted our loads, and waited.

And waited. Damn girls weren't coming out. Time for plan B. I told the Andersen brothers to get ready and handed my dripping paper balls to Paul. I grabbed Morrie.

"Get a mouth full of water from the fountain."

Morrie ran over to the shiny silver steel water fountain. He came running back a minute later, his cheeks filled like a squirrel storing nuts in his mouth. I dragged him over the window on the Women's side of the washroom and hoisted him up. He peered into the open window. A second later he sprayed his load through. Screeches and screams reverberated. I dropped him and ran around to the front.

"We give! We give!" cried the girls in unison.

They were a pitiful sight indeed, dripping wet and the dry dirt now wet and muddy.

We pointed and laughed mercilessly. Kids like us can be such little shits. And we were, no doubt about it. The decent thing to do was to have given the girls a ride on the merry-go-round, but in those last days of summer, before Junior High, girls still had cooties, and to admit that you actually liked them would've risked your reputation and led to endless teasing and taunting. And that wasn't only your peers. Parents have a wicked sense of humor too and I think at times derive great pleasure from torturing their kids about things that they know kids are embarrassed to admit or talk about. Girls were one of those things. So it was better to pretend that you weren't really interested in them, which of course I was. In fact I'd always been interested in girls, having crushes on whoever took my fancy like Sally or Penny or April or Mimi, or whoever caught my momentary fancy. I'd admire from afar, or sometimes actually talk to them or do something nice, like for Pam Zelman, who was in my fifth grade class and who loved horses. I drew a picture (having inherited the ability of drawing from somewhere in the family genetic structure) of a horse and rider and left it taped to her front door. The acceptance and delight of this gift allowed me to have her company walking home from school—but only if no one saw me.

The battle won, we marched away from the playground.

"I'm going to rest a bit. I'll see you guys at home."

Paul nodded. "I'd stay but I know Mom'll want us to get the chores done before dinner."

"Drop Morrie off?"

"Yeah, no big deal."

I waved to them as they disappeared over the crest. The bronze statue of Lincoln holding a book stared down at them.

A breeze rustled a chorus of flapping leaves from the copse of elm and ash trees dotting the rolling green hills of the park. The odd chirp of birds sighed a soft note. In a state of blue vertigo I lay on the soft green grass mattress staring up at the drifting clouds and wondering what it would be like to fly like Superman. The warm August sun baked my face and bare arms. I often came up to the park to think about things, and lately my mind was filled with apprehension about the start of Bar Mitzvah lessons. There was so much to learn, and I knew I had to do it perfectly. Not only because I was the first Cantor's son to have my Bar Mitzvah here, but because of the Hebrew school fiasco.

It had started about a year and a half ago. The Jewish community had an after-school Hebrew program held at the Jewish Community Center, which was a big yellowish two-story brick building down on 16th in-between Pierce and Nebraska Streets. The classes were held for students ages eight through thirteen, three times a week: Sunday morning from eleven until twelve-thirty in the afternoon, and Tuesdays and Thursdays after school from four-thirty until six in the evening. The first two years were spent learning the Hebrew alphabet, basic reading skills, and some Modern Hebrew vocabulary. A middle-aged spinster named Miss Joanna Bresden--or as we boys who noticed her well-endowed chest called her, "Miss Boobsden"—taught first and second grade. Rabbi Solomon and his wife taught the other two intermediate and advanced classes. They were really nice, and that was their problem. It was easy to get Mrs. Solomon off topic and thereby waste most of the class. We actually did little Hebrew and mostly read Bible stories. Rabbi Solomon, nicknamed Rabbi Showers, because of his wet lisp, caused small showers whenever he spoke. Now my father wanted me to not only be able to recite the prayers accurately—his motto being pronunciation first, fluency with practice—but also to understand what I was saying; having enough knowledge of Hebrew to translate the prayers. He also expected I would have a full class with no goofing off. At any rate, working with me and overhearing conversations of what was really happening blew my dad's short fuse. He confronted Rabbi Solomon, the result being that I was pulled out of the community school. Dad taught me privately at twice-a-week sessions. So the pressure was on. My father had to prove that he was a better teacher and that I'd be better prepared than the other kids. Problem was, languages were not my forte. I could read pretty well, but translating and learning vocabulary just didn't seem to sink in, causing my father no end of frustration. Of course it was no piece of pie for me either. I thought back to my sessions, sitting alone in a sea of empty wooden right-handed desks in one of the newly refurbished classrooms, most disconcerting since I was left-handed. I seemed to spend forever conjugating Hebrew verbs, and translating excerpts of prayers and Bible stories. I wasn't sure how this helped prepare me for the task coming up. And then I'd hand in my work and Dad would take this red ballpoint pen out and the knots in my stomach felt like chain links on a ship's anchor as I watched him mark the assignment. The high point of my studies was when Dad took me into the Youth Lounge and bought me an orange or grape Crush from the pop machine. It was just as good as the Oreo cookies and chocolate milk I got for twenty-five cents at the JCC (Jewish Community Center) before I used to go to Rabbi Solomon's class, that and the fact that I usually picked up some red licorice at Mr. Klages on my way to the synagogue.

Below me the white concrete band shell stood like a silent mausoleum among a sea of green. On Saturday evenings the city orchestra's music echoed out and filled the surrounding neighborhoods. People came with blankets and folding chairs since the twenty-seven brown wooden benches filled quickly. Ice cream vendors plied their trade to a ready market, and families visited.

I turned and looked up at the twin circular concrete water towers that sat like military bunkers on top of a hill opposite the band shell. There was a tunnel that led between them and exited to the next street. Once Paul and I had ventured up to it, but bogeymen stories of demented drunks kept us from entering. In truth, it was a popular make out spot for neighborhood teens. I picked myself up, brushed the dry grass off my jeans and sauntered down the hill toward home.

On the following Friday night we walked, as usual, to services. As soon as we left the house, the smell hit us like wet fish in the face. The hot humid air was permeated with the stench of raw sewage. It was like sticking your head down the hole of an outhouse; but to the farmers, the stench of rendering stockyard fat was the smell of money. Many a warm humid Friday night, we walked to the synagogue, while wafting the fumes that permeated the air. The first time it happened, almost four years ago, I thought Mom was going to be sick right on the spot. Morrie burst out laughing, to him it was like someone had let go a huge fart. But I guess like all things, you get used to it.

We lived eight blocks from the synagogue, two or three blocks of which was up hill, but if we cut a block over to Douglas Street the incline wasn't as steep. Most of the time it was a pleasant walk. We'd continue to talk about our week. In the winter if it was too cold, only Dad went and we got to stay home which was great because all the good TV shows like the Flintstones and The Adams Family-were usually on Friday night.

Built in 1951, the synagogue was a huge white granite and sandstone colored brick regal neo-Grecian style building with two big stone columns dividing the three main dark wood doors at the top of a half a dozen steps. Above the doorway, carved in stone was the name Beth Zion. At the top of the building near the roof was a carved representation of the Ten Commandments. A new one story social hall, built in sandstone colored brick, had been dedicated last year and was attached to the old part. Inside was a lobby with Grecian columns and black and white marble floor. Another set of doors on the other side led to the main sanctuary. A white carved arch enclosed the opening of the bimah. The area above the bimah was domed. The inside of the dome was painted blue and had gold stars. Four stained-glass windows on the sanctuary's walls allowed sunlight to stream in during the day. On either side of the bimah were two teak colored lecterns: my dad on the left, Rabbi Silverman on the right. The Torah reading table was in the middle. Smack center against the back wall was the Ark containing the Torah scrolls, above it hanging down like Aladdin's brass lamp was the Ner Tamid, the Eternal light that symbolized God's divine presence, just as the Menorah did in the ancient temple. On either side of the ark were spaced three high-backed wooden chairs with red velvet seat cushions where my dad, Rabbi Silverman and a couple of synagogue board members sat during the service. Chandeliers with wrought iron menorah decorations hung from the high ceiling. In the back of the sanctuary was a balcony section that was used only when the choir sang Friday night or for High Holiday services when it was really packed.

We always arrived a half an hour early, so Dad could warm up his voice, check that everything was laid out properly, and get himself centered and in the proper mindset to pray. During this time we either sat in his old office off the bimah, or wandered around the building. Sometimes Morrie and I would check to see what we were having at the Oneg Shabbat, or for coffee and dessert, after the service. Usually for Bar or Bat Mitzvahs, or special occasions they had punch with this huge floating brick of sherbet in it. It was my favorite, along with chocolate chip cookies.

One time Micah Woodrovitch, a disreputable little cretin of nine, came early and stacked a bunch of prayer books on the ledge of the balcony, planning to shove them on the top of some unsuspecting old ladies. Thankfully Rabbi Silverman came out to put something on his lectern and looked up and saw what the little bastard was planning to do. He rushed back and up the stairs and grabbed the kid by the ear and led him downstairs and into the arms of his father, who was not happy. I suspect that Micah couldn't sit for a week after that incident.

Another time, when Morrie was little, he fell asleep during Rabbi Silverman's sermon and started snoring. Mom was so embarrassed; but there was nothing she could do. If she woke him, he'd just be crabby and make even more of a ruckus.

I went to the door that led on to the bimah from Dad's office and peeked out. The sanctuary was starting to fill up. I saw a couple of buddies come in and turned to my parents. "I'm going out. Larry and Mark are here."

My folks nodded. I went out through the main office door, in through a small landing and out the door leading to the sanctuary with its rows of padded wooden pews arranged in three sections.

I'd met Larry Schaffer the first weekend we came to services. We were both in third grade then, though at different schools. We hit it off instantly. Larry's dad owned a men's clothing store downtown, which he'd inherited from his father and which his great-grandfather had started. Often Larry would help out there on weekends. Larry's dad was also president of the shul.

Mark Weiner went to my school. He was a tall gangly fellow with rust red crinkly hair and a turned up nose. The three of us were like the musketeers, having gone to Hebrew school and Junior Congregation services together. Mark's dad owned an office supply and business furniture place downtown and was on the board of the synagogue.

"So what's up?" asked Larry. Larry was around my height but slimmer. He had short wavy brown hair and black horned-rimmed glasses just like me. He was dressed to sartorial perfection with a tweed sports coat, dark brown slacks with a crisp crease and shortened to the proper length with cuffs. A solid blue tie, done with a Windsor knot, its ends perfectly matched. Shiny wingtips just about blinded me when I looked down.

"Same old," I replied. I wore cordovan penny loafers, gray flannel slacks, white shirt and a tan blazer. I had borrowed a brown and yellow striped clip-on tie from my dad.

Mark asked, "Ready for going to Junior High?" Mark was dressed in crisp gray slacks and a navy blue blazer, white shirt with a blue and yellow striped tie. We looked like miniature adults.

Larry and I glared at him like he'd said something blasphemous.

"Have you no respect? There's still two weeks of vacation left." Larry turned to me. "So how was the southwest?"

"Hot. We ended up stopping at this place called Hell, Arizona. Population seven, and I'm sure that included the rattlesnake I saw. Car overheated and we ended up sitting there schvitzing for almost an hour. There was a small store, well actually a battered mobile home with an awning. They charged Dad a buck for one Coke-and it wasn't even cold."

"Guneffs," spat Larry using the Yiddish word for thieves.

"Grammy was with us too," I said, " Did you know you can't bring fruit into California?"

"How come?" asked Larry.

"Don't know, but Dad had to dump the fruit before we hit the border station. And on top of that, he also threw out this salami sandwich Grammy had made. It really stunk up the car. She was really pissed too. Yelled at him about wasting food. Anyway, if they catch you bringing anything in, it's a five hundred dollar fine."

Mark whistled.

"So," I continued, "we get stopped, checked and as were pulling away, my grandmother reaches in her purse and pulls out a peach and offers it to my dad."

"Your dad must've gone ballistic," said Larry, knowing my Dad's temper.

"They were shouting at each other in Yiddish and German for miles."

In July we took our annual road trip. My dad's philosophy was that the only way he'd get a good vacation was to get as far from the congregation as possible. This year we spent a week in Phoenix visiting my great-Aunt Rose and Uncle Herman, then drove to Los Angeles and stayed with cousins of my mom. They had kids Morrie's and my age. It was too expensive to go to Disneyland, but we did go to Knotts' Berry Farm and saw a lot of old L.A. The best part was driving home. We sighted a tornado as we whipped through the northwest section of Texas and it continued to dog us through the Oklahoma panhandle and into Lawrence, Kansas. It hit the edge of town about twenty minutes after we checked into our motel. All I remember is seeing the funnel cloud eating up prairie miles as my dad just about slammed his foot through the floorboards speeding away from it. I honestly didn't know our 1962 Ford white station wagon could go that fast. We managed to make it into Liberal, Kansas and to the motel before the tornado hit the outskirts of the town.

People started coming in, so Mark, Larry and I headed inside to sit with our parents during the service, well, in my case, my mom. My dad and the Rabbi entered from a hidden side door on the bimah. The chattering of conversation softened to whispers. My Dad, dressed in his black robe and high black yarmulke, tallis gleaming in white and silver, went to his lectern and started chanting Lewandowski's *Ma Tovu* -How Goodly are your tents, o' Jacob-and silence hushed over the congregation. Morrie, as usual, fell asleep part way through. At least he didn't snore during Rabbi' Silverman's sermon this time.

Like ganza machers, big shots, or maybe junior mobsters, we met after the service. We shook hands, playfully crushing each other's hands, and wished each other a "Gut Shabbos".

"Well boys, what'll it be?" asked Larry, eyeing a tray of dark chocolate drenched short bread cookies.

Mark looked at the fruit tray and cheesecakes. "Tough decision."

"You Slim?" asked Larry.

Slim was my given nickname and somewhat of a misnomer considering I had a weight problem, though not as bad now. Dr. Katzman had me on diet pills, and during the summer I'd been swimming several afternoons a week at the Erickson pool. But I still had a ways to go and Dad was hoping I'd fit into an off the rack suit for my Bar Mitzvah.

"Fruit for me."

"And a far thinner man you'll be soon," said Larry as he popped a shortbread cookie into his mouth. "This cookie is soooooooooooo good."

"You bastard," I hissed.

"Now, now, remember where you are," said Larry as he wagged a finger at me with his left hand and reached for another cookie with his right.

I glared at him.

Mark cracked a grin. "Sucks to be you, man." He took a big bite out of a chocolate chip cookie.

After services we walked home, which proved to be more eventful than usual. Slashes of light from the streetlamps streaked across the darkened sidewalk like the stripes of a tiger. The shadowy branches of leaves fluttered like bats in the night. Walking down tree-lined Douglas

Street my mom clenched my dad's arm and shouted, "Stop!"

"What's the matter?" asked Morrie.

"I've lost my contact lens. You have to look for it."

"How'd it come out?" asked Dad. I could tell Dad was upset. Those contact lenses were expensive, but it sure made mom happy to have them, so I guess it was worth it. Thankfully Dad got a discount from Dr. Sherman who was a member of the congregation.

"I blinked. My eyes must be dry," replied Mom.

"Ok boys, stay still and squat down. Use your fingers to feel around. It's got to be around here." Dad took the lighter from his coat pocket and flicked it on. "Look for a reflection."

So there we were squatting on our haunches, reaching out and lightly touching the sidewalk. We tilted our heads to try and catch the light reflecting off the lens.

Mom had gotten the contact lenses a couple of months ago and rarely wore them. Usually just for when she and Dad had some special function to go to. I couldn't understand how anybody would want to put something in your eye. I'd watched Mom practically pressing her nose into the mirror and holding her eye open with one hand as she delicately balanced the glass lens on the tip of her finger to place it on the eye. Truthfully it looked pretty gross.

"Morrie! Don't move!" snapped Dad. He then bent over and wetting his forefinger with his tongue plucked the lens up off the cement. "We found it."

He handed it to mom who wrapped it in a tissue and put it in her purse. "I'll clean it at home."

"Do you have your glasses with you?" asked Dad.

"No, I left them at home because I put the contacts in."

"Well then blind-eyes, best grab my arm. I'll guide you." He nodded to Morrie and me and we continued.

Sunday we slept in, except for Dad since he had morning services to do. During the school year I'd go with him. After services there were bagels and cream cheese, and coffee, which I was allowed to have. In fact, I'd been weaned on the beverage. When we lived in Chicago my Aunt Rose and Grandma Sara (Grammy) would come over on Shabbos afternoon. Grammy usually brought a cake from this German bakery on Broadway. My favorite was a chocolate torte with whipped cream frosting covered in shaved chocolate. When I came back from the Saturday matinee, we'd sit and have coffee, though mine was more milk with just a splash of coffee. After sometimes we'd go for a walk with her, Morrie and I conveniently leading her by a toy store on Diversy. On rare occasions it was worth it.

Dad told us that when he was growing up his mother never bought toys, she thought they were useless. Dad had grown up during the Depression, in Germany, when Hitler was in power. Dad and my grandmother immigrated to the States in 1939. Being divorced and a single parent she worked hard. She put in long hours as a scamstress at a shirt factory. As well, her parents lived with her. I still remember my great-grandfather sitting on the radiator looking out her living room window. He was a tall spare man with plastered silver white hair and wire-rim glasses. He always dressed in gray flannel trousers and a crisp white shirt. He looked at Morrie and me as if we were annoying cockroaches, something that had to be tolerated because no matter how hard you tried, you couldn't get rid of them. On Passover he led the Seder and seemed to drone on forever. He had passed away four years ago. I vaguely remember the funeral. It had been a cold drizzly October afternoon.

Sundays in River City were like living in a ghost town. The town was quiet like a morgue at midnight. Most stores were closed. People attended Church, and those who didn't headed out to the lakes. The Andersen clan dressed up and went to church. When they came home they had dinner, so Paul wouldn't be available to play later in the afternoon. I had hoped that Larry would be able to play, but it turned out he was helping his Dad do some inventory at the store. And that's when Mom informed me that the Blackmans were coming over. Oy.

July 2012: Monday

"Are you okay Mister? Do you need some help?" asked a grating deep voice.

I snapped out of my reverie and looked at the man in front of me. Dressed in paint splattered dirty white overalls and black sneakers that looked like it had collected a menagerie of colorful dead bugs, he looked at me with concern in his warm brown eyes. He was in his thirties, with unshaven stubble, which seems to be the fashion today. A backwards-blue peaked ball camp was clamped down on his head. Black hair with the odd strand of gray peeked out from beneath.

"I used to live in this house. I grew up here as a kid," I explained. "Guess I sort of got lost in old memories. I'm fine."

"Well, we're painting the house. The realtor has it up for sale soon. Tell you what, if you want, why don't you go wander through, it's empty."

"Thanks, I appreciate that." I looked at the house.

I took a deep breath and slowly walked up the walk and up the three steps of the narrow front porch. I opened the door and entered. The house was a small, narrow three bedroom. Inside the entranceway, on the right was a shelf with a hanging clothes bar below. When we lived here, a comfortable armchair was in the livingroom on the left beneath the front window. Against the left wall were two windows, along which used to be our ten-foot sofa. We'd gotten most of our living room furniture from my dad's aunt when she remodeled her apartment in Chicago. Mom and dad had the couch cut down a bit and redesigned in a more modern way with new cushions, but there was nothing to do about length. On the right wall across from the couch was an upright piano. Grammy had bought it for my dad's 30th birthday. He'd always want one, and when he was young they couldn't afford it. Against the back wall, on either side of the fireplace, was a built-in mahogany shelf unit with a pull down desk on the left. The fireplace had a wrought iron black screen.

I turned right and went through an entranceway to the hall. To the right, facing the front of the house had been my parent's bedroom. I looked inside. The window faced the front. Next to it was a closet. My parents had kept the TV here. It was on a stand and we'd roll it out into the living room when all of us were watching Ed Sullivan or other family shows. I turned and went out.

The next door on my right was the bathroom. Next to it had been Morrie's and my room-well at least until I was in Jr. high when I got the upstairs bedroom. The built in desk unit, toy box, and another built in shelf and drawer unit were still there against the back wall. Above the toy box was the window that I'd help Morrie sneak out of when he got grounded. Across from the bedroom was a small dining room with a doorway into the kitchen and a door with steps leading to the back enclosed porch and another set leading to the basement. I turned to the hallway and opened the door directly in front of me. A staircase led up to the refurbished attic. I climbed the stairs, stopping on the landing. I looked out the window and could see the garage. When the elm tree stood next to the porch roof, Morrie used to climb out the window and down the tree. It was another escape route for him. I continued up the stairs, my feet silent on the worn gray carpet. I walked down the hall. To my left was a door to the L-shaped storage closet. We used to keep the rollaway bed and suitcases in there. It was also one of the hiding places April Blackman, my first girlfriend of sorts, and I used to go to get away from our annoying siblings. I could remember the smell of wood and the smell of April's hair as we sat huddled together, barely breathing. I hesitated at the closed door, then gripping the knob, turned and opened it.

To my left was the bathroom with a shower. The linen closet, against the wall next to the toilet, used to house my comic book collection. Each title stacked neatly on the shelves. DC comics on the middle shelf- at that time I read: *Batman, Detective, The Flash, The Atom, Green Lantern,* and *Hawkman*; the few Marvels like *Daredevil* or *Captain America* or the Gold Key comics, *The Phantom* or *Dr. Solar-Man of the Atom* on the bottom. The top shelf was actually used for spare linens, bars of soap and extra rolls of toilet paper.

I walked down the short hall and into the bedroom. To my right was a long closet. I used half. My parents had used the other half for storage. As my eyes swept the empty room, I pictured the layout of my furniture when I lived here.

Against the left wall of my room had been my dresser. My bed was on the right wall stretching towards the closet. Next to the bed I'd had a gray metal typewriter table with the old Royal typewriter I'd inherited from my Uncle Jake. On the other side of it was a metal pole desk with two shelves, painted with fake brown wood paneling. It was here, in this room, that Larry Schaffer and I had many sleepovers and pondered over which celebrity females we'd want to have sex with. It was here that I studied and practiced my guitar. It was here that I first really kissed April Blackman. I leaned against the wall as a flood of emotions and memories overwhelmed me. I stood suspended between the reality of the world I knew, the open doors portals to a part I was desperate to reclaim.

In Judaism we have the belief of free will. We have choice. And yet there is also a belief in b'sheret-that some things are meant to be. It's a curious paradox, but one that life experience has taught me is very real. There are times where I've felt that I've been nudged in a particular direction. Is it my subconscious or is it God, giving me a gentle push because God knows what I should be doing, or which path would be better for me. Looking back at my relationship with April Blackman, though I had an inclination of possibilities between us back then; I was not truly aware of them. (There were other opportunities that cropped up over the years after I left River City.) Looking back now, in the middle years of my life, the paths are clearer, the patterns more distinct. Yes we have free will. We make choices in our lives that put us on particular paths, and each decision we make either keeps us on the same path or diverts us to another. Hindsight is a wonderful teacher, and most often, if we knew then what we know now, who knows what possibilities might exist, or how things turn out. But in that year of my Bar Mitzvah, my hormone-induced state was not concerned with hindsight, foresight or anything in between. I lived in the moment, for the moment. My mind and body a kaleidoscope of feelings and sensations.

August 1964

The Blackman family were neighbors until last year when the new house they were building in the north end was finished. They initially lived in the Belleview Apartments behind and across the alley from us. Mr. Blackman and his brother Stan owned Blackmans Grocery Store on the south side of the city. Mr. Blackman and his wife Lois had two daughters: April and Susie. April Blackman was two years younger than me, while Susie was a year younger than Morrie.

Lois Blackman had dreams for her daughters. They were going to be prim and proper young ladies. They were going to go to the right schools when they got older, and marry the right men. She ensured that they looked like young ladies too. On the first day that April attended school, she dressed her in a white dress, white socks and black patent leather shoes. On April's hands were little white gloves. It was my job to take her to school. And I did, having her walk four or five steps behind me so I wouldn't get teased or laughed at. The fact was I was a bit embarrassed about having to take a little girl to school. It was bad enough I had to take Morrie. He and Robin walked behind Paul and me.

I hated going over to the Blackmans. Playing Barbie's was not my idea of a good time, and somehow I don't think it was April's either, but it's not like they had plastic army men or toy guns. However, Susie delighted in playing 'house' with Morrie as her husband who kept telling her he had to go to the office.

The fact is April, though I was hesitant to admit it, was actually pretty cool. At our place she'd strap on a holster and was ready to pretend to be Dale Evans or Annie Oakley when we boys got together to play cowboys. She could jump and climb and hide in bushes when we played army. And she'd swing a piece of clothesline rope over her head pretending to be Wonder Woman when we played superheroes. She had imagination and she wasn't afraid to be one of the boys.

I should've liked her, and maybe I did; but it was hard to admit it to myself. She was slim with shoulder length dark hair and big brown eyes set in an oval face. She had a great smile that lit up her face when she was happy. She was smart and creative. We had similar interests in writing. Sometimes she'd color the homemade comic books that Paul and I made. She was one of the gang, and yet not. But we kids can be cruel, and we boys are stupid at this age, and the stigma of acknowledging that you liked a girl could be deadly. When I found out the Blackmans were coming over Sunday afternoon, I was filled with dread and a strange comforting feeling of anticipation.

Mrs. Blackman didn't drive and Mr. Blackman was at the store as usual. They came in a yellow cab that pulled up in front of our house at one in the afternoon. Mom had coffee brewing. She and Mrs. Blackman would have a nice afternoon gabbing about the doings in the community and synagogue, and whatever else women talked about.

At this time I shared a room with my brother. Grammy, my dad's mother, lived upstairs in the guest room, which had its own bathroom. She had recently retired from the shirt factory that she had worked in for the past couple of decades or so, and was moving here to be near us. Anyway, against the back wall was a white built-in desk and shelf unit attached to a built-in toy box and another drawer and shelf unit. Being older, the desk and shelves above were mine. Our two single beds were pushed together against the left of the door. Opposite the beds were two dressers. A closet was to the right. The girls, knowing the layout of the house came into our room.

April's sister Susie was maybe four feet tall, slim like her sister with auburn hair and green eyes. She wore, surprisingly, a yellow sundress and yellow canvas sneakers. I don't know what her Mom thought she'd be doing here, but knowing Morrie, playing Barbie's or house was definitely not on the agenda.

"Hi," I said to April. I noticed April was dressed a bit more practical-plaid shorts and a green T-shirt. Her white sneakers were scuffed a bit, just like the ones I wore. Clean tennis sneakers were not cool. "So what do you want to do this afternoon?"

Morrie had already started strapping on his six-gun. "We're playing cowboys." He plopped his white hat on his head. "Here, you can use this," he told Susie. He handed his shoot 'n shell carbine to her. "You joining us?" He looked hopefully at April and me.

I glanced at April. "Well?"

April sighed and smiled, "Sure."

I dug out my Red Ryder air rifle out of the toy box and gave it to her, and strapped on my Mattel Shoot and Shell. "You and Susie against me and April. We'll head out first." I nodded at April and we went out, through the kitchen, out the back door and out of the attached screened in porch.

"We'll head for the lot and ambush them," I said to April.

We ran between the garages and down the alley.

The Belleview apartments had green terraces across from our garage. We ran out the back door, through the backyard to the alley. Turned left past the apartment building and further down on the east side of it, past the garage entrance, was an empty lot that sloped up to Summit Street. April and I clambered over the white cement retaining wall, and dashed into the jungle of shrubs, trees and uncut grass. We stopped, taking refuge in some bushes. Our hearts were beating. Sweat dripped down my brow, smeared my glasses, and stung my eyes. It was hot and humid out, a typical Iowa summer. I looked at her. She was watching the alley. The lever cocked on the air rifle. It'd make a popping sound when she pulled the trigger. I glanced at the alley and turned and looked at April. She was crouched next to me. I could feel her body heat.

"Anything exciting with you?"

"Mom's going to have a baby."

I didn't say anything at first. The thought of parents having sex was not an image I wanted burned into my brain. I looked at her. "Really? Damn, so you want a brother or another sister?"

April glanced at me. "Might be fun to have a baby brother. One sister is enough."

"So is one brother," I replied. "Uh-your parents give you the sex talk?"

Her face reddened a bit. "I guess. My mom talked about it a bit and explained her tummy would get bigger as the baby grew, and when it was ready, she'd go to the hospital."

My parents didn't really talk to me about sex, about a year ago they got some books from the library and told me to read them. Afterwards my dad asked if I had any questions. Like yeah, I really wanted to have a discussion with my parents about sex. But it did eventually dawn on me that on Saturday afternoons when they locked themselves in their bedroom and told Morrie and I not to disturb them, that were doing more than just 'having a nap'. I shuddered and pushed the thoughts from my mind.

"So they tell you how she got pregnant?" I was curious to know how other parents handled this stuff.

"Not in great detail, no. Do you know?"

"Of course."

"So?" she looked at me with curiosity in her eyes.

My mouth dried up. It was like I was sucking in the Mohave Desert. Sweat dripped down my face. I wiped it away and turned my head and stared towards the alley and listened for running footsteps. So far the only thing I heard were flies and mosquitos. The hot humid air saturated us. My shirt stuck to my back. I could feel April's eyes boring into me. I took a deep breath and could smell the small purple flowers that bloomed on a bush near us. I looked at April. Our eyes met and locked like hunters on their target.

"They probably are in the lot," yelled Morrie.

The spell was broken. April and I aimed our guns, ready to ambush our bratty miserable siblings.

Chapter Two

September 1964

Summer closed. On the September long weekend we had a BBQ at Rabbi Silverman's. We walked down Grandview and then up again. The Rabbi's ranch-style house sat on the corner of Grandview and 18th streets. The yard was tiered as 18th sloped down to Douglas.

Rabbi Silverman had a thick head of dark hair, going a bit salt and pepper at the temples. He was of average height and built. His father had been a Rabbi in Belgium, as had his grandfather. A lot of his family had been killed in the War. He had been a chaplain in the Korean War and from what I understood this was his second pulpit.

The Rabbi's family consisted of his wife Julia, a flamboyant Texas girl with Cadillac tastes, big boobs and flaming red hair. Julia was known as being brash and outspoken, something that didn't sit well with many of the congregants, especially the women. They expected the Rabbi's wife to be demure, involve herself with synagogue and women's organizations and to keep her mouth shut. To her credit, Julia was heavily involved in Women's League, but she also had a university education, and the role of traditional housewife was hard for her to handle. They had two spoiled daughters, in the Jewish American princess tradition: eight-year-old Terri who had dark hair, and four-year-old Sari who was a miniaturized version of her mother-minus the breasts.

The relationship between my dad and Rabbi Silverman was an important one. While the Rabbi was the main spiritual leader of the synagogue, the real conducting of the service, seventy-five percent of which was chanted or sung, the music was my dad's. Trouble was, Silverman thought he could sing. My dad had no problem with him singing along with congregants during prayers and hymns that were participatory; however the solo pieces were something else. My dad had a temper, but knew enough, and had control enough to never let it out on congregants or the board of directors. However, a spiritual colleague, which seemed to undermine his responsibilities, was something else. I overheard my parents talking a couple of years ago. Dad had sat Rabbi Silverman down, and gave a tongue-lashing, and after that, their relationship improved immensely. The boundaries had been drawn and respected.

We were welcomed and as was typical, dinner wasn't quite ready. Rabbi Silverman did have the BBQ fired up, but the coals weren't white hot yet. Terri, being the same age as Morrie, latched on to him like a leach to a sick person and dragged him off. I snickered gleefully. Instead I went outside with my dad and the Rabbi to supervise the grilling. Mrs. Silverman had prepared thick burgers, coleslaw and potato salad. And for those of us who weren't into the latter, French fries were sizzling on the stove in a pot of oil. I sniffed deeply on my way out the back door and into the yard.

I found a chaise lounge and sprawled out while my dad and Rabbi hovered around the grill.

Rabbi Silverman turned to me, "So you, Larry and Mark will be in the B'nai Mitzvah class this year."

"Guess so." I nodded.

"Big class this year, I believe there'll be a dozen." He looked at my dad. "Going to be busy for us."

My dad agreed. Typically the Rabbi helped us with our speech and gave a general introduction to history and rabbinic literature. My dad was the one who had to tutor us on our Torah portion, Haftorah and service parts. I was a bit apprehensive. People would be waiting to see how well I did, and the idea of getting up in front of the entire congregation was overwhelming to say the least.

Their talk continued about the congregation and I tuned out. I turned my head and watched the traffic. A steady stream of cars headed south towards Pierce. At the corner of 18th and Pierce was the Green Gables restaurant, which just happened to be owned by one of the Temple's members. It was a popular eating-place and they made great apple pie. We went for dinner there occasionally, but obviously because we kept Kosher, we were restricted to fish or dairy items on the menu.

Suddenly I heard yelling coming from the house. Both Rabbi and my dad turned. Julia Silverman burst through the door looking like a mad bull in a china shop. She stormed up to my father. I could see my mom running behind her, dragging Morrie by the hand.

"Your son is a degenerate miscreant!" she shouted. "Do you know what I caught this little pervert doing? Why he had his hands all over my innocent Terri. What the hell do you teach your children?"

Dad and Rabbi looked at each other, then back to Julia. I swear you could see steam streaming out her nostrils. Her face was red and her eyes blazed like hellfire- that is, if we truly believed in a concept of hell.

My dad glanced behind Julia to my mom. "What happened?"

"Morrie and Terrie were playing doctor. He had her shirt rolled up and was listening to her tummy."

"And what sort of perverted game is that?" demanded Julia.

"It's innocent. Kids are curious. I talked to him and he understands what he did," said Mom.

"I should hope so." Julia glared at Morrie who hid behind my mom.

"I'm sorry," he whispered.

Rabbi Silverman rolled his eyes at my dad then, turned to Morrie. "It's ok. Apology accepted. Now, where are those burgers?"

"That's it?" queried Julia.

"That's it," replied Rabbi Silverman. "It's over. Crisis averted. Apologies accepted. It's time for dinner now." The tone of his voice gave Julia a clear message not to push it or him further. She glared at him, then turned and went into the house. I suspected that Rabbi Silverman would be paying penance to her for the rest of the week.

School started just before Labor Day weekend, which was good considering Rosh Hashona, the Jewish New Year, was beginning Sunday night. It was strange not walking with Paul as I had the past several years. On the plus side Grammy, moved into the Belleview Apartments, leaving the upstairs bedroom free. My parents, in a stroke of mental insight, decided I should have my own room. We'd moved my stuff upstairs. Dad got me a metal pole desk that I helped put together. To boot, I had my own bathroom with a shower.

Northside Junior High was the opposite direction from my alma mater of Huntington Elementary School. I walked up Grandview underneath a protecting canopy of green elm. Mostly wood frame or a mix of brick and wood frame two-story homes lined both sides of the street. The air smelled of morning coolness and dappled sunlight marked the way. A robin hopped on the grass looking for breakfast. It was a good neighborhood. A place for couples to raise families. Everyone was a neighbor. Some didn't bother to lock their doors. There was no need to be afraid of anything. Paranoia did not run deep. At the top of the hill I followed 24th street three blocks to Jackson then turned left. I joined the cattle trail of students moseying on to Northside. We were young and the world was ours.

Northside Junior High was a three-story red brick building with light gray trim. Around the school was a gray cement retaining wall. Two sets of steps led up to the main wood doors on either side of the building. The school's track field was across the street and took up a full block. A chain link fence surrounded it like a giant kennel or prison yard. At eight-thirty the double wooden doors opened and students stormed the building as if they were breaking into the bastille. All of us entering for the first time were directed to the auditorium where we'd find out where our homeroom was along with other administrative information.

We were herded into the auditorium and asked to take seats. I folded my wooden chair bottom down and sat. I looked around for Mark. A tall spare man with glasses and dressed in a gray suit took the stage. "Find your seats and settle down."

Someone plopped into the chair next to mine. He was a string bean of a fellow with a mop of brown hair and black horn-rimmed glasses, like mine, that sat on a long face. He thrust a hand out, "Tim Shaunessy."

"Jeff Reimer," I returned as I shook his hand.

"Wonder if we'll be in the same homeroom?" wondered Tim.

"Wouldn't mind if she was," I said watching a tall rather mature young lady sit down two rows in front of us.

Tim grinned. "Yes, pleasant distractions, wouldn't you say?"

I grinned back.

"You know," said Tim as he gazed about, "the difference between men and women?"

"What?"

"Women have zippers up the back."

I looked at the girls wearing dresses. Damn, if he wasn't right. Junior high was definitely going to be interesting.

My first day at Junior High was fine. A lot better than my first day of elementary school in Chicago where I got the shit beat out of me. I remember it was January. I was four and a half. Alan, Louie the janitor's grandson who was in fourth grade, walked me to school. There was a crowd of kids milling around the front door. Nettlehorst was an elementary and junior high combined. The junior high kids used a different entrance on the other side of the school. Anyway this kid is standing next to one of the stone columns that lined the door. He pointed towards me and yelled, "That's the kid who did it!" Now maybe I was in the wrong place at the wrong time. Maybe it was a case of mistaken identity. Maybe he was just a little shit. But I got trampled and beaten by a stampede of kids. I think I actually lost consciousness for a bit as I crawled towards the steps, seeking shelter. I remember being led into the classroom, crying. The kid's name that yelled was named Bobby Miller. He denied everything. But on the other hand he did end up going to the principal's office for fighting. Sometimes you take the justice you can get.

Anyway, once my schedule was done, we did a walk through. Mrs. Madsen, an attractive blonde woman in her thirties was my homeroom teacher. There wasn't a guy in class who had any desire to make trouble. A number of classmates from elementary were in my homeroom too. Turned out Mark was in my Math class, and Tim was in English and Social Studies. According to my schedule I had woodworking every other day last period for the semester. Gym was after lunch on alternating days, and I had one study period before lunch. Orchestra after. I'd been playing the violin since third grade and was taking piano this year, but what I really wanted to learn was guitar. All the groups like The Beatles, Dave Clark Five, the Rolling Stones, and Herman's Hermits used them. And they were portable. It's not like you could lug a piano around. Hopefully I'd be able to use some of my Bar Mitzvah money to buy one.

After school I walked down Pierce Street past homes and a few apartment buildings until I hit the beginning of the business district heading to 16th street, where I would turned right and go up to the synagogue. Dad was starting my Bar Mitzvah lessons. Nervous didn't quite describe my state. I'd been to enough Bar Mitzvah ceremonies to know what was expected. I just hoped I did as well as the others before me.

It was a pleasant walk. Along the way I passed Klages Drugstore, which sat on the corner of 20th and Pierce. I stopped in for a couple of pieces of strawberry licorice and to check the comics.

Klages was an old fashioned drugstore. It smelled like a compote of antiseptic, perfume, and medication, with a hint of candy. As you entered, on the right there was a long glass counter. An assortment of health devices was displayed. Behind there were wooden cabinets with glass doors holding a variety of drugs on its shelves. An old fashioned cash register sat at the end of the counter. The other side of the counter held three shelves of penny candies. To the left were two wood and glass display cases. One filled with women's perfume and lotions, the other with men's shaving stuff. Along the back wall was another counter cluttered with toys and models. An old unused soda fountain spread out along the back wall. Across from the cluttered toy counter were three green wooden tiered racks filled with comics. DC comics and Gold key on the first, Marvel and Dell on the second, Charlton comics on the third. I scanned the shelves. I picked up the new issue of *Detective* and *The Flash*. I went to the counter where Mrs. Klages rang in my twenty-seven cents for the comics and licorice. I put the comics in my binder and left the store.

My love of comics came from my dad. When I was little, he used to read me the comics from *The Chicago American*. I remember following the adventures of *The Phantom*, *The Lone Ranger*, *Flash Gordon*, and *Tim Tyler's Luck*, among others every Sunday. At Nana's I'd read the comics strips from the *Chicago Tribune*: *Dick Tracy, Prince Valiant, Snuffy Smith*, and *The Katzenjammer Kids*. I'd marvel at the artwork and loved how the words and pictures worked to make a visual narrative. When I was six and seven I was sick with spells of bronchitis. Dad would pick up a stack of comics: *Batman, Detective Comics, The Cheyenne Kid* and others to read while I lay in bed. I usually had a pencil and paper and would spend hours copying scenes and drawing. Comic books were my comfort reading, my stress release. When I grew up, I thought about how neat it'd be to write and draw comics. But I also liked the characters, the concept of a hero fighting to correct wrongs and make the community a better place. I often thought what sort of superpowers I'd like, which ones would be the most useful.

I went in the side door of the synagogue and waved to Mrs. Levin the secretary, whose office was the first door on the right when you entered. Behind her was the Rabbi's office with an interconnecting door. I entered the second door on the right that was my dad's office. My dad's new office, was downstairs in the synagogue. It was a windowless, square room with a desk and two chairs and a small credenza. I plopped down in the first one to the right of the door.

"How'd your first day go?" he asked. My father had an oval, clean-shaven face. His skin was a light olive brown, and his wavy black hair was starting to recede a bit. He looked at me with his deep-set dark brown eyes. He wore a pair of gray slacks and white shirt with the sleeves rolled up. His gray and red striped tie was loose. Dad's herringbone sports coat was draped over the back of his chair.

"It was okay. Sure different from elementary school."

He nodded, and reached into his top right desk drawer and took out a small booklet, two 45 records, and a handout. He pushed them across the desk. "Take this, you're going to need it."

I looked at the red covered booklet. It was my Haftorah book, Parshat Shabbat Hagadol. It contained the special haftorah for the Sabbath before Passover. I looked at the records. One was marked Haftorah, the other: Musaf. Musaf was the additional Amidah, a section of prayers that we did on Shabbat morning. It represented the additional sacrifice that had been made on Shabbat during the time of the Temple.

The handout had a series of symbols on the left side of the page. On the right were a couple of bars of notes. The handout was labeled: Haftorah trope.

"I'm going to teach you trope, the cantillation melodies so you'll really know how to chant your haftorah. We'll take a couple of symbols a week. Practice plunking them on the piano. You have to memorize them and each musical code."

I looked at him in disbelief. Oh shit! This was going to be trouble all right. Why couldn't he just notate my haftorah and use transliteration? I wondered how often I'd have to study or how long it'd take me to learn this. I opened my haftorah book and counted the verses. There were twenty-three. I looked up at my dad like a deer caught in the crosshairs of a hunter's rifle.

He saw the expression on my face and sighed. "It's average length. We're going to start with you reading it through a few verses at time, while you learn the trope. Then we'll go back and put the two together." He sat back and pulled a package of Kent cigarettes from his shirt pocket. He took one out and lit it. A curl of gray smoke drifted up towards the ceiling. I hated cigarette smoke. It stank. I couldn't understand why my parents did it. But, everyone did. Radio and TV ads showed how pleasant it was. I knew kids who smoked. Yet, my parents certainly didn't promote or encourage us. One time I was puffing away on a candy cigarette and Dad asked if I wanted to try his. I was pretty wary. At least candy tasted good. But he gave it to me and told me to take a puff. So I did. I choked and coughed. "And that's why you shouldn't smoke," he said, adding, "It's too late for me."

"What about the service stuff?" I asked.

"You'll work on that as well. Some of the prayers I suspect you already know from coming to Junior Congregation every week for the past five years."

Dad assumed a lot. Oy vey.

The High Holidays descended upon us. Rosh Hashona is the Jewish New Year. Now we know the world is billions of years old. But according to the Rabbis, who started counting days from the beginning of Genesis and down through the generations, the current date, according to the Jewish lunar calendar is: 5725. I remember asking my Dad about this and he said that a day in God's time could mean billions of years. So having created the Earth and universe and all in seven days, is looking at it in God's terms, not mans'. And some Rabbis say that this is when our current world, the world of the Jewish people began. According to the Torah, God created and destroyed many worlds prior to this one. So if God is perfect, then this concept sort of shoots the idea in the foot.

For Erev Rosh Hashona I sat in the balcony (my mom, Grammy and Morrie sat below in assigned seats). Lot of kids sat up there and tended to go in and out of the service, including Mark and Larry. But I knew better. Dad's eyes would rove to see if I was there. During the daytime services for Rosh Hashona and Yom Kippur I went to the Junior Congregation Services. They were held in the youth lounge, part of the renovated basement. The youth lounge was a huge white cinderblock room with linoleum floor. Our USY youth group held meetings and dances there. The carved mahogany portable Ark containing the Torah scroll had been rolled in from the chapel, along with two lecterns. Folding chairs were set up in neat rows, ten chairs wide. A former student of my dad's, David Katzman acted as Cantor. Mr. Learner, our advisor, gave a sermonette. Gary Schindler, the president acted as Rabbi and announced pages. The services were a scaled down version of the main service upstairs. We had seventy kids in Junior Congregation, and several parents also attended. The youth lounge was jammed with one hundred and twenty five people.

Yom Kippur is the Day of Atonement. It falls ten days after Rosh Hashonah. It's a fast day, and a day spent in prayer and reflection. Supposedly this is the day when God sits in judgment, deciding who shall live and who shall die. But I have problems with that. Kids like Bobby Miller and Tom Bernstein who tormented me in Chicago are still around living and breathing. I saw them two years ago when we went back. I remember once at Fullerton Beach when a body washed up on shore. People said he was a fisherman, but I never saw a fisherman wearing a three-piece suit. And, I don't think God uses a gun to kill people. The dead guy had three bullet holes in him.

Dad says that this is the time of year when we can change our behavior. We should look at how we lived our life the past year and try to do better in the new one. That makes a lot more sense to me. If God really decided who should live and who should die, I suspect there'd be a lot of lightning bolts flying down to earth.

This was also the first year I actually fasted. According to Dad we concentrate on our spiritual life and not pay attention to the physical one-except Grammy who had to eat so she could take her diabetes and blood pressure medication, though I knew she still tried to fast. Erev Yom Kippur (the evening of the holiday) was on Shabbat this year, so instead of the usual Shabbat dinner of roast chicken or brisket, Mom made steaks, baked potatoes, salad and green beans. It lasted me until around eleven o'clock the next morning and my stomach growled in the middle of services. Larry and Mark looked at me. "You'll be a pale shadow of your former self by evening," whispered Larry.

I knew he would have lunch after services; technically we're not responsible for the mitzvot, the ritual commandments, until after we turn thirteen; but Dad figured I was old enough to start trying.

Four weeks of our holidays zipped by-after Yom Kippur came Sukkot, which is sort of the weeklong Jewish version of Thanksgiving. According to tradition, the Israelites would camp and grow crops and then harvest them before moving on. A Sukkah is a temporary shelter that provided a place to sleep for those doing the harvest, as well as a shelter for the harvested crops. It's customary to build your own Sukkah and live in it; but I don't think the ancient Rabbis ever imagined Jews living in the northern hemisphere. In the fall it can be cold and rainy. The synagogue had a sukkah and after services we would have a light meal in it, thereby fulfilling the mitzvah.

A few years ago Morrie and I built this roofless fort using a corner of the house and porch as two of the walls, and then building two walls each attached to the big elm tree next to the back porch. We got some branches we spread over the roof, and invited Mom and Dad to share in our sukkah, but the entrance wasn't big enough and Mom was afraid of snagging her dress on a nail. But that year, Morrie and I had lunch in the Sukkah.

The holidays ended with Shimini Atzeret, an eighth day of feasting after Sukkot, and Simchat Torah, where we finish reading the Torah and begin the prescribed readings over again. During the service we'd march around with flags and carry the Torahs around in a procession. In past years the little flags were topped with apples, but kids kept bonking the person in front of them while marching around and so my dad and the Rabbi stopped doing it. Anyway with the holidays over, I had a lot of homework due to the fact that I missed school because of the holidays.

Also, after the holidays, religious school started and so did my attendance at morning minyans. Jews are required to pray three times a day; morning, afternoon and evening, though often the latter two are done in close time proximity. A minyan is a quorum of ten men. This is the minimal number of people that constitute a sense of community, and communal prayers can't be said if there is less than ten.

The Shacarit, or morning service, is relatively short and made even shorter by lay people leading it, and davening, chanting the prayers, at super speed. I don't know how those old guys rattled off the Hebrew prayers so fast. I'd be still reading the top of the page and they were finishing. Larry and Marks' dads schlepped them to minyan too. One time there were only nine men plus Larry and myself. The Rabbi asked how old Larry and I were. We told him we were twelve. Then he said that between the two of us, if he added our ages together, we counted as one adult. And with just ten men neither one of us had better leave to go to the bathroom during the service. Eleven was better. That way you had a pisher. If someone had to go to the bathroom, you didn't end up short. Anyway we followed along as best we could. The service was over before an overtired teenager could blink.

Morning services were in the new Chapel downstairs. It had light colored wood paneling and comfortable wooden pews. We had Junior congregation on Saturday mornings there as well. It had a nice fresh smell, not like the old Chapel that had a musty smell with an overlay of whiskey, herring, sweat and Old Spice. Following services we went into the youth center where coffee and bagels with cream cheese were spread out on a table. Larry and I each helped ourself to a cup of coffee and a bagel then wandered back to our classroom.

We had a good size B'nai Mitzvah class that year. Surprisingly, there were more girls than boys. We boys had Bar Mitzvah ceremonies on Saturday morning; but girls, who were seen as not having the same religious obligations, nor could they be called up to the Torah, had their Bat Mitzvah ceremony on Friday evenings.

The other kids turned as Mark, Larry and I entered the room.

"Hey, how come they get to bring food in here?" demanded Scott Berman. Scott had gone to Huntington Elementary School with me. His father worked for Mr. Shaeffer.

Dr. Sherman, an optometrist and a volunteer teacher, sighed. "They went to services this morning, so they didn't have time for breakfast."

"It's not fair," gripped Scott.

"Life isn't fair. Get over it." Dr. Sherman seemed a bit grouchy this morning.

"I think we should be able to have snacks too," said Julie Fine. She was a raven-haired girl whose grandfather had been the rabbi at the synagogue for forty years. Her grandparents had made aliyah to Israel two years ago when Rabbi Bolotnikoff had retired.

Dr. Sherman seemed to shudder. In a minute he'd have a full-scaled uprising on his hands. Dr. Sherman was a slight, mild-mannered balding man in his forties. His wife Betty looked like the Librarian from hell with glasses perched on her nose and a frizzy short hairdo. They had three children. Josh, who sat quietly in the back row of our class, his older brother David who was in high school, and Janet, a mousy brown-haired girl who was in Morrie's split grade three-four class. Everyone in the Sherman household wore glasses. Sherman looked nervously at all of us. You could feel the nervousness and fear. Kids can sense this. It was as if we were a bunch of sharks circling our intended victim. His eyes scanned the class.

In the first row were Larry, Mark and I along with Sue Glass, whose father was a lawyer and on the synagogue executive. Sue had short dark hair and glasses. I wondered if Sherman had prescribed hers too. Next to her sat strawberry blonde Debbie Stein whose blue orbs kept making goo-goo eyes at Mark.

Behind us were Janet Greenstone, who I had an instant crush on, with her pageboy cut brown hair, Cindy Davidson, in short pigtails, her heavy auburn eyebrows down as she glared at Dr. Sherman, and Molly Weiner. Molly had blue eyes, light freckles and white blonde hair. The Weiner's had adopted her as an infant. She never said much in class. Next to her was Beth Levine, who was Larry's cousin. She was a small dainty girl with shoulder length light brown hair and a perky nose.

In the third row was redheaded Scott Berman, Julie Fine and Marilyn Scheckter, a dark haired willowy girl who had just moved to River City. Her father was the director at the local blood bank. Some of the boys referred to her as that 'vampire girl'. She was shy and quiet.

"Now let's get started with history. Please take your books out," said Dr. Sherman.

"I still don't think it's fair that they get to eat," muttered Scott.

"Maybe you should come to minyan then," said Larry.

"Enough! Open your books." Dr. Sherman's face seemed to be turning a bit red.

I reached down and took the book from the shelf under my seat. I put it on the spit of a tray, careful not to spill my coffee. And so, class began.

I ended up going for morning services at seven-thirty on Tuesday because I had an eye doctor appointment at nine-fifteen and it didn't pay to go to school then get pulled out. Morning services are short, maybe twenty-five minutes. The old guy leading it, Mr. Nussenbaum chanted very quickly and ended every sentence with an oy oy oy. We finished in twenty minutes. The men took off their Tefillin, or phylacteries, and tallit, both worn in the mornings as reminders of the six hundred and thirteen commandments we're obligated to do and to help concentration on the prayers.

Afterwards Rabbi Silverman suggested get something to eat, and since we had about an hour until my appointment, Dad agreed. Fact is, we would've gone somewhere before, because no way was I going to school without breakfast. Rabbi locked the side door of the synagogue and went to his Chevy Caprice. We got into our Ford station wagon, and followed, heading downtown. Dad turned off Pierce and pulled up at a small restaurant that sat between a stationery store and a menswear shop. The neon light sign read 'Bishops' and there was the sign of a chess piece. We got out and went inside. I knew Dad had coffee here a couple of times a week.

We walked in. It was dimly lit, most of the light came from outside through the large picture window scrawled across with Bishops' name. A row of booths was affixed to the wall on the far left. The rest of the room was scattered with square tables and chairs. There was a counter with a few stools. I saw the two waitresses bustling to fill coffees. A dim greasy haze hung over the entire place. You could smell bacon frying mixed with tobacco from cigarettes and cigars. I lost a bit of my appetite. A couple of men waved to us to join them. Tables were pushed together and we sat down. I sort of did a double take when I saw Father Victori, a tall dark haired man wearing a black suit. He was an ex- Catholic priest who'd gone over to the protestant side. His daughter Mary had been in my class in elementary school. Dave Litman's dad, a Lutheran minister, was there too. Dave and I had been in elementary school as well and shared homeroom class this year. In fact the truth was, this was the place that all the clergy gathered. We sat down. I sat at the end of the table and tried not to be noticed. Dad and Rabbi seemed on very friendly terms with the others. A waitress came over and laid down menus.

Rabbi and Dad ordered coffee. Dad got a hot chocolate for me.

I looked at the menu and decided on oatmeal. I knew Dad would order scrambled eggs fried in butter, and toast with marmalade. The waitress came back with coffees and my hot chocolate. She was a skinny middle aged lady with bleached blonde hair piled high on her head. She wore a black dress with a blue apron. I noticed a dollop of whipped cream floating on top of the hot chocolate and smiled.

The door opened and a cold wind blew into the restaurant scattering the blue haze of cigarette smoke. A short tubby man wearing a black suit with a white collar barreled up to our table. He was swearing profusely under his breath. "I swear the nuns need to beat those little bastards harder in class."

"Hi Father Mike, tough morning?" asked Mr. Litman.

"Ah Reverend," he nodded, then looked around the table and acknowledged the rest of us. "I went to do a christening and got me bottle of holy water and it smelled off. So's I look at it and I never seen yellow holy water before. When I find the little bugger that peed into the bottle of holy water, I'm gonna wallop him. The problem, men, is that the kids today have no respect "

"Well didn't Jesus turn water to wine?" said Rabbi Silverman. There was a grin on his face.

"Maybe, but I sure as hell know he didn't turn water to piss!"

Father Victori and my dad burst out laughing.

"On top of that, I think the altar boys have been getting into the wine."

"We can loan you a bottle of Mogen David," offered the Rabbi.

Father Mike looked at Silverman, "Well now Rabbi, that's mighty Christian of you."

Everyone burst out laughing.

Lots of people forget that clergy are human like anyone else. The profanity didn't surprise me. Dad swore when he was angry. He just didn't want to hear us doing it. It was sort of hypocritical. I remember when I was in second or third grade he heard me use the F-word. He'd been passing me in the cleaning delivery truck (back then he was going to Cantorial school at night to finish his degree) and heard my friends and I when we were walking home from school. I didn't realize I had been that loud. When he got home from work I got my mouth washed out with soap and a spanking-the spanking for walking through puddles with my new corrective shoes. The shoes were expensive and my parents didn't have a lot of money. That was the last time I did that, walking in puddles with new shoes. Anyway the fact is that priests, ministers, rabbis and cantors are people too. No one is perfect. We all have our idiosyncrasies. But people tend to put clergy, and other professional people, up on a pedestal. They are to serve as examples to their congregants and the community. Word spreads quickly if something is off kilter. People notice where you eat, what you eat, how much you drink. You are under the magnifying glass; my mom says that life is lived in a fishbowl.

The food came and the conversation settled around complaining about congregants. It didn't matter if you were Catholic, Protestant, Jewish or otherwise. If you had a board of trustees or directors, there was no way you could keep everyone happy. If you could please the majority then you were doing okay. And hopefully those congregants who liked you would put a bug in the board's ear when your contract came up. After the complaint session discussion moved to the Halloween UNICEF drive. Every year on the weekend of or near Halloween all the youth groups went out to collect for UNICEF. The city was divided into sections and each religious institution organized their youth to collect. This would be the first year I could do it since I was now in Junior High.

After breakfast Dad drove a few blocks and parked in front of a sandstone colored brick building where Dr. Sherman had his office. I hated wearing glasses. I'd been diagnosed and given a pair of bifocals in fifth grade. But then every patient of Sherman's had bifocals-even his three kids. He also made me do a bunch of goofy eye exercises, supposedly for strengthening the muscles, but I don't think it did squat. Fact was, I couldn't see worth shit without glasses. But maybe this time I could get some cooler frames. I was thinking black.

Chapter Three

The leaves dried, became brittle, and layered the green grass that was turning brown as October rolled through. The wind blew crackling dried leaves against fences and corners of houses and garages where they huddled together. Wood smoke subtly colored the cool air. Jack-O-Lanterns, crepe paper black cats, sheet ghosts blowing in the skeletal branches of trees dotted the neighborhood. It was my favorite time of year.

On the way home from school, I walked with Tim Shaunessy. Tim lived in a blue-framed house on Nebraska Street.

"You want to check the haunted garage?" he asked.

"I don't think ghosts come out during the day."

"You never know."

We walked past Tim's house and turned left on 21st street. There was a dark blue Victorian home with white trim and a gabled roof on the corner of 21st and Pierce. On the 21st street side was an old carriage house that had been converted into a garage. There looked to be a small apartment above. Metal mesh covered the windows, which were always dirty. We rubbed some of the dirt away with our hands and pressed our noses to the window. It was empty. You could see on the right a support beam that had separated two horse stalls. In the back, still up on hooks were some old harnesses. Local schoolboy rumor had it that a man had been hung there, supposedly for fooling around with the owner's daughter. At night a few guys claimed you could see the victim's body hanging from one of the rafters, his eyes wide staring at you as he tried to whisper, "Help me."

One year Paul Anderson and I went there on Halloween, hoping to see the hanging man. We never got the chance. Some neighbor's boxer got out and chased us halfway home. We ran like the hellhounds were after us. It took us a half dozen candy bars to recover from the fear and shock.

Halloween was in the air. Being in junior high, I figured this would be the last year I would go out trick'r treating. Though he didn't appear in the Journal comics, when I'd lived in Chicago I'd been a big fan of The Phantom. I had a stack of Gold Key comics to prove it. So, I had a navy blue hooded sweatshirt, Lone Ranger style mask, my old Fanner 50 holster and a black plastic automatic. The only problem was my glasses that I needed to see with. Mom suggested I wear the glasses over my mask. Yeah, right... one geezer hero coming up. In the end I opted not to wear glasses and just keep them handy in my sweatshirt pocket. I should've been Daredevil, Marvel's blind superhero.

This year Halloween fell on Saturday night. Typically we'd do all up and down Grandview for about a four-block stretch, then go over one to either Douglas or Summit and do the same. My parents took a ten percent cut. But that still left enough to last me until winter break. Luckily Paul's older sister Paige had agreed to take Robbie, Draytin and Morrie out, which left Paul and I to go with a couple of other kids in the neighborhood: Robby Cramer and Mike Patterson. Robbie lived across the street and up four houses. He had an older sister Janice who was quite the looker. Mike had moved to River City the previous year. Both he and Robbie were a year older than me. He had a younger sister, but she didn't hang with any of the kids in the neighborhood.

"So who are you supposed to be?" asked Rob.

"The Phantom, he's a comic strip character."

"I've heard of him. But doesn't he have two guns?" asked Mike.

"It's what I had."

Paul was dressed as the Lone Ranger. In previous years he'd gone as Superman. His mom had dyed a pair of long johns blue, and a pair of white briefs red. She'd gotten material from a fabric store and made him the cape. His yellow and red "S" had been made of felt and sewn on. His mother made a lot of the kid's clothes, so Halloween costumes hadn't been a problem. Thankfully the briefs covered up the trap drawer in the long johns. Otherwise it might have been a bit breezy.

Mike was dressed up as a gangster. He wore one of his dad's old black suits and had his old black plastic Tommy gun. Rob was dressed as Frankenstein. He'd enlarged the holes in his rubber mask so he could actually see where he was going. We set off down Grandview at a good pace, wanting to hit Sunny Hermman's house before all the good stuff was gone.

Sunny Hermman, a middle-aged bachelor, was a local attorney. He lived in his late parents' home, a modest two-story frame house down the street. Sunny loved kids and every year he put on this fantastic Halloween party for all the kids in the neighborhood. His maid laid out tables of treats and every kid picked their goodies. In addition to the store bought candy bars, licorice and waxed candy, there were popcorn balls, brownies, chocolate chip cookies and cupcakes. It was like hitting the mother lode at Virginia City during the silver rush.

By the time we got there the line was out the door and down the steps to the street, but we waited and were well rewarded for our patience. I snatched a couple of popcorn balls, one turquoise and the other red, along with a chocolate chip cookie and some red licorice.

"Let's go over to Summit," said Mike. We walked back to the corner of 21st Street, turned left and walked over a half block, hitting another five houses in the process. A couple of years ago a tornado had ripped down Summit Street. It deposited a car in someone's driveway, ripped off a roof of one house and hit the park and split a tree in half. We spent that night huddled in the basement with an old kerosene lantern for light. Our dog Shadow cowered on a blanket in the corner as we listened to the freight train winds and machine gun hail pocket the neighborhood like a Nazi blitzkrieg.

We were wandering down the street collecting the statutory loot as expected when Mike stopped us and asked if we wanted to do a Halloween trick.

"What'd you have in mind?" asked Rob.

"Mike pulled out a small paper back from his pocket.

"What's in it?" asked Paul.

Mike opened it up and told Paul to look. Paul barely peeked but the odorous smell wafted up like a genie out of a magic lamp. His face scrunched up and he back-pedaled fast. "Shit!"

I couldn't believe Mike had actually carried that in his pocket. Good thing it hadn't leaked. That would really have been shitty.

"Exactly," said Mike. He looked around and pointed to a white-framed two-story house across the street. "How about there?"

"So, what do you do?" I asked.

"We're gonna light this bag on fire and ring the doorbell. The guy will come out see the fire and stamp on the bag getting a foot load of shit," laughed Mike.

Well it certainly sounded fun. Hopefully we didn't burn the house down.

"When I ring the bell you guys run like hell," said Mike.

We walked across the street. Paul and I waited by the hedges that bordered the sidewalk. Rob kept an eye out on the street. It was already almost nine o'clock and the street was pretty deserted. I watched as Mike darted up the walk and placed the bag on the porch. He took a lighter out of his pocket, lit the bag and rang the doorbell.

'Run!" he gestured. It didn't take a second signal. We ran. As our footsteps echoed softly on the pavement, we heard the door creak open. A moment later we heard a gruff voice yell, "SONOFABITCH! SHIT! WHEN I GET MY HANDS ON..." The rest of it was lost on the night breeze. We stopped a block away to catch our breaths, laughing so hard our stomachs hurt.

"He might come after us," said Paul.

We looked at each other, ran across the street and down the steps next to the Belleview Apartments that led to the alley. We cross the alley and came through our back yard. In the shadows of the garage we felt safe. Mike and Rob continued on through our yard and across Grandview, heading for home. Paul peeked around the garage. It was quiet. He waved good-bye and headed down the alley to his house.

I pulled my hood off. My hair was drenched in sweat. I walked across the grass to the back walk and in through our enclosed porch to the back door. It was good to be home.

November 1964

November saw President Lyndon Johnson pound Republican presidential candidate Barry Goldwater, who had voted against the Civil Rights Act, in the national election. The Mars Mariner probe was launched to Mars. FBI Director J. Edgar Hoover declared Martin Luther King was a notorious liar. The Roman Catholic Church replaced Latin with English in American churches. The U.S.S.R. had another nuclear test in Eastern Kazakh.

On Sunday, November 1, we met at the synagogue. There were no religious school classes for the older grades. Instead, we were given a map and assigned a section to canvas for UNICEF. We received a small cardboard box with a slot in it and were paired up. Larry and I teamed up and would be dropped off into the ritzy area next to Grandview Park.

At first I let Larry do most of the talking. He was a schmoozer from way back. It was in his genes. You can't do sales unless you have the gift of gab; but actually it was pretty easy. The day was quite warm. I wore a light windbreaker over a plaid short-sleeved shirt, white jeans and tennis shoes. We walked along, up and down driveways, steps and front porches as we weaved our way around.

Larry lived in a different area and went to a different junior high. The only time we got to see each other was on weekends, mostly at shul unless we arranged for a sleepover. We usually chatted on the phone for a bit most nights unless our parents had a need. If you were lucky like I was, you had an extension in your room.

"Janet lives near you, right?" I asked as we walked up the steps to another front door. So far we'd been collecting a fair bit, except for one cheap bastard that after we rang the bell, tore out of his garage in his car and whizzed by us.

Larry smirked and glanced at me. "You got a crush on her?"

"She's cute."

"Hate to tell you this Slim, but she also prefers older guys-ones' that have driver's licenses. Most girls our age want guys a year or two older," said Larry. "That's what my brother said."

"So what does that leave us with?"

"Ferkacht. The problem is the tit factor. Those girls we're attracted to have tits, but we don't drive yet, so we aren't on their radar. The fact that girls tend to mature faster than guys means that they're attracted to older guys. Whereas the young girls have no tits, hence we have no interest in them.

The door opened and a frumpy old lady with glasses perched on the edge of her narrow nose and sagging breasts under her housedress looked at us. "What do you want?"

Chapter Four

Shop class was the bane of my existence in Junior High. It was required. We did wood working the first semester and were to do metal work the second. Our teacher was Mr. Woods-I kid you not, that was his name - he was slim, ramrod straight like a telephone pole and spoke in a monotone voice. He had brown hair crew-cut and wore black horned-rimmed glasses, and cotton checkered short-sleeve shirts. No sense of humor whatsoever, but then considering he was dealing with seventh grade boys I don't blame him. The first month we learned about all the power tools, safety requirements and warnings about cutting parts of our anatomy off. You do have to wonder what the administration was thinking putting heavy power tools into the hands of inept, immature young boys. Because you know telling us about the potential for danger isn't really going to sink in.

The second week we started projects beginning with drafting plans. We had two projects: a desktop book holder and a lamp. The book holder looked pretty easy, but it turned out I was sadly deluded. First I drilled two dowel holes in the wrong places having to fill them in, and then had to purchase an additional piece of wood because I managed to cut the piece the wrong way. Needless to say I fit the stereotype about Jews and tools.

I had shop either twice or three times a week depending on our alternating schedule. My stomach would tighten up and I'd get the sweats walking into class. Tim was in the class with me and he was worse at using tools than I was. If Mr. Wood could've transferred students, I'm sure we would've been among the selectees. But we persevered because we had no choice in the matter.

The rest of junior high was ok. English and Geography was easy. Math was hard. It was about as stressful as shop. This was a year of transition for that curriculum and the discovery of positive and negative numbers. My parents, in their infinite wisdom, as well after having a call from my Math teacher Mrs. Soleburg, hired a tutor. Mrs. Wright was an elderly white haired grandmother type retired teacher. She lived two blocks down from us. I went to her house twice a week after school and worked on math over a glass of milk and shortbread cookies. Yes, I was supposed to watch my weight, but math was very stressful. It's amazing how milk and cookies reduced that stress.

Physical Education was also required and my athletic skill was non-existent. Coach Pitt was a modern Samson. His biceps were bigger than my thighs. He had us running laps around the block for warm-ups. If it was rainy we ran steps in the auditorium and usually somewhere going across one of the aisles, some smartass would always flip a seat down and you'd rack yourself if you didn't keep alert. We played touch football (weather permitting), as well as basketball. I could shoot but couldn't run and dribble at the same time to save my soul. The most embarrassing part of gym was showering after. The penalty of not doing it, after one warning, was the paddle (of course not listening and horsing around-like snapping towels, theft or bullying got you the same thing). Coach Pitt had a two-foot long paddle with three holes drilled in through it so there was no slowing from airflow. You were told to bend over, grab your ankles and brace yourself.

They had one huge stall with eight showerheads. I hadn't showered in a communal shower before. The basic rules were: look down and don't stare. Thankfully my body had begun to mature and I looked a bit older than I was. Others were not as fortunate and nicknames like 'Stumpy', 'Baldnuts' and 'Dinky-doodle' stuck.

I had started learning violin when I was in third grade. We had an excellent music program at Huntington Elementary School lead by Mr. Israelson. He was a tall man with salt and pepper hair and a very gentle demeanor. He was a member of the Reform Temple, Shir Shalom. We had a school band and orchestra and did a concert in the spring. I had continued with violin and orchestra at Northside under the direction of Mr. Chestnut, who also taught music for student enrichment. This meant you sang. He taught us how to do warm up scales, and we'd usually do a couple of songs, mostly folk songs. He'd built a harpsichord from a kit and would accompany us with it. It sounded pretty cool. However he did want to hear us sing and occasionally would have us sing a line or two individually in front of the class. I'd never sung in front of others solo before. And of course somehow he knew my dad and who do you think his first victim was when he decided to have us sing? Yup, you got it. I was nervous. My mouth felt dry. My heart was pounding. Yet another place to be ridiculed or so many thought. Looking around the class, there were a few faces sighing in relief, and a couple of assholes that couldn't wait for me to open my mouth. But thankfully I had my dad's genes. I could sing. My voice was changing gradually and I didn't squeak, grunt or crack. So I sang. I impressed Mr. Chestnut and apparently a few of the girls. One in particular who I later found out was named Barb Zeffman, a cute sloe-eyed brunette, with a nice tight figure.

After enduring such trauma during the day after school, twice a week, I continued Bar Mitzvah lessons with my dad at the synagogue. He expected me to practice every night. Dad had given me a record of my Haftorah and another one with the liturgy. He had a recording machine that made recordings on vinyl disks. Standard recording speed was 33 and a 1/3 rpm (revolutions per minute). So even though the records were the same size as 45's, they played like albums. By mid-November I was a quarter of the way through learning my haftorah. My ability to read music was a plus as I practiced and memorized the cantillation symbols. However, I struggled learning Musaf (an additional part of the morning service symbolizing the extra sacrifices that were made in the Temple on Shabbat) with a section in the Amidah called Tikantah Shabbat. There was a Hebrew word *'Vat-tzah-vame'* that I kept tripping over. The word meant: and you commanded us'. I kept saying: *vuh- TITS-a vame*. Must've been my hormones affecting my thought processes; but it drove my dad to distraction which meant he'd yell and pace around his office not comprehending how I could keep making the same mistake week after week. But at least I wasn't spending hours conjugating Hebrew verbs.

Chapter Five

The air grew crisper. Some mornings hoarfrost covered the trees like fairy dust. The grass dried up, its life-blood sucked to death, turned brown and crunchy. The trees stood naked like skeletons along the street. Though bright in the sky, even the sunshine was cold. Thanksgiving weekend was approaching. I learned that the Blackman family was coming for Thanksgiving dinner. We got Thursday off and Friday morning, but we had classes Friday afternoon. There was an Underdog cartoon special on Thursday morning that I hoped I'd get to watch. It was Beth Zion's turn to host the non-denominational interfaith service that year. And of course we had to go. But at least we could drive to shul.

The service consisted of several English readings and a few songs sung by one of the church choirs and ours. Dad did America the Beautiful and another prayer of Thanksgiving from our liturgy. Rabbi Silverman and one of the pastors spoke briefly. It was over in an hour, and then everyone rushed home to get their turkeys in the oven.

One of the countries' kosher slaughterhouses was in River City. The word Kosher means ritually fit and refers to the idea that being made in the image of God, we need to be aware of what we put in our bodies. In fact, in chapter eleven of Vayikra, or Leviticus, a whole chapter tells us which animals we can eat, and which we can't. Kashrut is a way of keeping the Jewish community closer. (Dad said a lot of Christian versions had this part edited out.) You don't have to worry about what you're going to be served at someone's house. But the main thing Kashrut does is to teach self-discipline.

Kashrut extends, because of the expansion of the laws in the Talmud, to how an animal is slaughtered and what dishes it can be served on. The animal must be killed humanely and with as little pain as possible. A shoichet, a person trained in ritual slaughter, cuts the jugular vein quickly. According to the Torah, blood is a symbol of life, and we are commanded to not eat meat with blood in it or it is an insult to God. Therefore the animal is drained of blood, most kosher meat is soaked in salt water to draw the blood out, and the meat is de-veined.

Dad had the opportunity to make some extra money and be trained as a shoichet. He was invited down to the kosher facility. I'm not sure what happened, but apparently he decided it wasn't a job for a nice Jewish boy. Guess he didn't have the stomach for it.

Saul's Kosher Meats was two blocks down on Grandview in a basement shop with a side street entrance. His shop was part of the Indian Hotel Apartments, a tall six story red brick building on the corner of 16th and Grandview. Saul Schwartz, a middle-aged man with sad eyes, a Holocaust survivor, was owner and sole proprietor. When Saul had his sleeves rolled up, you could see the concentration camp number tattooed on his arm. Dad always spoke either German or Yiddish to him. My Dad was from Germany as well, and was almost shot crossing the border out of Germany. He and Grammy, in September 1939, left Holland on the one of the last boats before the Nazi's invaded. Saul was a 'landsman'.

Saul was a nice guy, but according to Dad must've learned to cut meat at the hacksaw school of butchering. I don't know where Dad learned or accumulated the skills, but somehow he knew how to cut meat and Saul would let him cut our own steaks. Anyway, for Thanksgiving we got a turkey from one of our members, the Fishbergs who owned a turkey farm outside town. Dad would go down to the kosher slaughtering plant, and then he'd take it to Saul's to be prepared. This Thanksgiving we had a massive turkey- around twenty pounds.

As soon as we got home, Mom set the table and ordered us to bring some folding chairs from the basement. Then she shooed us out so she could cook, with dad helping. I knew she was making Brussels sprouts, mashed sweet potatoes and carrot tzimmis. Dad was making a salad.

Morrie and I wandered into the living room and watched the *Underdog* Thanksgiving TV special on our 19" Zenith black and white TV. It sat on a TV stand in a corner of the living room near the fold out desk. Afterwards I left Morrie to his own devices and took my bike for a ride down to Klages. It was Thursday and I hoped that his store might be open and that maybe the new shipment of comic books came in. It was the perfect day. Cool enough for a jacket but not so cold for gloves or a hat. The wind tossed my hair around as I pedaled down the street, turning left on 20th to Pierce two blocks over. The ride was good exercise but for naught. Klages was closed tighter than a tavern on Sunday. But I couldn't blame him. It was a holiday. So I returned home.

The Andersen kids weren't out. They always had a big Thanksgiving dinner and I knew they had family driving in from outside the city. I sat on the front step of the walk. The street was deserted.

I went around back, got the leash and Shadow and together we went for a walk. I loved walking in the neighborhood. The homes were neat, well cared for, and gave a feeling of security and order. However when Shadow had to poop, I always tried to steer him to an inconspicuous spot. He could have some pretty good-sized poops. If a little kid stepped in it, it'd be like being swallowed in quicksand.

It was a safe town and a safe neighborhood. Unlike Chicago, no one locked their doors. Neighbors knew each other. You didn't worry walking in the neighborhood no matter the time of day. Though one summer Dad parked in front of the house and when he went to go to minyan in the morning there was an Indian sleeping in the back seat of the Buick. Dad woke him up and gave him a quarter to get a cup of coffee. He thanked dad for letting him sleep in the car.

And another time, a couple of years before, Sonny Hermann had his house broken into and some stuff stolen. Paul Anderson and I went over and dusted for fingerprints with stuff I made from my chemistry set. At the time we were die-hard Hardy Boy readers and figured if they could solve mysteries, so could we. I even had a copy of the *Hardy Boys' Detective Handbook*, which was our bible. The fellow had jimmied a side window and climbed in. Sonny had been away on business. The guy took some jewelry. The police investigated and had descriptions of the stolen articles sent to the pawnshops. I don't know if Sonny ever got it back. Paul and I didn't find the crooks either. Of course not knowing where to look or what to do with the fingerprints we found probably didn't help any.

Shadow and I walked up Grandview then down 24th until the road curved onto Solway Drive and edged around Grandview Park. Shadow was having a good time, stopping and sniffing trees, bushes, grass. He had a really good time last year when Mrs. Rosenberg and Mrs. Broitman came to visit. The ladies liked checking up on Mom. Anyway they were sitting on the couch when Shadow came over. They were afraid of him and sat like rigid statues. Shadow took a liking to Mrs. Rosenberg and started humping her leg. I mean he was going at her like she was a piece of steak. He was shaking and shimming faster than a Go-Go dancer. Mom called me to take Shadow outside. When I came in, it was very hard to control myself. I felt the laughter about ready to burst out of me like an overcooked hotdog. Mrs. Rosenberg was absolutely petrified. She was sitting stiff as a board and Shadow was humping her leg with everything he had. In fact, I'd never seen a dog smile until that moment. I managed to drag Shadow off her, with Morrie chiming in to Mrs. Rosenberg, "You know he only does that to people he really likes." I could hear Mom apologizing profusely, though I knew she was having a hard time keeping a straight face.

The dog pished at almost every lamppost and made a humungous dump next to some hedges that bordered the sidewalk of a fieldstone ranch house. After that he seemed to move more quickly. And so did I.

It was mid-afternoon by the time I got back to the house. I could smell the turkey baking in the oven. Morrie was playing in his room. He had his Northwest Mounted Police play-set up, a gift from Cousin Toby in Minneapolis last year. The metal store front- the town was set up on the desk, the prospector's camp up on the toy box top. He was directing a blue molded Mountie on a brown horse out of town. No doubt some claim jumpers had just shot the prospector and it was Sergeant Preston to the rescue. I had the urge to play with him, but kids in Jr. High didn't play with toy cowboys or soldiers. I went upstairs to my room and dug into a couple of issues of *The Flash* and settled down on my bed to read.

Footsteps creaked on the landing. My door was open and I turned my head right to see April Blackman coming up the stairs. I could hear my heart beat faster. I put my comic down and sat up, hoping she wouldn't notice the sudden hard on I got when I saw her.

April wore a red plaid tartan skirt, white knee socks and a white blouse. She had a red hair band in her dark brown hair. She looked pretty, but of course, God forbid, I actually compliment her.

"Hi."

"Happy Turkey Day," I responded. "Come on in."

April walked into the room and sat on the edge of the bed. "How many comics do you read?"

"Several titles. Mostly DC." I put down *The Flash*. "I like the art work. It works for the character and the story."

I handed April the comic. She looked at the cover. *Flash* #149 had a dramatic picture of the Flash on TV unmasked. "Hmmmm."

"It'd be pretty neat to be the fastest man alive," I said.

She looked at me. "I can think of other superpowers that'd be neater."

"Like being able to fly? "

"Yeah, and maybe super-strength."

"X-ray vision would be cool."

"X-ray vision is over-rated," said April.

"Not if you want to find out what your parent's got you for Chanukah or your birthday." (Or look at girls' underwear I thought.)

"Good point," she said.

I sat up, pulling my legs up and giving April some room. She looked really cute. God, I was such an idiot. "So-uh-how's school going?"

April looked at me, her eyebrow arched. "Really?"

"Did you see the Man from U.N.C.L.E. last week? With the two Napoleons?"

"Yeah, it's one of my favorite shows. I really like Ilya."

"Really? It seems all the girls say that. I prefer Napoleon Solo."

"David McCallum is cute."

I rolled my eyes.

"What?" demanded April.

"Nothing," I said.

She continued to stare at me, then huffed, and rolled her eyes.

We fell back into an easy silence, both reading comics. I went to the bathroom and dug out the latest issue of *Detective Comics* that featured Batman and Robin fighting the Zodiac Master.

I put down my comic. "Do you want to help me with the comic I'm making?"

"Okay, but do I get to use the ink this time?"

I paused for a moment then said, "I guess."

I'd been making homemade comics for several years, usually giving them to my cousins. I created a couple of DC rip-offs like Speed, a super-fast hero who got his powers from being transfused with alien blood.

And Nightowl, a former soldier turned vigilante in the Batman and Hawkman motif, but whose wings allowed him to glide. I was working on a story of Speed, using techniques that Carmine Infantino, the Flash artist used. I really liked his style. I penciled the story, then used India ink, and colored the stories with watercolor or colored pencils. I would type the dialogue in the balloons after penciling. I had a natural knack for cartooning. I guess I got it from my mom's side. My Aunt Eileen was a professional painter in Chicago. But Audrey was better at coloring, and she would help me on the times she came over. Usually it was just Paul Andersen and myself doing them. Paul was a good artist. He took after his mom who was studying art at the local college.

I got the finished pages I'd penciled and put them on my desk. I got the pen and ink out. I took my drawing pad and sat down on my bed to pencil the rest of the fight scene. Nightowl was after a purse-snatcher.

We sat quietly apart working. Smells of turkey and stuffing drifted up from downstairs. Occasionally I looked up and stared at April. I thought about what Larry had said about girls. April had no tits, but she was cute, and I still couldn't help watching her. It was a conundrum.

April turned and caught me. "What?"

"Nothing."

"Then why are you staring at me?"

"Uh-no reason."

She huffed and turned and went back to inking.

Sometimes she irritated me. Other times, well...

"Dinner!" Mom called up.

April capped the inkbottle and went into the bathroom to wash her hands. Fat chance of her getting India ink stains off in one wash. Her mom would be angry.

"Do you have a scrub brush?" asked April.

I went into the bathroom and reached into the shower stall and took out a short nailbrush. I tossed it to her. "Here."

I stood there and watched as she scrubbed her hands. She turned and looked up at me. "Do you mind?"

I stepped outside the bathroom and she shut the door. I heard the lock click.

Not bothering to wait, I went downstairs for dinner.

Mom's turkey and stuffing were great. We sat crammed around the dining room table. Dad and Mom on the ends, Mr. Blackman, Mrs. Blackman, and Susie on the side closest to the kitchen, and Morrie, April and I across from them. Dad said Hamotzi, the blessing over the bread, and we started passing around mashed potatoes, breaded cauliflower and peas while Dad carved the turkey.

Mrs. Blackman looked across the table at her daughter. "What did you do to your hand, April?"

April glanced at her hand; there was a smudge of India ink on the fingertip of her middle finger. She looked back at her mother. "I was helping Jeff do some work on the comic he's making."

Mrs. Blackmans dark brown eyes zeroed in on me.

"It's no big deal, it'll wear off in a few days," I said.

"Oh for heaven's sake!" she muttered.

I glanced at April. She looked at me and shrugged.

"Well, how's the turkey?" asked Mom. She was a master at misdirecting.

Chapter Six

Things settled down into the usual routine after Thanksgiving: school, Bar Mitzvah lessons, piano lessons, violin practice, and occasionally getting together with Larry, Mark and David. We were looking forward to the new James Bond film *"Goldfinger"* that was due out in December and made plans to see it during winter break.

The first Chanukah candle lighting was on November 29th. Mom had set a TV table up in front of the fireplace and put the menorah on it. Below were a few wrapped packages. Years ago, our parents had given us the choice to get all the gifts of one night or to have them spread out over the holiday. I opted for the latter, while Morrie, greedy little bastard he was, wanted it all. And that's what he got. He ripped into those gifts like a fat kid searching a cupboard for a box of Oreos. And then he sat in glory amid shreds of wrapping paper. As for myself I was content with a new Hardy Boy mystery, *Sign of the Crooked Arrow*, and a 45 of The Beatles' *I Feel Fine*. In the nights that followed I got another book, pajamas from Aunt Rose-she sent me a new pair every year, and some other smaller items like socks. My grandparents sent Chanukah gelt-money. That would keep me in supply of comics and a couple of movies until my birthday in April. Morrie on the other hand got nothing. Nada. Zip. And there he sat night after night looking forlorn as I slowly opened the gifts. He'd look up at Mom and Dad with those sad puppy dog brown eyes, and all my parents would say was, "Well you made your choice."

Lots of people think Chanukah is the Jewish Christmas, but nothing could be further from the truth. Chanukah has nothing to do with Christmas. Christmas celebrates Christ's birth, in their belief that he was the

Messiah, and was combined with the pagan winter solstice holiday by the Church to make it more popular among the pagans, which is why it falls on the 25th of December. A lot of Biblical scholars think Jesus was actually born in the spring.

Chanukah celebrates the concept of religious freedom, and the victory of the Hasmoneons over the Assyrian-Greeks. Around 165 b.c.e. Israel was under Greek control and like North American society Greek culture was very popular. To be 'in', you had to be Greek. Sort of a play on Tim's joke, that you're either Irish or want to be. Some of Israelite society, mostly in the urban areas, followed the Greek lifestyle. They were called *Hellenists*. But more traditional Jews, those living in the rural areas want none of it. The Maccabees (Hammers- because they pounded their enemies), as the rebels became known, in the onset were the sons of the high priest Mattathais along with a number of followers. They won the rebellion in three years, using guerilla tactics. Thankfully the Romans were rattling their upstart swords. Egypt and Greece didn't have troops to support the soldiers stationed in Israel. Anyway, after their victory, they re-dedicated the Temple and restored Jewish practices and religions.

Later in Jewish history, the Rabbis had a hard time supporting the concept of Chanukah and tried to ban it for three reasons: First, at that time Israel was under Roman rule and the last thing you wanted to do was piss off the Romans. They tended to tie people to crosses, among other nasty tortures; Can anyone say 'sedition'? Also, Chanukah celebrated a military victory. The Rabbis were uncomfortable having a holiday that celebrated a war. It's just not the Jewish way. We don't take pleasure in taking lives. But the holiday was too popular among the people. So the Rabbi's wrote a Midrash, a story, to solve this problem. They came up with the concept that when the Maccabees went to rededicate the Temple, they found only enough holy oil to light the Menorah, the symbol of God's divine presence, for one day; but a miracle happened and the oil lasted for eight days which gave them enough time to process more holy oil. And that's why Chanukah is celebrated for eight days according to the Midrash. In actual fact, it was probably because when Solomon built the Temple, he celebrated it for eight days because when the Temple was completed, it fell around Sukkot, the Jewish Thanksgiving that was a weeklong holiday. At any rate, it's considered a minor holiday on the Jewish calendar, but a very popular one among us Jews-especially kids.

Initially, children would get sweets or a few coins, Chanukah gelt, as a reward for being a good student. Later, as Christmas got more commercialized, Jewish parents felt that they didn't want their kids to be present deprived so the tradition began of giving small gifts on each night of Chanukah. Unlike Christians, we weren't about to blow our yearly budget and go into debt. Usually Morrie and I got a game, some books, maybe a small toy. Now the Andersen kids got gobs of stuff. One year, our parents realized that we'd been nosing about looking to see what we were getting. So they conspired with Paul's parents and they did a hidden present swap. When Morrie and I came upon a wrapped doll, we were stunned. But then Paul and Robin reported that they found gifts with Chanukah wrapping in their house and we figured it out. Apparently so did our parents. The next year Dad locked our presents in the trunk of his car.

December 1964

In early December police arrested eight hundred students at Berkley who were advocating Free Speech. The Beatles released their "For Sale" album. Dr. Martin Luther King was awarded the Nobel Peace Prize, and later the U.S.

detonated another A-bomb in Nevada. But for me it was December and winter break couldn't come fast enough.

In River City, it snowed the first week of December. A good, mid-western snowstorm that dropped a foot of heavy white stuff and covered the gray brown lawns and bare trees. The city was transformed into a snowbound frozen world. Cars and buses had a hard time making it up Grandview. And for us, that meant that sledding season was in. But that would have to wait for the weekend. After school I stomped and sloshed down Pierce to the synagogue for my lesson with Dad.

At the synagogue I sat in his office and recited what I had learned of my Haftorah. Dad leaned back in his chair and said, "Looks like you've been studying. You're making progress."

I smiled. Getting praise is better than getting yelled at. And then he rewarded me by assigning two more verses to learn. We went over them, Dad breaking them down into musical phrases that I repeated several times before moving on to the next one. Then we looked at the Musaf section of the service, most of which I already knew, but he had me review everything and then assigned me another section of prayer to learn.

"After the winter break," he said. "It's time to start working on your speech."

"That shouldn't be too hard," I replied. Writing in English was easy. Little did I know what I was in for.

***

In English class, we were assigned to write a script about a job interview. It was a section we were studying in English, God knows why, since we couldn't legally work until we were sixteen. But a few kids did have paper routes or worked in their parent's store. Anyway, Tim Shaunessy and I walked downtown to his Uncle's radio station to write and record a job interview. It was a Saturday afternoon and the offices were empty. Tim took me into an empty sparsely furnished office containing a brown metal desk, a filing cabinet and three metal and vinyl straight back chairs. On the desk was a reel-to -reel tape recorder. Our interview ended up straight out of vaudeville. But then both Tim and I had watched a lot of Marx Brothers, Three Stooges, and Abbott and Costello movies on TV. Tim used the tape recorder to record the skit when we were done. We listened to the playback and paid attention to our delivery. We ended up rehearsing it a few times until we could do it without laughing.

A week later, we were on. Most of the kids who came before us spoke in stilted voice. They were nervous getting up in front of the class. A couple of kids in drama and could act actually presented what we guessed were realistic scenarios. I wonder how much help their parents had given them.

Tim and I got up in front of the students. Tim sat at Mrs. Anderson's desk. I waited by the classroom door, pretended to knock. I made a knocking sound effect with my mouth.

Tim as Mr. Wolfman: Come in.

Dr. I.M. Nuts (me): Are you Mr. Harry Wolfman?

Wolfman: Yes, I am. Please come in.

Doctor Nuts: Thank you. I am Dr. I.M. Nuts and I'm here to apply for your morticians' job that you advertised in the Saturday Evening Ghost.

(Some kid groaned from the back of the room)

Wolfman: Take a chair.

Dr. Nuts: No thank you, I have enough chairs already.

(A few kids laughed and snickered)

Wolfman: No, I mean sit down.

(I sat down in a wooden chair on the opposite side of the desk and Tim and I continued our interview.)

Wolfman: Do you have a high school education?

Dr. Nuts: Yes, I graduated from the Morgue Public High School in Transylvania.

Wolfman: I take it you graduated from college?

Dr. Nuts: Unfortunately not really. I was expelled for bodysnatching.

Wolfman: I see. So where did you work first?

Dr. Nuts: I first worked for Mummy's Home-made Tomb Company.

Wolfman: What happened to that job?

Dr. Nuts: I got so wrapped up in my work I was embalmed.

Wolfman: And where did you work next?

Dr. Nuts: At the Dracula Dynamite Company.

Wolfman: Did you enjoy working there?

Dr. Nuts: I got a bang out of it.

(A couple more kids laughed)

Wolfman: I see, do you have any references that are alive?

Dr. Nuts: Yes, I once worked with Dr. Stein- Dr. Frank N. Stein. His telephone number is Transylvania 13131313.

(Tim pretended to write down the information.)

Wolfman: Well, I'm not sure about hiring you.

Dr. Nuts: Mr. Wolfman, Oh please, hire me. You don't know what it's like being a failure all your life.

(I slid off the chair and went down on my knees. I glanced over and saw Mrs. Anderson staring at the floor and shaking her head.)

Wolfman: Well, you've had a long time to get used to it.

(The class burst out in laughter.)

Tim paused and pretended to think. He stroked his non-existent beard. Rolled his eyes and looked cross-eyed at the class that got a smattering of chuckles.

Wolfman: Well I guess you're hired. I will contact Dr. Stein. As for your salary, you will receive fifty dollars a week, and if, as we say it, you should drop dead, you'll receive free burial services in the plot of your choice. Will that be satisfactory?

Dr. Nuts: Yes, and thank you.

Wolfman: Okay, report to work at midnight. And remember our slogan: We'll be the last to let you down.

Dr. Nuts: You won't live to regret it. Good-bye.

Wolfman: Good-bye.

We finished. The class was in an uproar, and it took a lot that we didn't break up laughing too. Our teacher, Mrs. Anderson, just rolled her eyes again and looked at the ceiling. It wasn't quite what she had expected. After all, she really didn't know us all that well. I suspect it was something she probably started to regret too.

In Geography class, as I've said, I noticed a sloe-eyed auburn young lady whose name was Barb Zeffman. She was Jewish. Her parents were members of the Reform Temple, and she lived one block over on Summit and maybe two blocks down from me. Not that I was following her or anything. Barb was short, but had nice curves. Falling head over heels for a girl without really knowing her was typical of me. I'd been noticing girls since I was four and had a few crushes during my relatively short existence. Girls, it seemed, were always on my mind.

When Larry came over we used to play a game called, 'Which would You rather Do', where we'd create some sort of sexual or erotic scenario and have to pick which female celebrity we'd like. Usual choices were Leslie Gore, Petula Clark, Stella Stevens, Sandra Dee, Sally Fields, the girls on *Gilligan's Island*, one of the Bond beauties or the latest heartthrob, Diana Rigg who played Emma Peel on the Avengers. The fact is that we had girls and, more specifically, naked girls on our minds. Puberty, hormonal overload, call it what you will, we were horny with semi-permanent erections. But we were also totally inexperienced. At least Larry had an older brother who could share knowledge and tips. I had no one. However, what I did have was a stash of some of my dad's old girlie magazines that were squirreled away with some old music that he kept in a box in my closet. He'd probably forgotten they were there. But I discovered them when I was nosing around after I moved into my room. Larry and I studied them religiously. We should've studied for our Bar Mitzvahs so well. But then, they were more interesting than our Bar Mitzvah material.

My nosiness also helped me discover a stash of Playboy magazines in my parents' nightstand drawer along with a paperback copy of Ian Flemings' James Bond novel *On Her Majesty's Secret Service*. Now I'd seen *Dr. No*, the first Bond movie-Dad had taken me when I was ten. We went to an early evening showing-actually for once, getting there on time; but I didn't realize that the movie was based on a book. I 'borrowed' the book; since it was obvious Dad was done reading it. It turned out this was much better than the Hardy Boys.

Another time when Larry came over, we were fortunate when my parents left with Morrie. We stole into their bedroom and perused through the issues of Playboy magazines. It was like discovering buried treasure. When we were done, I made sure the magazines were put away in the same order that they were. No one was the wiser. And so, began my descent into the phase of raging hormones.

***

December moved on like a glacier. As its end drew near, teachers cowered and bribed us with candy canes. Like starving wolves we could scent blood as Christmas holidays approached. We were ravenous for freedom. No more assignments. No more studying. FREEDOM! And so on Wednesday December 23 we burst out the school doors like a herd of charging rhinos, and were released for Christmas break. Snow swirled down upon us. The wind whipped the flakes, shooting them like shrapnel. My face stung as I walked into the wind. I pulled my parka hood down and slogged on, like Sgt. Preston in an arctic storm pursuing claim jumpers. At the top of 24th Street I turned left down Grandview. The snowdrifts were higher than my boots, I moved onto the snow covered grass strip that lay between the street and the sidewalk. I had no intention of falling on my ass and sliding down the snow and ice covered sidewalk.

When I got home, Shadow greeted me and followed me down to the basement. I hung my parka on the clothesline to dry out. Then I went upstairs to my room and flopped on the bed. My red Haftorah book lay on top of the old Royal typewriter, which sat on the stand next to my bed. I stared at it; but learning by osmosis wasn't going to happen. I sighed and snatched the book. I pulled out the portable record player from under my bed, and started studying. I reviewed what I had learned and began on the new verses that Dad had assigned me. Over and over I listened, sang along with Dad's voice on the record, like searching for oil, I tried to drill it into my head. Half an hour later I turned off the machine and stared up at the ceiling. Oy. I rolled over and went into the bathroom. I dragged out the new 80 page Giant, a 25th anniversary issue of *Batman* containing a variety of reprinted stories mostly from the '50's, and the latest issue of *Green Lantern* #33 that showed Dr. Polaris blasting Green Lantern. Now this would relax my brain. I knew I had more studying to do for my Bar Mitzvah, but it could wait until after dinner.

Chapter Seven

On Sunday, it snowed again. Chained tires churned and rumbled down the street like mini-tanks. The sky was a dismal gray and all thoughts of sledding vanished as a cold wind whipped the flakes around like bullets smacking against the windshield. The wipers on our car became encrusted and tended to smear rather than clear the snow off the windshield. Dad had to stop and manually clean the wipers off. The churches had let out, and the streets were clogged. We stopped at a traffic light on 18th and Douglas and watched as cars crawled up the hill. I had gone to minyan with my Dad, and then had an extra lesson. It hadn't been that great, despite my studying. Afterwards,it turned out we weren't going directly home. Dad had to drop off another Haftorah record to Arnie Levitz who'd managed to break his. The Levitz family lived out on Country Club Blvd. We turned right on to Pierce at 20th street, Dad not wanting to chance sliding down 18th Street. At 25th street we turned and headed down Country Club Boulevard, past the Sunset Shopping Center and back into the ritzier part of town with large lawns and sprawling ranch homes. The car clanked along. Traffic thinned. I looked out the window and into the gray and white landscape.

Dad was quiet as he drove. Occasionally he'd glance at me. I guess this was quality father son time, but neither of us knew quite what to do. I smiled, then turned my head and stared out the window at the snowy street. A few minutes later he pulled up in front of a red brick ranch house with white trim. "I'll only be a minute." He grabbed the record that sat on the seat between us and got out. I watched him trudge up the snow-covered walk to the front door. I couldn't see who came to the door. A few minutes later he walked back, got into the car and we drove home.

There was a time, right after Morrie was born that my parents split up for a few weeks. We went to live with Nana and Grandpop, my mom's folks. My parents fought a lot during that time. It had been pretty hard to keep from hearing the yelling at each other. Dad wasn't happy with his job or jobs. Mom was frustrated with Grandma Sara and Aunt Rose. They always came over on Saturday afternoons to see if Mom was living up to their expectations. Thankfully Mom and Dad made up. I remember the day Dad came to bring us back home and I got this neat army play set with plastic soldiers, trucks, tanks and planes. It was shortly after that Dad went to night classes to finish his Cantorial school. Things were better then, even though we saw less of him during the week.

When we got home, Morrie was sprawled out on his bedroom floor playing with his toy cowboys. I was a bit envious. I wasn't sure what I wanted to do

I went upstairs to my room. I looked out the window and watched the snow whirl around. The snowflakes were like dancers in the air moving to complicated rhythms.

***

Larry and I were supposed to get together this afternoon at his place, but given the road conditions that wouldn't happen. I hadn't seen much of Paul lately either, but Sunday after church his family had their main dinner. He'd be busy. Boredom looked to be staring me in the face. Though I know I had some reading to do for science class, and, of course, Dad would expect me to spend at least a half an hour or so working on the new Haftorah verses. All I wanted to do was goof off. Hopefully the snow would stop and then we could go sledding. Sledding was my winter sport.

I didn't ski like the Rabbi, who had broken his arm the year before when he hit a tree at the park. I didn't ice skate-though my parents did try. When I was little they took me to the lagoon at Lincoln Park. It was a popular skating place. They put my skates on and took me out on the ice. Holding my hands they let me glide with them. Then they let go. My balance alone was not great and I fell smack down on my ass. After falling a few times I decided that skating wasn't for me. However, sledding was. There were two hills overlooking the lagoon and a path on the smaller one was fairly open. My buddies and I would go up on the top and slide down, skidding over the walking path and onto the lagoon. We'd whiz across to the opposite bank-skaters beware.

River City was built on the hills and bluffs overlooking the Missouri river. The street stretched up steeply for three blocks from where our house was, with only 21st street breaking it. We'd haul our sleds up the alley and take off back down, building a fair bit of speed. Of course the problem was three-fold when we did this. We'd usually come to a stop in front of the Belleview Apartment garage door; or have to skid around a car coming down the little used 21st street. But the biggest danger was cars and trucks coming up the alley. A couple of years before, a milk truck was coming up, stopping to make deliveries. Funny it hadn't been there the last time we'd gone down several minutes before; but we were undaunted. I'm sure we scared the crap out of the driver. We were whizzing down the alley; the truck had just stopped. There was nowhere to go. No way I could fit under it. I spotted a snow bank next to a telephone pole by a garage. I rolled off into a snow bank, as did Paul. Morrie was coming up fast behind us. But he was so small and skinny that he slid right under the truck and took off unscathed down the rest of the hill. Good thing our parents never found out. We'd be standing for dinner instead of sitting-or worse.

The park was better, though there were a lot more trees. The wooden sled with steel runners I'd gotten when I was eight had a crude steering bar on the front, that with shifting my weight made me able to steer it a bit and allowed me to dodge the trees. Lots of kids sled at the park and the hill across from the playground was busier than O'Hare airport. With no traffic controllers; but somehow we usually survived unscathed.

The thought of going out and sledding added to my restlessness as I watched the snow whirl before my eyes. I was trapped at home this afternoon. I put the latest Beatles single on my record player and plopped down on my bed. I heard the phone ring. One of the things my parents did was get me an extension- a white princess phone- for my bedroom. I heard my mom call from below. "It's Larry."

I picked up my phone. "Hi. Eh, what's up doc?"

"Just called to tell you I can't come over. My dad got stuck in the snow coming down the hill by our house. Marshall and I had to help push him out."

"I sort of figured that. Dad took me to drop a record off for Arnie. We got through ok, Dad had chains on, but coming down Grandview, I thought Dad would put the brakes through the floor. We had to park in front, couldn't even get into the alley for the garage."

"Anyway, we are off for winter break. The Bond movie starts on Thursday."

"So what, maybe on Sunday afternoon?"

"Yeah, you want to call Mark and see if he's game?"

"What about Mainard?"

"It's good for him."

"Streets'll be cleared by then too."

"So, you working on your Bar Mitzvah stuff?"

"Must you remind me?" I rolled over on my side.

"Your Bar Mitzvah is months before mine." Larry's Bar Mitzvah was next September.

"I know. Just hard to concentrate today, and I do have homework for school to do as well."

"And yet you are spending your valuable time talking to me."

"You called me," I retorted.

"I haven't called you anything."

I closed my eyes. Here we go again, and I thought it was just Tim and I who did the Abbott and Costello routine. "What's that yelling going on in the background?"

"Max is running around throwing his clothes off as usual."

Max was Larry's younger brother. I swear he was a nudist. At five he was always running around the house in his underwear. When Mrs. Shaeffer tried to get him ready for services she practically had to hog-tie him just to get his pants on. Obviously another fight to get Max dressed was going on.

"You want to sleep over this week? Marshall's going to AZA convention in Omaha. Please come, otherwise I'll be stuck with Max." Desperation. I did pity Larry. I'd been over lots of times and seen Max in action. He could be an obnoxious little bastard for sure.

"I'll talk to my folks. Don't think it'll be a problem once the roads get plowed."

"I hate having a younger brother. He's such a pain in the ass."

"Well there are times Morrie gets under my skin too," I admitted, "but he's not bad." But I'd never let Morrie know that. The fact is that despite the four year different in ages, we got along pretty well. Yes, there were disputes, but we watched each other's backs. There were times when the only people we had to play with were each other. But Larry's relationship was different. He was the middle child. Marshall was two years older and so they were a bit closer. Max was eight years younger. But then Max was also a pain in the ass. He'd get into Larry's stuff.

He was always hanging around. It's a wonder that Max had survived as long as he had in that household.

Mom made breaded veal culets and mashed potatoes for dinner along with salad and peas and carrots. She kept a careful eye on Morrie. He always tried to hide the peas and carrots under the mashed potatoes, and slip them to Shadow. Shadow would rest his big head on Morrie's lap and suck in anything that fell off the fork either accidently or accidently on purpose.

During dinner I caught Dad staring at me.

"What?" I asked. I was chewing with my mouth closed. I hadn't spilled anything.

He turned to my mom and said, "Looks like it's time."

Mom looked at me, studying my face. "I think you're right."

I huffed air out of my mouth.

"You're developing a caterpillar under your nose. You need to shave."

I looked at him. I had noticed the growth of facial hair, but I figured it made me look grown up. In actual fact, I'd been sprouting body hair like a new lawn.

"With a razor?" I asked.

"Well," replied Dad, "that's usually how it's done."

"If you're not careful, you'll slit your throat," piped up Morrie.

Mom glared at him. "You know when you get older, you'll have to learn to shave too."

When I was little, I remember getting a toy shaving kid. It had a plastic cup, a bar of soap, a plastic safety razor, and some cardboard blades. Sometimes I'd go into the bathroom and pretend to shave. I'd lather the soap and look at myself with a white bubbly beard. Occasionally I'd do it while Dad was shaving, watching his every move.

Dad had lots of safety razors. Every Father's Day, we'd get him a new razor and a tie. Last year we got him a new adjustable double-bladed safety razor. I wonder if that's the one he'd show me how to use, or maybe the electric razor mom got him for his birthday.

We finished dinner. Mom loaded the dishwasher and Morrie and I helped dry the pans and pots that wouldn't fit in. Afterwards, Dad led me into the bathroom.

"Take off your shirt."

"Now first thing you have to do is make sure your face is wet. Use warm water. It'll soften the hair."

"Do I get to use shaving cream?" I asked.

"Well, I think maybe it's better if we start with a safe method for you." He opened the wooden door to the vanity and took out his electric razor from the cabinet. He plugged it in.

"Now take it," he said.

I took the razor as he plugged it in.

"I'm going to guide your hand."

I felt the vibrations as it buzzed under my nose, my dad guiding my hand in short circular motions. He pulled my hand back and inspected my face, then directed my hand to my cheeks.

"You got a bit of fuzz coming in," he said. "Blow your cheek up with air."

I did. He guided the razor over both cheeks.

"Keep the skin taut like this and it's a smoother shave. Later when you use a safety razor you're less likely to cut yourself."

Morrie poked his head in the door. "Did he slit his throat?"

Dad turned and grimaced. "You're a blood thirsty little momser. Go on. Jeff is fine. You're out of luck."

"Poop." Morrie vanished.

"How often should I shave?" I asked.

"As much as you need to. Probably not every day for now, but once or twice a week. Unfortunately, the more you do it, the more you'll need to do it."

"Cool." I dried my face off with a hand towel by the sink and put my shirt back on.

"You won't think so twenty-five years from now," said Dad.

***

Bond day finally arrived on Sunday the twenty-seventh of December. Larry, Mark, Mainard and I were going to see the new Bond film *Goldfinger* at the Capital Theater. Better yet it was a double feature that included *From Russia With Love*. Dad had taken Mom to that one when it came out the previous year. It had been a riotous winter holiday so far: sledding with the Andersen kids, sleepovers at Larry's and vice versa. Playing army in the snow. We built this massive snow fort that curved out from the garage. We stockpiled snowballs and then had a great snowball fight with the some of the older kids in the neighborhood. And yeah, I did spend some time studying my Bar Mitzvah stuff. Dad still met with me at the synagogue twice a week, except the lessons were late in the morning, so Dad would come and pick me up, then I'd walk home, usually stopping off at Klages Drugstore to check the new comics and maybe buy a piece of red licorice as an energy boost.

The movie began at one. Dad was going to drop me off at twelve-fifteen where we'd get in line, hopefully early enough to get good seats. At eleven o'clock I was counting my money. It was a buck to get in. I had thirty-five cents for popcorn and a dime for a coke. At eleven-thirty Mom invaded my room and informed me that April Blackman was going to the movie with me.

"What?" Horror spread over my face.

"The Blackmans are coming over and April doesn't want to be with the younger kids. I happened to mention that you were going to a movie, and her Mother thought it'd be nice if she went with you."

"But I'm going with the guys."

"I'm sure they won't mind." My mother smiled and went downstairs. I think sometimes parents have a sadistic streak.

Shit! I'd be teased and mentally tortured for weeks over this one. I could see Mark and Larry grinning and making snide remarks. Mainard wouldn't give a shit. Being a year older and being a bit cooler he looked at things differently.

At noon the Blackmans showed up. Mom had made the kids hotdogs and put out a basket of potato chips. I came downstairs and put on my parka and pulled on my galoshes. April smiled at me. She wore a long, red wool coat, black leather gloves. Her feet and legs were covered in black leather winter boots. She had a small red purse slung over her shoulder

"Your Dad's waiting out front in the car," said April.

"Your Mom knows we're going to a James Bond movie?" I asked.

"Sssshh." April shot me a warning look.

We left the house quickly. I hopped in the front and April got in the back.

"Wish I was going with you," Dad said.

"Guess you and Mom will go later," I said.

He nodded. "Uh huh." He put the car in drive and carefully pulled out.

There was quite a line by the time we got down to the theater, but I spotted Mainard closer to the box office. He was leaning against the building reading a paperback. Dad pulled up, we hopped out and went over.

"Where's Mark and Larry?" I asked.

"Not here yet," he replied. Mainard wore a gray parka and had black cords on. He was a couple of inches taller than I was and had dark curly hair and metal-framed glasses. He lived with his Mother and Uncle. His dad had died in Korea. He peered over at April. "Who's the chick?"

"April Blackman. Her mom and sister are visiting us today."

"How cute."

I wasn't sure whether he meant April or the fact that she'd come with me. I was embarrassed.

A minute later Larry and Mark pulled up. They got out of Mr. Shaffer's tan Chevy Bel-Air and bounded over.

"I'll pick you up when it's over." he called out.

Larry noticed April right off and grinned at me. "You sly dog."

"Asshole," I muttered.

April looked at me. I introduced her to Larry and Mark. Being a couple of years older, they might have seen her at shul, but not known who she was. The line started to move and we headed to the box office. Once inside we got our snacks, popcorn and pop for April and I (Dad had slipped me a buck to pay for both our treats), Mainard opted for Milk Duds. Larry and Mark got licorice and popcorn, and we each had an Orange Crush to drink.

"Let's go up to the balcony. It won't be crowded and we'll get a better seat," said Mainard, leading the way.

We got settled. We let April go into the row first. April sat next to me on my right. Larry was on my left with Mark next to him and Mainard on the aisle so he could stretch his legs. April took off her coat and hung it over the back of the seat. She wore a black turtleneck sweater and a pair of dark blue stretch pants. She looked really cute.

Mainard pulled out his Matt Helm paperback and began to read. He always had a book with him. Sometimes he wasn't overly sociable.

Mark and Larry worked in their Dad's respective stores during the Christmas season. It was busy and the extra help was needed. I knew they, too, were studying for their Bar Mitzvahs as well. Larry had just started and met with my father on Monday evenings. Mark had been at it a month or two and met with Dad on Wednesday afternoons. Mark's Bar Mitzvah was scheduled for the end of August. What we all dreaded was meeting with the Rabbi about our speeches in January. Don't get me wrong, Rabbi Silverman could be very nice, but he was strict and would expect us to spend time researching in the synagogue library. We were expected to speak for three to five minutes about the Torah portion and about what it meant to become a Bar Mitzvah. I was still trying to figure the latter part out. I really didn't see an advantage. It just meant you had more responsibilities and obligations to the synagogue. True, we'd count as part of a minyan, the quorum required for a full prayer service. We could participate in an adult service, not that I had a whole lot of desire to though, and it was expected we'd take leadership positions in our Junior Congregation. I was a bit uncertain about that. Chanting the service stuff was easy, but preparing Torah reading certainly wasn't.

Larry leaned over to me. He glanced briefly at April. "Remember you two, behave. No making out."

I blushed and felt a wave of defensiveness.

Larry snickered and elbowed Mark who also glanced over. "They do make a cute couple."

Mainard groaned and turned a page in his book. "God."

The lights dimmed and the trailer started. We saw previews to a new spy movie, *Our Man Flint.*

"This looks cool," I said.

"Definitely gotta see this one," said Mark.

Another trailer came on for a spy film with Richard Burton called *The Spy Who Came in From the Cold.* It was in black and white and looked rather depressing.

After the trailers was a plug for the snack concession and then a Pink Panther cartoon came on. We laughed. The theater went dark. The James Bond theme started. A white circle moved across the screen. It opened up into a gun barrel. A man in a suit walked across. He turned, did a little jump and fired. The red gun barrel circle moved down, faded and opened up into garden scene with James Bond moving stealthily through it. I glanced at April. She was glued to the screen. Suddenly on the screen a man leaped out and garroted Bond! April clutched my arm. I felt my heart palpitate. I sipped my Coke and glanced at her. She was still staring at the screen. She'd put her drink down by her feet and her right hand squeezed her popcorn box.

During the movie she leaned towards me and rested her head on my arm. It felt sort of good. At one part of the movie the Bond girl slipped naked into bed. There was a glimpse of a naked woman running behind some sheer curtains. I saw Larry and Mark lean forward scrutinizing the screen for whatever detail they could obtain. I felt a bit embarrassed and glanced over at April. She watched as Bond entered the room.

"He's kind of cute, but too old," she said about Sean Connery.

"Uh huh," I grunted.

"But I'm glad I came," she whispered.

The movie ended. We stood up and stretched but barely had we done so then the lights dimmed and the 007 theme music came through the speakers. We settled down for Goldfinger. Mainard missed the first five minutes. He had made a quick dash to the can.

The movie held our attention. When Honor Blackman gave her name as Pussy Galore, Mainard snickered. "God, this is great."

Mark and Larry looked at me. "Pussy Galore."

"I got it, I got it."

April glanced at me with an embarrassed look on her face. "Never mind," I told her.

During the movie she leaned against me again, and put her hand over mine. I froze. I didn't know what the hell to do. I glanced over at Larry and Mark. Thankfully, they weren't paying attention to me. I put my empty popcorn box under the seat, and stretched, putting my right arm around April, who automatically snuggled in. I couldn't believe I was doing this. I mean April, was well, April, younger by two years, just a kid. What was I thinking? I had my eyes set on Barb at school and at Janet in Religious school. Shit, I had my eyes set on any well-developed teenage girl around my age. April's mom was best friends' with my mom. And yet, sitting there, watching the movie I felt cool and suave like James Bond. And it felt natural to have my arm around her. I glanced over to see if the guys noticed, but they were glued to the screen. A gangster had just gotten crushed in his car. I looked at April. She was watching the movie. I just hoped she didn't expect me to kiss her. I had no idea how to kiss a girl. And besides, it was April. I turned my attention back to the screen. One could learn a lot from watching a James Bond film.

After the movie we stumbled outside into the neon lights and shining streetlights. Traffic chugged along slowly. I spotted my Dad and said good-bye to Larry, Mark and Mainard. Larry's dad was taking them home since they live further away. I checked to make sure April was there and we headed to Dad's car and slid into the back seat.

"How was the movie?" he asked.

"Great. The next one they're doing is *Thunderball*."

He smiled. I could see part of his face in the rearview mirror. Then Dad turned his attention to the road and seeing it clear, pulled out. Cars were moving slowly. Throngs of people jaywalked across the street, weaving in between the lines of traffic. Snow flurries sparkled in the streetlights like tiny gems. April was looking out the window.

"What'd you think of it?" I asked her.

Her face in shadow, she turned to me. I could see her eyes sparkle. "It was good. Mom usually doesn't let me see movies like that." She grinned. "Definitely glad I came."

We sat back in silence. In my mind I said, "So was I."

July 2012 : Monday/Tuesday

My eyes focused on the window. I could see the sunlight had shifted. I checked my watch and couldn't believe how much time had passed. I'd been in another world. I took one more look around my old bedroom and headed downstairs. As I went out of the house, I thanked the painters for allowing me my nostalgic visit. I still had time to kill, so I walked around to the back of the house. I paused where the old elm tree had towered over the screened in back porch. Nothing was left of it but a stump.

I remembered when we had built a fort there in the corner of the house, using the tree as one of the supports. From there we had shot renegade Indians, hidden from armed assassins, and held secret meetings. That fall we used branches as a roof and turned the fort into a sukkah. We invited Mom and Dad, and they bent over and squeezed through the doorway. But they refused to sit on the hard packed dirt floor.

I remember hot summer nights and camping out in the screened back porch. I remembered too being terrified when a bird got trapped in there. Dad used a sheet to capture it and release it outside.

The garage was divided into three separate spaces with adjoining walls. When the synagogue owned the house they rented two of the stalls and we had use of the middle one with the door that led to the back walkway. When I was in eighth grade one of the units was empty, so Dad parked there and I turned our garage into a gym using it for weight training and working out, as well as storing our bikes.

One year the Andersens gave us some corn seed and Morrie and I planted a stalk of corn. It liked it there. Every day Shadow would 'water' it. By fall we had a seven-foot stalk of Indian corn, which wasn't good to eat but fine for livestock. And then came time to take it down. Dad sweated and swore for a couple of hours as he hacked at the stalk with a small hand axe. Needless to say we didn't grow corn again.

I remembered baseball games. The three trees: Plum, Apple, and Cherry were still there on the property to the right of the house. The Apple tree was first base. The garage doorway was second, and we picked a spot midway on the left of the porch near the short retaining wall next to Mrs. Hutchinson's garden for third base. Home plate was the cement pad in front of the porch. Any ball hit over the garage was an automatic home run.

I sighed. Before we left River City, I had taken a picture of April and her sisters standing in front of the elm tree next to the porch. I still had that picture in an old album. The other picture I had of her was when Jerry and I were there in '70. Larry shot a picture of the three of us sitting on the curb next to a fire hydrant in front of his Dad's store. April was in the middle, leaning on my shoulder. She was sixteen at the time. She wore bell-bottoms, a light sleeveless top, and her hair was long, pageboy style. Those were the only pictures I had of her.

The Andersen's rambling two-story 1920's yellow wood framed house that was on the other side of the Hutchinson's was no more. It'd been torn down several years ago to make room for angle parking for the Belleview Apartments. I walked across the back yard and around the garage. I looked up and down the alley. Across from me was the terraced backyard of the manager's house for the apartments. In winter we had sledded down those terraces, which seemed mountainously huge as kids. It was still steep, but the terraces were a lot smaller now. I turned around and went back into the yard.

We never picture ourselves getting old. When I was a kid, I couldn't imagine being a teenager and learning to drive. When I was a teen, I wondered what it'd be like to be twenty-five and out of college. Time seemed endless when I was a kid. And now, as I approached the eclipse of my life, I shuddered to think how swiftly time moved and pushed away thoughts of my mortality. I wasn't tired of life, and in fact didn't feel old-except my when back acted up. I told my wife that age is a state of mind, and that she should love my youthful exuberance. She'd grin and say, "Well maybe if you still weren't twelve..." Ha ha ha. "Age is as old as you feel—I feel with my fingers"...wiggle eyebrows. I'd get another laugh.

Here I was again in River City and I couldn't help the nostalgia, the memories. In fact it was comforting, bathing in them, remembering things that had made me who I had become. And I wondered what the future would hold for me here, now.

I left the room. The painters were cleaning up. I thanked them and left. On the walk, I took one last look at the house, then headed to my car.

From the house I drove down Grandview to 20th street and made a left. At the corner of Pierce, I stopped for a red light. Klages wasn't there anymore. I had heard that he had retired. His son took over, but modernized the place. I guess he had retired too. A flower shop had taken over the space. The barbershop was still there, but I doubt Bill was still cutting hair. The light changed and I turned left onto Pierce. The tavern that had been next to Klages was now a pizzeria. I drove home. Tomorrow was a working day.

***

On Tuesday, I pulled into the parking lot at Temple Beth Shalom with my CD player blaring The Beatles' "Revolution." It was a sand colored stone building with tall thin stained glass windows on top of a hill that looked out over the countryside, though most of it was now built up. The drive led around to the parking lot where the main entrance was. River City's Jewish population had declined from six hundred to two hundred and fifty families since we'd left in 1968. The Reform and Conservative congregations had combined. My friend Larry Schaeffer had been Beth Zion's president during the negotiations. Beth Zion got sold and the congregation renovated and expanded the Temple since it was slightly newer. Most of the Jewish families lived out on the north end, so location was a factor.

I put a black leather yarmulke on my head, a leftover from my son's Bar Mitzvah years ago, and fishing out my keys entered the building. The main office was to my left as I entered. Mrs. Fishbein was busy at her desk. She was a slight, silver haired senior with big 1980's glasses, but no slouch when it came to getting things done. She'd taken over for Bessie Rabinovtich whose husband had worked for Gateway computers. When the plant closed he'd gotten a job in Seattle. They moved and Mrs. Fishbein, now widowed, came out of retirement. She'd been the secretary after Mrs. Levin and her husband had moved to Chicago decades ago.

"Cantor...or should I call you Rabbi? Mrs. Bernstein called about her son's Bar Mitzvah rehearsal."

"I answer to either Mrs. Fishbein," I replied.

"Well I remember your father aleva shalom (may he rest in peace) so you're Cantor Reimer to me."

"I'll give Mrs. Bernstein a call. We're supposed to rehearse Friday morning."

"Maybe that's inconvenient for her." Mrs. Fishbein rolled her eyes.

I went into my office and turned on my computer. I'd been here for less than a week and already I was besieged by congregant requests. It had been unfortunate that my predecessor had died unexpectedly. The congregation had been in panic. It was July and the High Holidays were coming early. Small congregations, not having the financial resources, also find it harder to get professionals. But a friend of ours in River City, Rhonda Eisenstein, found out that my contract was coming up and that my wife and I were looking at moving. It was time for a change, and I was leaning towards smaller congregations where I got to know the people better. We'd been in communications with her, and the board, finding I was available, phoned. I'd been back to River City a few times over the past twelve years as a Cantor-in-Residence and to officiate at friends' B'nai mitzvahs and weddings, so I wasn't an unknown commodity. The fact I'd gotten my smicha as a Rabbi five years ago was a definite plus. We talked it over, and took the plunge. But our daughter Marissa and her husband Brad had booked a four day Alaska cruise and needed someone to take care of our grandson Joseph. We had promised at the time and then, when this pulpit came up we were at odds. So we moved, and my wife went to Seattle to look after Joe while our kids went on their cruise.

My new office is a conglomeration of old furniture. The Board told me I could purchase new furniture, but looking in the storage area, I discovered a treasure trove. My desk was a beautiful cherry wood double pedestal. My file cabinets were wood. I had retrieved them from a storage area in the basement. My bookcases that lined two walls of my office were mahogany. An old upright piano was on the wall opposite my desk. Mrs. Fishbein had arranged for a piano tuner to come next week. I liked natural furniture. The modern stuff seemed too cold and impersonal. I also had a small wooden worktable that I could use for meetings or teaching in the center of the room. The only modern piece of furniture was my desk chair, which I had purchased at Staples. Last year the synagogue had purchased new computers. I had a new HP computer and inkjet printer. Thankfully the synagogue not only had Internet, but wireless Wi-Fi, so I could use my MacBook Air laptop and iPhone.

I reluctantly picked up the phone and pressed the digits of the Bernstein's home.

The phone rang three times before going to voicemail. I left a message that I had returned their call and that they could reach me on my cell.

I spent some time working on my sermon. The parsha was V'etchanan in D'varim, or Deuteronomy. It had the second version of the Ten Commandments and the Shema and V'ahavtah in it. Lots of material to think about. When I got bored researching and writing-my mind was blocked up more than a constipated senior, I turned my attention to the piano. It was a bit off, and a couple of keys stuck, but I played some scales, did some vocal warm-up exercises, then pulled out a few volumes to practice and vocalize from and maybe make some decisions about which pieces the congregation and I would sing on Shabbat. Forty minutes later I was back at my desk going through the Siddur, the prayer book, outlining the service for Friday night. Saturday morning was the Bar Mitzvah, and the Bernstein kid was doing part of the service. I had a rehearsal scheduled for Friday morning, but who knew if that would take place now.

I spent the rest of the day catching up on phone calls and messages. Before I knew it, it was four o'clock and I had one more thing to do. I checked my Daytimer. Tomorrow I'd do hospital calls at St. Luke's and try and wrap up my sermon. I opened up the calendar on my phone and reminded myself again that I had to be at the airport Thursday.

I left the Temple and drove to St. Luke's. Laura and Mark Koplowitz had a son last week and they'd called me while we were on the way up to ask about the Bris. Dr. Murray Smith (a relation to the late Mort Smith of the confectionary store next to one of the movie theatres) was doing the actual surgical work.

The B'rit Milah, or Covenant of Circumcision, has been part of the male entry into the Jewish faith since Abraham four thousand years ago. According to tradition God commanded Abraham to circumcise himself and all the males in his household as a sign of the covenant. For infant males it was to be done on the eight day after birth. It was also the ceremony where the boy received his Jewish name.

***

Both Mark and Laura's parents were there, both middle-aged couples. Mark's dad was a radiologist and his mother a physical therapist. They worked at a clinic in North Sioux. Laura's parents were from Minneapolis. I think her Dad, Jacob, was a dentist. They were a nice young couple in their late twenties. Mark owned a cell phone franchise for one of the carriers and had a place at the Southland Centre Mall. Laura worked as a receptionist for her father-in-law.

The ceremony was done in the non-denominational chapel. Murray was there with a portable circumcision kit. There were a couple of young couples there to witness the event as well.

As Laura, a petite brunette with short hair and red-framed glasses, brought their son into the room, I chanted "Baruch Haba" (Blessed comes he who is to be blessed.)

She and Mark helped get him undressed and on the molded plastic circ board where Velcro straps held the baby down at the arms, legs and stomach. I had Mark's dad, Phil, open a bottle of Manischewitz Kosher wine and pour some into a plastic wine cup. Laura's dad, Jacob, would dip some gauze into the wine and give the baby a taste.

Murray took a syringe and injected some freezing into the area. Mark turned green and looked like he was ready to pass out.

"Maybe it's better if you sit down," I suggested.

He looked down at me and then went to sit at the back of the room. Laura joined him a minute later.

I then went and did a couple of English readings, which discussed the tradition of B'rit Milah. I nodded to Murray. He took off the baby's diaper and the kid showed his displeasure. He peed. The pee arched high over his head like an Italian fountain in Rome, and landed with the accuracy of a U.S. military drone smack into the Kiddush cup.

"See that!" cried Phil Kotlowitz. "With that kinda aim he's gonna make one helluva basketball player."

"I've never seen anything like this," said Jacob. He turned to his wife, "Miriam, I think we need a fresh cup."

Both women were laughing their asses off.

When decorum had restored and everyone had dried his or her eyes from laughing too hard, we continued. Murray loosened the foreskin and put the bell clamp on over the penis. Murray recited the blessing: 'Baruch Atah Adonai Eloheinu Melech Ha-olam asher kidshanu b'mitzvotav vetsivanu al ha-milah. (Blessed are you Lord Our God, Ruler of the Universe who sanctified us with your commandments and commanded us concerning circumcision). Murray cut the foreskin off using a small scalpel and then we timed the clamp for three minutes.

I then called Laura and Mark forward and they recited the blessing praising God who commanded them to bring their son into the covenant.

Afterwards Murray removed the clamp and took two pieces of gauze and shmeared them with Vaseline and wrapped the tiny penis in it. I knew he'd give Laura and Mark extra gauze and Vaseline and instructions on how to change the dressing over the next week. I let Laura and Mark dress the baby and then we continued with the naming ceremony.

The Mi Sheberach blessing is sort of a standardized fill-in-the-blank blessing we do for numerous occasions. In this case the wording blessed the child. The baby's name was David Ben Kotlowitz or in Hebrew, David Benjamim ben Mattathias v' Leah. I finished with the three-fold Priestly Benediction and then Laura's father brought out a bottle of fifteen year-old Oban single malt scotch. We had a couple of l'chayims. Some honeycake and Mandelbrot was served on paper plates.

Simchas, joyous occasions, were better than funerals.

Chapter Eight

January 1965

President Johnson declared his "Great Society"; NASA was getting ready to launch Gemini 2; and the Vietnam War was heating up. School started back and it was like dropping into a frozen lake. I was numb. My brain didn't work. I'd forgotten half the stuff they'd crammed into me in the first semester.

In Wood/Electricity shop class we were going to continue making a lamp; this class would alternate with metal work, which bode as well as wood shop. I still had to put up with Mr. Wood again. Part of the course would be textbook stuff where we learned to read schematics. I wasn't too worried about that, given my wood making skills; but making a lamp was a challenge I didn't want to think about. Last semester I had barely managed to complete a desktop book holder. The project was marred by the fact that I mis-measured a couple of dowel holes and had to use wood filler to plug them up and re-drill them. I planned to give it to my dad on Father's Day. It was stashed up on the shelf in my closet.

Mr. Savick, a short, hairy man with thick glasses, ran metal work. He talked like a cross between a drill sergeant and a cheerleader. He was also the uncle of one of my elementary school rivals named Louie Morrison, a wry skinny kid with a face like a chimpanzee's. Maybe it was his size, or the fact that he'd hung around with these giant football players, but Louie had more chutzpah than a Jewish stand-up comedian. He was loud, obnoxious and for me, a general pain in the ass. One time in fifth grade he tried to butt in line. I pushed him out and we started to fight. I had him in a headlock. He was hitting my stomach, but I had strong stomach muscles and didn't feel it. His face was turning purple by the time two supervising teachers pulled him away. He collapsed on the ground heaving. Of course we got sent to the office and thankfully got nothing more than a stern warning from the Principal. My dad had given both Morrie and I ground rules. Fighting never solved anything; but if someone starts a fight, make damn sure you finish it. I think with Louie gasping for breath and rolling on the ground, I finished it. And as it turned out, Louie was in the metalworking class; thankfully so was Tim Shaunessy. And he was about as good making stuff with his hands as I was. I definitely didn't take after my Dad. Dad was good with tools, but then all those years working for his Uncle's construction company as he readied to go back to cantorial school helped. Anyway we were told we'd be making several projects: a money clip, a sugar scoop, and a tin box. We'd learn to cut metal, file, solder and screw things. Too bad there weren't any girls in the class. Not that I had any experience to speak of, but I was eager to learn. Hormones.

In gym I stuffed newly washed black shorts, white socks, and a white t-shirt into my locker that still stunk of sweat and body odor. I didn't see the point of it; but when I'd brought my gym clothes home last semester, I'd left them stuffed in a brown paper bag on the kitchen table. Mom came in and thought it was some grocery stuff Dad was supposed to pick up. She opened the bag, shoved her face close to it and almost passed out. What? It'd only been a month since she'd last washed the stuff. Needless to say she was not impressed, and reminded me, rather sternly for her, that I should've taken it right down to the laundry area in our basement. She said she couldn't smell anything properly for a week after that incident.

In science class Mr. Rassmussen had switched the seats again and Tim and I sat behind Karin Miller whose father was a minister and had done missionary work in

Africa. Karin was a very shapely brunette who wore tight knitted sweaters.

"Now you notice my son," began Tim, "that this female has no zipper up the back. But she has bumps in the front."

Karin turned around, grinned fiendishly and said, "Little boys with little toys, should not be heard."

At that point we got a "harrrumph from Rassmussen who inquired if he had permission to start the class. One look at his flat stern face as his beady black eyes bore into us like a sniper's gun barrel diminished any further retorts.

***

On Tuesday I was happy that mom and dad didn't push me to get straight to my homework after dinner. *The Man from U.N.C.L.E.* was on. Next to James Bond, it was probably the coolest spy show to watch, though I still didn't understand why all the girls, like April for example, liked David McCallum's character of Ilya. He was brainy, but Napoleon got the girls. We had a six-foot TV aerial on top of the house, and sometimes, if we were lucky, we'd be able to pull in Omaha. Occasionally we got really good reception. A few years ago one of the stations there was showing old movie serials late at night. Dad, being a fan of them when he was a kid, let me stay up late on Saturday night. I'd snuggle in bed between him and Mom and we'd watch the snowy images of *"SOS Coast Guard"*, *"The Mysterious Dr. Satan"* and my favorite, *"Zorro Rides Again"* which took place in the 20th century with Zorro leaping from his appaloosa onto a moving truck.

After school I trudged through the wet snow and tromped down to the synagogue, as usual, for a Bar Mitzvah lesson. But this time instead of seeing my Dad, I was told to see the Rabbi.

Rabbi Silverman's office had a large L-shaped desk with a typewriter table. Along the far wall were two bookcases crammed with volumes of Talmud, Judaica and oddly enough several Mathematic books. I later found out from Dad that the Rabbi had a bachelor's degree in Mathematics. He peered across the desk at me through black horn-rimmed glasses. His thick dark hair was combed back as usual. He wore a black and gold yarmulke. As always he was dressed immaculately in a dark blue suit, white shirt and red and silver striped tie.

"We have to start your D'var Torah," he said. "Or more familiarly known as 'The Bar Mitzvah speech'."

"I thought my Dad was going to help me with it," I replied.

"Your father decided that it might be best if I work with you on this."

"Oh."

"Now, your Haftorah is Shabbat HaGadol, the Great Sabbath. Do you know why it's called that?"

"It was the Shabbat before the Israelites left Egypt."

Rabbi Silverman smiled. "Good. Now it's a special haftorah. The week's regular parshat is Metzora, which is not the most ideal parsha for a Bar Mitzvah."

"Why is that?" I asked.

Rabbi Silverman hesitated a moment. "It talks about our ancestor's rituals for those people who contracted leprosy."

"What's that?"

"It's a skin disease, which if not properly treated could allow people's limbs to get infected and basically rot off."

"So they became like zombies?"

Rabbi Silverman rolled his eyes and stared at the ceiling as if praying for deliverance. He sighed and peered at me. "No, not like zombies. Leprosy is a bacterial infection that can produce sores or lumps. It causes numbness in a person's limbs. People get cuts or infections and without treatment they develop diseases that causes them to have their limbs amputated. It occurs in tropical or subtropical climates. Today we have medicine that can cure, but in ancient times they didn't."

"Ick."

"Yes, well," continued Rabbi Silverman, "the portion also talks about a woman's impurity when they have their—uh—monthly women's issues."

"Oh." I wasn't quite sure what he was talking about, but then I thought back to all the sex education books my parents had piled on me last year and suddenly I got it, and then I didn't want to get it, because it was totally ewwwwwville. Robby Cramer used to talk about his sister being on the rag, and yeah, totally ick.

"So what should I talk about?" I asked. Hoping like hell I didn't have to write about women's issues.

"Well it is Shabbat Hagadol and I think it best if you concentrate on that great Sabbath before our ancestors left on their journey to Canaan."

"Ok." I breathed a silent sigh of relief.

"Now I'd like you to go to the library and do some research. I'll help you find some texts. I want a rough draft in two weeks."

"How long?"

"Two or three paragraphs would be good. We'll fill it out a bit and have you talk about the meaning of becoming Bar Mitzvah and we'll add in your thank yous."

"Ok," I agreed.

The rabbi pushed back his chair and stood up. "Come with me."

I followed him out of the office, past Mrs. Levin, and down the hall to the library.

"Do you have a lesson with your father today?"

"Yes." I checked my watch. "In about a half an hour."

"Ok." Rabbi Silverman perused the shelves and pulled out a couple of large books. He flipped through them, and placed them on the table. He pointed to the sections he'd left open. "Read this. This should give you some ideas."

I sat down and stared at the books. The Rabbi left. Yeah, right. I stared at the page. I took a deep breath and began to read.

At five o'clock I left the library and walked down to my dad's office where I was mentally tested on my Haftorah and more drill and practice learning the Musaf service. Finally either my dad could tell I'd had enough, or maybe he had. We packed it in and went home.

By the end of the month, I'd narrowly avoided getting stitches for a nasty cut from a file that slipped out of my hand. Tim almost passed out from the sight of blood as I got carted off to the nurses' office. I heard Mr. Savick order his nephew Louie, whom he'd caught goofing around, to get a mop and clean up the blood on the floor so no one else would slip on it. On the plus side I didn't have to climb ropes in gym, which was a major embarrassment at the best of times. I also got to sit out a few basketball games.

I was still going for math tutoring once a week and my grades had improved slightly. I had managed a C- on my last test and thereby justified the money my parents were spending.

Mom and Dad were busy during the evenings looking at invitations and creating an invitation list. Dad was exasperated. They were sitting at the dining room table. There was a small cloud of gray smoke over them. The ashtray was overflowing.

"I don't know how we can limit the number of people. We have to invite the community." I overheard him say.

"Well, we'll send invitations out to the family and we can put a general invitation in the synagogue bulletin.

Women's League will help cook the lunch. How many people do you think we'll have?"

"I don't know. And I sure as hell don't want to think what's it going to cost to feed all these people."

"We don't have a choice, David. We'll have the lunch and then we can just have an open house here. I'll make pastries and some simple hor d'ourves. I can store stuff in the freezer. I'm sure some friends will help too," said Mom.

Dad sat back and lit another cigarette.

"When are you going to get his suit?" asked Mom. She tapped her cigarette ash into a small green glass ashtray.

"I'll take him to see Morrie next month. His blue blazer still fits, he can wear that Friday night. Saturday he'll wear the suit. I just hope he doesn't outgrow it between the time we buy it and the time he wears it."

Chapter Nine

February 1965

Whthis they called the counter-revolution was beginning in the war as U.S. Troops were sent to Vietnam and people started questioning our involvement. Down south in Selma, Alabama Rev. Martin Luther King Jr. and around 2600 others were arrested for protesting against voter registration rules. By the end of the month Malcolm X would die from a gunshot wound. Medicare would become law this year. Dozens of UFO sightings took place. Although I watched the CBS news at 5:30 pm regularly, the events seemed secondary as more mundane items concerned me. Some of which actually had to do with my Bar Mitzvah; the other of which had to do with Valentine's Day.

In elementary school we gave out Valentines to everybody in class. Boys gave to girls and vice versa. Sometimes I didn't get Valentines from all the girls, but always looked out for ones from girls that I liked. By Junior High there was no real card passing in class. It was of a more personal nature and there was to be a dance Friday after school on Feb. 12th since Valentine's Day fell on Sunday. Now being a good Jewish boy, Valentine's Day certainly isn't on any Jewish calendar nor would any Orthodox Jew celebrate it. But for me it was secular like Halloween and I wasn't Orthodox. It was a fun time to get candy hearts with quaint sayings on them and give cards out that you'd be too shy to give to a girl at any other time.

At home, Mom and Dad had finalized the invitation list. Dad had talked to Sam the butcher and had ordered briskets for the Kiddush lunch. I told them I wanted a bottle of Ketchup at the table. Surprisingly they agreed. I never ate meat without ketchup.

I met with Rabbi Silverman the first Thursday of the month and handed him my D'var Torah. He glanced at it, then up at me. "Why don't you read it to me," he suggested, which of course was no suggestion.

I shrugged. I took the sheet of paper from him and began to read aloud:
Rabbi, Dad, Mother, Morrie (*my folks made me put his name in, God knows why, the little cretin*), Grandparents, Relatives and Friends,
Today is my Bar Mitzvah. It's supposed to be a day of joy and seriousness. I've often wondered what this day would be like. And now, I know. After today I'll probably wish that I could go through this ceremony again (*yeah, like when hell freezes over*), but it only comes once in a lifetime.
Today is also Shabbos HaGadol, the great Sabbath before Pesach. This Sabbath became great not only because of God's greatness, but because Israel showed they had greatness too. Israel performed the miracle of renouncing Egypt and aligned themselves with the teachings of Moses. They demonstrated their devotion to God, though risking the unknown future.

(*The fact is they kvetched for 40 years and I'm sure there were times Moses regretted taking them out. Not only that, they made the Golden calf, and God slaughtered a bunch of them for that one.*)

It is only fitting, this being my Bar Mitzvah day, that I too devote myself to the teachings of the Torah which has been an important part of our heritage for forty centuries.
What does Bar Mitzvah mean? It means that I am re-dedicating myself to my Jewish heritage. It means that this is the beginning of my full membership as a Jewish adult. It means that I am not only part of a minyan (*yep, every time they're short one*), but part of the synagogue as well. It means that all the training I have had to this point was in

preparation for the future. It means that from this time forth, it is to be put into practice and not to be forgotten. (*Like I actually would have a say in this*)

I want to take this opportunity to thank Rabbi and Mrs. Miller and Miss Bresden (*God help me if I called her Miss BOOBSden*) for all they taught me, and to you mom and dad for guiding and teaching me what it means not only to be a good Jew, but also to be a good American.

And thank you to our dear relatives and friends for coming, some of you traveling great distances to make this day such a joyous one, not only for me but for my parents as well.

Our God and God of our Fathers, I pray that you give me the strength and wisdom to continue in the ways of my people and that you grant peace to all mankind. Amen.

I looked up at Rabbi Silverman.

"You might want to expand it a bit when talking about Shabbos HaGadol, but otherwise it's pretty good."

"Thanks." I sighed with relief.

"Next time we'll get you practicing it from the bimah and work on expression and projecting your voice." He glanced at his watch. "You'd better go on and see your Father."

And so I went, the sacrificial lamb to the slaughter.

In the winter we rarely went out after lunch if the Principal thought it was too cold. Instead we'd be herded into the auditorium and shown old black and white 16mm news reels, documentaries and, if we were lucky, the occasional cartoon or comedy short from the 1930s, 40s or early 1950s. Tim and I sat staring at a film about the lumber industry in the Pacific Northwest. Talking was kept to whispers, so as to not earn a detention.

"You going to the Valentine's Day dance?" asked Tim.

"It's the beginning of our Sabbath. I have to get home for dinner and services."

"Your parents wouldn't let you have a night off?" Tim gazed away as Karen came down the stairs and sat down in the row below us. "Love those sweaters," he murmured.

I followed his gaze and sighed. Karen had great tits. I wondered what they looked like naked and exposed. Were her nipples big or small? Such questions were more interesting than pondering geography or algebra. Of course algeBRA had the word BRA in it. I snickered and let Tim in on the joke.

"Then in alge-BRA we should be studying the circumferences of the breast. Does X=Y?"

"Hell if I know."

"But it'd be interesting to find out." Tim rolled his eyes and I burst out laughing.

Karen turned around and looked at us. She rolled her eyes. "First of all, that'd be geometry, not algebra. Second, you're idiots." Karen turned around, but I sort of caught a half smirk forming on her mouth.

Mrs. Anderson didn't approve of my book report. It was because the book I chose was Ian Fleming's *Thunderball*. She was a big woman and peered down at me with judgmental eyes from behind her glasses. "Do you really think this is an appropriate book for you to read?"

"It's my favorite series. Dad got the entire series in hardcover through a book club."

"And your parents let you read these?" She looked questioningly at me through her glasses.

"Kids stuff is boring. Last year I read *The Three Musketeers, Count of Monte Crisco,* and *Tale of Two Cities*. They were ok, especially *The Three Musketeers*. The sword fights were cool."

"And you understood those novels?" she asked.

"Yeah. If I didn't, I wouldn't have bothered reading them."

Mrs. Anderson rolled her eyes, shook her head, and went to the next student.

Friday night rolled around. At five o'clock we sat in the dining room. Mom lit candles and Dad chanted the Kiddush, the blessing over the wine. We did hamotzi, and each had a nice chunk of Challah. As usual we had our usual chicken soup with egg noodles, roast chicken, kishke (sort of like Jewish vegetarian haggis), and peas and carrots. Mom kept an eye on Morrie to make sure he ate his vegetables. Morrie had a habit of smuggling them to Shadow, who sat with his head on Morrie's lap so that any spilled food would not go to waste. After dinner, mom put the dishes in the dishwasher and we got ready for services. If I hurried I could watch a bit of the Flintstones before we left.

For a lot of kids, religious services were boring. They didn't understand the prayers. The Rabbi's sermon lulled us into a comatose state; but for me, it was the music that stirred me. Dad sang several pieces that I enjoyed. I also enjoyed listening to the choir hum a niggun during the Amidah, the silent meditation that gave us time to communicate privately with God. I sort of read the prayers, some in Hebrew, some in English and I felt a serene calm. No matter what sort of crap I had faced during the week, it was washed away. Compared to other kids my age, I'm sure I was weird. But for me, it was a good weird.

The choir stopped. The Rabbi signaled people to be seated then began his sermon. I glanced around to see who was there. I noticed the Blackman family sitting on the pews along the right wall. I sort of craned my neck but didn't see Mark or Larry. Most likely I'd see them tomorrow at Junior Congregation. Post B'nai Mitzvah students, trained by Dad and the Rabbi, led Junior Congregation services. Typically one person did some Torah reading, one acted as Cantor and the elected President announced pages. The girls did a d'var torah or story. On average we had about fifty to seventy kids attending the one-hour service. The best part was the candy bars that we got at the end of the service. Next year I'd be expected to help lead some of the services. It was part of the responsibilities that were expected after having a Bar Mitzvah. Kids, other than being in the youth choir for Kol Nidre and N'eilah on Yom Kippur, didn't participate much in the adult services.

The services ended with the singing of Yigdal, a hymn thought to be written by Daniel ben Judah in the fourteenth century and sung to M. Leoni's 18th century popular melody.

After services, I exited the sanctuary and went through the adjoining corridor to the social hall for the Oneg Shabbat. There were cakes and some chocolate dipped short bread sugar cookies along with tea and coffee served out of silver urns by the Women's League members. I waited patiently eyeing the cookies. I knew not to start until some of the older adults hit the table first.

"Hi," said a female voice behind me.

It was April. She stood there in a blue and white striped dress, white stockings and black patent leather shoes.

"Hi."

"Happy Valentine's Day. She pulled a card from the small purse that was slung over her shoulder.

I felt embarrassed. I hadn't gotten her a card. To be truthful, I hadn't even thought about giving her one. Not that I had given one to anyone else, either. "Uh-thanks. I'm sorry, I didn't know you were coming."

"It's ok. I'll get yours on Sunday. Apparently we're coming over."

"Cool." She kept standing there, watching me. I looked around.

"Well, aren't you going to open it?" she asked. April cocked her head when she asked the question.

I looked around, then back at her. "Here?"

She rolled her eyes. "Are you embarrassed?"

"Uh—surprised. I didn't expect it."

"Sometimes you're a real idiot, you know that?" She turned on her heels and huffed off.

I followed her. She left the social hall and headed down the hall towards the ladies' bathroom. I caught up with her right before she entered. The hallway was deserted.

"April, wait."

She stopped and turned around. There was a trace of a tear in the corner of her eyes.

"I'm sorry." I held up the card and opened it.

It was a heart shaped card. There was a picture of two little bears kissing. Inside it read: *Valentine, I can't bear to be without you.* It was pretty cheesy.

"Do you like it?"

I took a deep breath and smiled at her. "Yes, thanks."

A smile broke across her face. She took two steps, leaned forward and kissed me on the cheek. Then she turned and went into the bathroom. I stood there. Frozen to the spot. Holy Shit!

Well tomorrow, I'd go and make a Valentine for her. But I had no idea what to say. I mean it sort of dawned on me that I did kinda like her; but then again, I liked lots of girls. April was the only one though that I could actually be comfortable talking to.

Saturday morning, as usual, we went to services again. Afterwards we walked home and had lunch-leftovers from Friday night. I spent the afternoon doing homework and spending a bit of time studying my Bar Mitzvah stuff. That evening Mom and Dad were invited out. I left Morrie downstairs watching Flipper on TV and went to my room to make a Valentine for April. I don't know if I felt the same way about her that she did about me. As I've said, I had my eyes on a few girls and hopefully more to come. But I didn't want to hurt her feelings. I took a piece of drawing paper and folded it in half. On the cover I drew a picture of a Skunk, sort of Pepe le Pew. He had a bunch of flowers in his hand. Inside I wrote, using my calligraphy pens, 'You scent (send) me.' And signed my name. Pretty lame and corny, but hey hopefully she'd like it.

Sunday morning was religious school. We continued to study about the Jews in the middle ages. The crusades were just a hotbed of anti-Semitism. We learned about Rashi, the 12th century French scholar. Most of the kids found it boring. Even Larry was doodling in his notebook. But for me, I was fascinated. I mentioned this to Larry, who concluded that all the stress was making me meshugge in kop (crazy in the head). After class Larry informed me that he had to work at the store, same with Mark. I went home to face April Blackman.

The Blackmans came over right after Sunday school. Mom made grilled cheese sandwiches, cutting them diagonally the way I liked them. They seemed to taste better if they were cut diagonally. She even pulled out a bag of potato chips, a rarity in our house, and cut up slices of apple. We ate well-balanced meals in our house.

Afterwards April's sister, Susie followed Morrie who headed to the basement to play with the electric train we had set up down there. My Uncle Jake had given us our cousin Paul's old train set. Dad had gotten a huge plywood board and we set up the tracks on it, along with creating a town scene, which Morrie and I had expanded by using some building sets and cardboard shoe boxes to make more of a city. Morrie had Lone Ranger and Tonto action figures and some others we'd collected over the years.

"So we're playing dolls?" asked Susie Blackman.

"Arrrgghh! I told you we're playing cowboys." Morrie stomped off with Susie trailing behind.

"Dolls are dolls Morrie!"

"Don't be a stupid girl! I play with plastic men." I could hear Morrie trot down the basement steps. His voice echoed in the stairwell.

Mom was getting coffee for Lois Blackman, so April and I vanished up to my room.

I went to my desk and pulled out the card I had made for her. I handed it to her and stood back.

She studied the cover for a minute or two then opened it.

"It's a pun."

"I get it, Jeff." She lifted her eyes and looked at me, then walked a few steps and awkwardly put her arms around my waist. "Thank you."

I looked down at her. I could smell her peppermint breath. Our noses were almost touching. I could feel my heart racing. She looked up at me, and well, it only seemed natural. I bent over and kissed her briefly on the lips. She stared at me. "What was that?" she asked.

"A kiss."

She arched an eyebrow and looked at me. "Really? Sort of hard to tell."

Hard to tell? Where'd she become an expert on kissing? There was more to April Blackman than I thought. "I could do it again."

She paused for a second, and leaned forward. "Okay."

This time I kissed her slowly. We got our noses properly arranged. Our lips pressed together. She stepped back and smiled at me.

"Wow."

"Yeah, wow," she agreed.

We both blushed a bit. April released me and took a step back.

"But I have to know," said April. "Why did you kiss me? Usually it seems you just tolerate me when I come over. I know you were surprised when I gave you my

Valentine. I didn't think you'd give me one. And, I remember walking behind you when you first took me to school."

Damn girl had a memory like an elephant.

I sighed. My heart was pounding like a locomotive and my mouth was drier than the Negev desert. I looked her square in the eyes. "April, I know I've treated you like shit at times. I'm sorry. Sometimes I can be a real jerk." I stared at the worn gray carpeting in my room. "But the fact is, well, uh… you're pretty. And, we like some of the same things. Fact is—" I paused, lifted my head and took a deep breath. My mind was a jumble. Words rushed to get out. Words that I'd never hear myself admit to or speak. The words exploded quickly after I exhaled. "I'll admit it, I like you a lot. Okay? There, I said it."

She smiled, grabbed my shirt, pulled me close and we kissed again.

"So does that make me your girlfriend?" she asked.

"Well, you're a girl and you are a friend, but I prefer to think of us as special friends."

"You sound like my Uncle Sid. He's a lawyer. Are you planning to be a lawyer?"

"I'd rather be a comic book writer and artist."

"Hmmm."

I didn't know what hmm meant, but it probably wasn't a good thing for a girl to respond that way. I looked at her, puzzled.

"You said that we're special friends. To me, that means you're my boyfriend."

"Don't expect me to hold hands when my parents are around."

"Agreed. Parents can act so goofy when their kids are attracted to someone. But you are my boyfriend—just remember that MISTER!" Her arms came up around my neck and next thing I knew, her lips crushed into mine and we held that way. My glasses steamed up. I felt the blood rushing to my head and into my groin. My heart was pounding. I got an instant boner and just about ejaculated in my jeans.

The rest of the afternoon was spent playing 'the spy game'. We'd come up with this game when we'd gotten roped into playing spies and guns with Morrie and Susie; usually this meant that we were hiding in the upstairs storage closet outside my bedroom. Basically we wrote a simple code message on a slip of paper, went into the bathroom, and hid it on our person. Then entering the room, one of us would 'knock the other one out' and search for the message. Truthfully, this game of 'spies', was really just an excuse to feel each other up and sort of answer our curiosity about human development and sexuality. When we first started this game, we'd check pockets and shoes. But of course things got challenging after that, though we were very respectful of each other's private areas.

Today, I was the first victim. The message was taped to the inside of my belt near the buckle. I came out of the bathroom, walked into my room and April pretended to whack me from behind with a pillow. I fell on the bed "unconscious". She checked the usual places first, shoes, pockets. I could feel her fingers moving in my jean pockets extracting keys, wallet and penknife. It was then I started getting a hard on. She rolled me over and plopped her hand on my crotch as she reached to check my shirt pocket. Her fingers pressed on my dick. She wasn't as naïve as I thought. She unbuckled my belt. I reached up and grabbed her arms, pulling her towards me. I rolled over on her. I could feel her hot breath. Her big dark brown eyes stared into mine. Our faces were inches apart. And then we did it again. We kissed.

I heard footsteps pounding up the stairs. Had I locked the door to my room? April and I stared wide-eyed at each other then rolled apart and fell on either side of the bed. When Morrie and Susie burst in-turns out I hadn't locked the door-the Beatles were singing *'I Feel Fine'*, and I was sitting at my desk 'reading' *Hawkman.* April was lying on the bed with the recent issue of *Detective.* We looked up at them, annoyingly.

"What the hell do you want?" I asked.

The next day Dad picked me up after school and drove me down to Morris Bernstein's Menswear. Their slogan was "Home of the Suit with Two Pants." The store was wedged on the main drag between Mr. Weiner's Office Equipment store and Yonker Martin's Department store. Dad tried to give both Mr. Schaeffer and Mr. Bernstein equal business. I'd gotten a Navy blue blazer and a pair of gray slacks in the fall from Larry's dad, so we went to Bernstein's for the Bar Mitzvah suit.

Mr. Bernstein was a big bear of a man with a shock of silver hair. He had a couple of other salesmen working for him, but when we walked in the store, he finished wrapping up something for a customer, walked around the cash area and strode over to us, cigarette hanging out of his mouth, the ash perilously long. The store was crammed with tables stacked with sweaters and ties in the middle and two long rows going to the back. On the right were jackets and overcoats; to the left were sports coats and slacks.

"So, this is the Bar Mitzvah bocher, eh?" he looked from my dad to me. A cloud of gray smoke left his mouth and floated above my head. I coughed.

"Yes. I was thinking something in navy blue or black." Dad took out his pack of Kents, selected one and lit up.

Like a heaving locomotive, Mr. Bernstein nodded and led us towards the back of the store where the suits were. He whipped out a measuring tape and measured my waist, now down to a 34, my inseam 27, and my arms. He then went over to one of the racks and pulled out a navy blue suit. "Try this on young man."

He handed me the suit and ushered me into one of the two changing rooms. It was smaller than our broom closet in the bathroom and I barely had room to move. I slid my cords off and hung them on a hook on the back of the door. I put the slacks on and tucked my checked flannel shirt into the pants. They were longer than my legs, so I rolled them up and put my shoes on. I put the jacket on and went out.

"It's a nice suit," said Dad.

"Navy blue goes with anything. Black, he'd look like a mortician." Mr. Bernstein winked at me.

"He's going to need a couple of shirts and a tie too," said Dad.

"Come with me young man." Mr. Bernstein guided me with his hand on my back over to a table of shirts. Dad walked over and started inspecting the stitching. He saw an ashtray next to a wooden armchair. Dad tapped off the excess ash into the ashtray. He knew material and how shirts should be made, thanks to Grammy.

Eventually Mr. Bernstein directed me to stand in front of the mirrors located at the back of the store.

The pants are a bit long," I said.

"It's ok, Mr. Bernstein can shorten them," said Dad.

"We'll need to take off three or four inches, but nothing serious," said Mr. Bernstein. He bent down and adjusted the pants legs. He took a few straight pins from his coat pocket and pinned the pants. He looked up at dad. "Well, what do you think?"

Dad nodded his approval.

Mr. Bernstein looked up at me. "Let me have a look at the jacket and then you can go and change."

It was going to be a bitch taking the pants off without sticking myself. He made some marks on the sleeves, and in the back of the jacket. "We'll just taper it a bit. It'll have a slimming effect," he explained.

In the end, which seemed to last forever, we bought a light blue shirt and a new white one. I got a blue and red striped tie that would go with either shirt. And I managed to get the dress pants off without sticking myself on one of the pins.

"You can wear the blue shirt on Friday night and the white one on Saturday," said Dad as we thanked Mr. Bernstein and left the store.

It had taken us an hour and a half, but we finally headed home where I had at least an hour or so of homework waiting for me.

***

The invitations my parents ordered came in at the end of the month. They were a one-fold. On the cover in Hebrew and English was a quote from Judges 13:24 *"And the child grew and the Lord blessed him."*
Inside the text read:
Our son, Jeffery Allen, on his Bar Mitzvah will be called to the Torah on Saturday morning the tenth of April, 1965. We cordially invite you to worship with us on this joyous occasion, at Congregation Beth Zion, Sixteenth and Douglas Streets, River City, Iowa. A luncheon will follow the conclusion of the services. Cantor and Mrs. David Reimer

Well, guess my Bar Mitzvah was really happening.

Chapter Ten

March 1965

The month came in like a roaring avalanche. The cold war was heating up. Tensions rose between East and West. Russia conducted more nuclear tests. A Leftist revolt in Iran protested British rule. The first thirty-five hundred troops arrived in Vietnam. Selma, Alabama had race riots. Later, Cosmonaut Alexei Leonov became the first man to walk in space and in popular news The Beatles were making a new movie.

Purim fell on March 18th. Purim is the craziest holiday in the Jewish calendar year. It's sort of like the Jewish Halloween. The evening prior to the holiday we read from Megillah Esther, the Book of Esther. It tells the story of how a Jewish queen ascended the throne in Persia and saved the Jewish people from Haman who sought to destroy us. Rabbi Silverman told us that the story was based on a Babylonian folk tale and given a Jewish twist by the Rabbis. It's said to mirror an actual event and the story gave ideas to the Rabbis and therefore it was decided that the book was written under divine direction and added later to the Jewish Bible. At the synagogue we were going to have carnival on Sunday March 14th, with the USY kids (United Synagogue Youth) organizing the gaming booths. Dad had gone around and schnorred lots of prizes that we could get by trading in prize coupons. There'd be a hot dog lunch as well. A lot of kids dressed up as the main characters of the Purim story: Queen Esther, Mordecai—Esther's Uncle, King Ahashvarous (linked perhaps to the historical character of Xertes) and of course, Haman with his three-cornered hat. But still a lot of other kids just used their Halloween costumes. Morrie was going as The Lone

Ranger. I wasn't sure whom I'd go as. Wearing a fake beard, a bathrobe and carrying a scroll for Mordecai didn't really appeal to me. Besides, I did that the year before. At least I had a couple of weeks to figure it out.

Around the house things were getting crazy as preparations for my Bar Mitzvah exploded. Dad booked rooms for out of town guests at the Sioux Apartments. Invitation replies from invited family and friends poured in. There were a lot of relatives coming, some I'd never even met.

We were going to have a family Erev Shabbat dinner before services. Our house just wasn't big enough. Saturday there'd be a brisket lunch after services. Mom and Dad were going to have an open house and serve hors d'oeuvres, cold cuts and desserts. Larry and Mark could come over too. Sunday we'd have a brunch for out of town guests, and then Dad and a couple of their friends would schlep people to the train station and airport.

The Purim carnival took place in Kaplan Hall. The extension had been built at the synagogue in '62 and was a long one-story building on the west side of the synagogue. It held a small stage, a meat kitchen, and enough seating for several hundred people. At the carnival, Larry, Mark and I did our utmost to win prize tickets. Mark was dressed as Haman. He wore black slacks, a black turtleneck sweater and an old pirate hat. He had a sword stuck in his belt. Larry had gone the traditional route and dressed as Mordecai complete with a fake longhaired wig and his dad's striped bathrobe. I'd gone non-traditional and dressed as Commando Cody, yet another character unknown to the youth of River City. I wore my dad's old black leather jacket, attached were two aluminum foiled round Quaker oats boxes as my jetpack. Using two pieces of shirt backing cardboard and painting them silver, I'd stapled them together and Dad had cut eyeholes and a mouth hole. In my belt I had a toy ray gun. Rocketman to the rescue!

I had to take the helmet off so I could see straight. So far I'd won five prize tickets. Mark had fifteen and Larry, athlete that he was, had twenty-five. Most of the small prizes: pens, pencils, and key chains, bubblegum were two tickets. The stuffed animals or sports equipment like a badminton set, a football, a soccer ball, or softball were more. Then there was other chazzerei like cheap plastic cap pistols, and some Barbie type dolls.

We took a break and looked at the prize table.

"Cashing in your ticket yet Larry?" I asked.

"Naw, I need another five for the football."

"I might get the harmonica," said Mark. Now what Mark would do with a harmonica would be anyone's guess. He couldn't sing worth shit, and he didn't read music. In fact, his voice was getting deeper. Pretty soon he'd sound like a bullfrog—unless Larry beat him to it first.

"You could get a necklace for Debbie," nudged Larry.

Mark glared at Paul. We all knew he had a thing for Debbie. "Piss off."

"Hey, it's ok to like girls," I said. "We're sorta like teenagers now."

"So why don't you buy something for April Blackman," shot back Mark.

I turned red. "Fuck you."

"Boys," said Larry, "we are in a holy place. Such language is offensive."

Mark and I turned to him. "Piss off."

One of the joyful booths at the carnival was the sponge throw. Both the Rabbi and my Dad volunteered. They had a sense of humor after all. I think that was the busiest booth at the carnival. I know lot of teenagers bought tickets, including Mark, Larry and I. Morrie thought it was hilarious seeing Dad's face soaked and his dark hair dripping. Of course Dad, being the practical joker, would get Morrie back when he least expected it. I couldn't wait to see that.

"Maybe we should go a bit easy on Rabbi Silverman," I said.

"Why?" asked Larry.

"Well, I gotta meet with him about my D'var Torah later this week."

"Tough tits for you," whispered Larry as he threw the soaking sponge and beaned the Rabbi right between the eyes.

April came over to visit during lunch. She was dressed as Queen Esther and wore a long white gown and white dance shoes. A small gold plastic crown rested on her head.

Long tables had been set up close to the kitchen. The lunch was set up buffet style with warming trays full of hot dogs, sliced buns, bowls of potato chips, egg salad and coleslaw. Bottles of pop and plastic cups were at a separate table. Most of the little kids were making swamp water, mixing several types of pop.

"Is it okay if I sit here?" she asked.

We looked up and I nodded, but not too enthusiastically. The guys teased me enough as it was. She sat down to my left. Of course. She didn't ask who I was supposed to be, like a lot kids did. We'd played Rocketman at our house. She of course was the female lab assistant. But, instead of being a screamer, like in the movie serial, she packed a toy gun and could join in pretend fights.

"Win enough prize tickets to get anything?" asked Mark politely.

"Actually I won a teddy bear and a hula hoop."

"I didn't know anyone still played with those," said Larry.

"What did you get?" she asked Larry.

"I need a few more prize tickets, and I'm getting a football."

"Then you'd better hurry, there's only two left," said April.

Larry looked up. "Back to work. Come on boys."

"I gotta finish my hot dog," I said. "I'll catch up." I had my eye on a realistic looking cap pistol.

Mark finished wolfing his down and stood up. "We'll let the love birds talk," he said as he left.

I flipped him the bird.

"You can go if you want," said April.

"It's okay." I took another bite out of my hotdog. Mustard oozed out the side. I used my finger and caught it and licked it off.

"You're not afraid of girl cooties?" She giggled.

"Already got yours." I grinned.

"True, and you can have some more if you want." She moved closer.

I looked at her and blushed. And then I looked around to see if anyone was looking at us. Mom and Dad's spies were everywhere.

Gifts started pouring in. I got a lot of checks and some bonds from some relatives. Congregants sent a variety of gifts. I received two clock radios, a desk set consisting of a desk pad, wastepaper basket and pencil holder. It was brown with a pattern of fleur de lis. I got a couple of ballpoint pens, and a pen desk holder with two pens. I also got a sixteen-pound bowling ball with my initials on it. All I needed was for Dad to take me down to the sporting goods store so they could measure my hand and drill the holes. It also came with a nice black leather case.

After dinner, mom and dad got me a spiral notebook and divided the pages into sections, along with a roll of stamps. The first was the gift, then name, address, and a space to check off when I wrote the thank you note. Mom suggested not waiting until after my Bar Mitzvah to start writing them. Dad suggested I write about ten a night.

"It'll take you about a half an hour. I think you can spare that much time from homework and studying. Make sure you check the name off once you've addressed the envelope. When you have a stack ready, put a stamp on them and give them to me. I'll take them down to the post office."

He was sitting on my bed. I sat across the room at my desk. "What about all these checks and things?"

"Tomorrow after school I'll pick you up and we'll go down to the bank. We'll open up a savings account and get a safety deposit box. All the savings bonds, we'll put in the box. It'll take about seven years before they come due. You'll be able to use them for college. The checks and cash we'll deposit."

"Don't I get to keep any of it?" I was thinking I should be allowed a bit for comics and movies, as well as buying a guitar.

"What are you planning to spend it on?"

"Well stuff… comics, paperbacks, movies, maybe some records… and a guitar."

Dad raised his eyebrows. "A guitar?" He nodded. "Well, we'll see how much you have, maybe five to ten percent. But the majority of it has to go into savings. You have no idea what college expenses are."

"Do I have to go to college?"

"You want to be something when you grow up? High school education doesn't get you much, and college will open doors for you, no matter what you decide to do. Your mother and I both went to college."

"I don't know what I want to do."

"Well you have until the end of high school to make up your mind." He got off the bed and reached into his pocket for his Kents. He took the pack and shook one out. Dad stuck the cigarette in his mouth and reached into his other pocket for his lighter. It was silver and had his initials on it. He lit up and took a drag. "Anyway, you have studying to do. And remember to write down all the gifts you got today."

I watched him leave the room. Jeez, how much time did they think I had?

It was during this time too I received invitations to some other Bar and Bat Mitzvahs. It was going to be a very busy spring and early summer. There weren't any during July and early August so my dad and the Rabbi could take vacation. I knew this summer we were going to Miami to visit my grandparents. Nana and Grandpop had moved down there a few years ago when Grandpop retired and closed his confectionary store at the Chicago train station.

As ordered, I wrote ten Thank You notes and addressed them. Afterwards I did my school homework and spent about half an hour on my Bar Mitzvah stuff. I had the haftorah down and most of Musaf. I still had to make corrections and additions to my speech, but I wasn't due to meet with Rabbi Silverman for a couple of days. I looked at the clock on my gold and white clock radio. It was ten o'clock, too late to call Larry and schmooze with him. Crap, I even missed *The Man from U.N.C.L.E.* Well that'd be an episode to catch on summer reruns, presuming I remembered.

At the end of the month Dad started rehearsing with me in the main sanctuary. We went over the Torah reading, my Haftorah and speech. I chanted the Musaf service. Then we'd go after the little bit I was doing Friday night: the Kiddush, the blessing over the wine, and the concluding prayer the Aleinu and Yigdal. I was still having trouble with that one   Vatz-a-vem (or I as I continually mispronounced it: v'tits-a vame), Dad was going ballistic. He voice went beyond thunder and his face turned red. Thankfully he didn't spank anymore. Actually spanking had ended for me when I was eight.

Dad used to enjoy playing with us. We played cowboys with Morrie and me against dad. We'd strap on our six-guns and run and hide around the house. Well at the time the upstairs was a guest room. We had the rollaway bed set up for when Grammy was coming to visit from Chicago. I was running away from dad and he grabbed me from behind. I guess I had the proper leverage and inadvertently used a judo throw. He sailed over the rollaway and landed flat on his ass—dazed. I remember him looking around, then back at me. He wobbled a bit when he got up and declared that we were done playing. After that if I got into trouble, he never spanked me.

In the end, he wrote the word out in transliteration in my prayer book. He figured there was no way I could screw up now.

***

July 2012: Wednesday

After morning minyan, I went to St. Luke's and visited Mr. Marcovitch who'd fallen off a ladder while cleaning out his eaves. He'd fractured his leg in two places. I tapped on the door to his room. "Up for a visitor?" I asked.

Mr. Marcovitch had his leg slightly elevated. He wore a maroon terrycloth robe over his bedclothes. He peered at me from above a copy of the River City Journal. "Ah, Rabbi, come in. I'd offer you coffee, but as you can see, this isn't my home."

"It's ok," I chuckled. I saw a blue vinyl chair in the corner and pulled it closer to the bed, and I sat down. "So, what's new?"

For the next fifteen minutes Mr. Marcovitch and I kibbitzed about the stupidity of his accident, goings on at shul, and the views within the Jewish community. He'd been a member of the Orthodox synagogue, Beth Joseph, when it had existed. Now however, most of the more traditional Jews did their own service in the chapel. He also remembered my father.

"I loved your dad's voice. I remember coming to a number of Bar Mitzahs at Beth Zion, including yours," said Mr. Marcovitch.

"That was a long time ago," I replied.

"Yes, and look where it got you," he laughed.

"Yeah, I know. I remember a colleague of my father's once told me: 'Being a Cantor is not a job for a nice Jewish boy."

"So is that what prompted you to finally become a Rabbi?"

"It seemed a good career move. It made me more marketable, and I wanted to be able to do everything," I answered. "Even though as an ordained Cantor I could."

"Well, I'm glad you're here. We need a guy like you, a mensch. Not that your predecessor wasn't, may he rest in peace. But you have a history here. You know us. You understand us. That's very important."

A few minutes later I made my farewell and left Mr. Marcovitch.

I had to go downtown to Shaeffer's, to get some pants altered.

I headed down Pierce. On the way, I had a sudden whim and turned off on 16th and drove up the hill to the old Beth Zion building. I pulled over and parked. The side street was still tree-lined. A light morning breeze rustled the branches. By the side door there was a small fenced in playground, so presumably the church had a pre-school program. I jaywalked across the street. The tall thin stained glass windows were still there I walked around the front and stood on the steps leading up to the main doors. A lamp hung over the middle one. The name above now read: Mount Zion.

A lady parked in front of the social hall and got out. She was a middle-aged black woman, tall, stately "Can I help you?" she asked.

"Just having a nostalgic look around. I'm Rabbi Reimer. My father was the Cantor when this was Beth Zion Synagogue."

"Are you visiting?"

"Actually I've just taken over as spiritual leader at Temple Beth Shalom."

"Well, welcome home. Would you like to see the inside? I'm Mrs. Beaumont. I'm the pastor's secretary."

"A pleasure to meet you." I shook her long-fingered dry hand.

"We'll use the side entrance," she said.

We walked around to the side and back down the hill. As we entered I saw the office looked pretty much the same. The office was on the right, and through it was now the Pastor's office.

"Pastor Davis is out doing hospital calls."

"And I'm just coming from mine."

Mrs. Beaumont led me around on a tour. My dad's former office was now the Music Director's. The chapel, library and classrooms were all the same. In fact, I don't think they'd even been redecorated. We went upstairs. The lobby was the same with white marble floors engraved with the Mogen David, the star of David, the same motif in the stained-glass windows above the dark mahogany doors.

We entered into the main sanctuary.

"As you can see, we've only made minor changes."

A smaller raised stage sat on the bimah with a bit of a railing. In front of the platform were four high-back straight armchairs. Where the ark with Torah table had once been, a small podium extended out. A small choir station was now at the bottom of the bimah with a music stand in front of it. I figured that's where the choir or organist sat.

I walked part and sat down in one of the pews. I took a deep breath.

"It is truly a beautiful place to pray," said Mrs. Beaumont. "I find there's a real feeling of spirit here."

"I agree. I had my Bar Mitzvah here. I was the first Cantor's son to ever have a Bar Mitzvah at Beth Zion."

"Really? So this place has a lot of memories here for you.

I nodded.

She put a hand on my shoulder. Why don't you sit here a while. I'm going back downstairs. Don't forget to say good-bye before you go."

"Thank you. I will. And thank you for your kindness and hospitality."

"We're all sisters and brothers, Rabbi."

I heard her soft footsteps go away. I sat there, the sunlight gleaming through the stained glass windows, making colored patterns on the pews. A feeling of serenity came over me. I took a deep breath and once again was swept away in a sea of memory.

Part II: The Bar Mitzvah

Chapter Eleven

April 1965

The Vietnam War was heating up and thirty-five hundred people marched in Washington to protest the war. There was rioting in Los Angeles. The weekend of my Bar Mitzvah saw the worst natural disaster to strike the eastern Midwest as twelve hundred people were injured and one hundred and thirty five people died in tornadoes that devastated Indiana. But in River City, the skies were clear, the sun shone down and I celebrated my Bar Mitzvah.

The week before me, Beth Levine, Larry's cousin, had her Bat Mitzvah on Friday. Beth did a Haftorah, a D'var Torah and the Kiddush, the blessing over the wine. Afterwards, the Oneg Shabbat was great.

They had two kinds of punch. Both with a chunk of sherbet in it, but the other bowl also had some liquor in it, which of course Larry, Mark and I tried to sneak when the adults weren't looking.

"So, you nervous?" asked Mark.

"I guess," I said. "I mean there's going to be a crap load of people coming. Dad had to invite the entire community."

"Maybe I should sell hotdogs and Coke during the service," joked Larry. "It could be profitable."

I rolled my eyes. "Typical capitalist."

Larry gave me a big toothy smile. "Damn right."

"We're having salad, brisket, roasted potatoes, peas and carrots. And Mom's letting me have a bottle of ketchup at the head table."

"Good menu," said Mark.

"We'll be there," said Larry. "But no salad for me. My dad says there's only two things you do with things that are green: save it or invest it."

"You guys coming to the house next Saturday night?" I asked.

"Yep," said Larry. "Someone has to help you celebrate."

"I can come for a short time," said Mark.

"Great."

"So, your girlfriend coming?" asked Larry.

I looked at him questioningly.

"April Blackman?" Larry turned to Mark. "How soon they forget."

I stammered a bit. "She's not my girlfriend. She's just—a friend. Her mom and my mom are friends."

Larry winked at Mark. "Right. It's okay, Slim."

"You looked pretty comfortable with her at the movie," said Mark.

Damn, they had noticed. I ignored the jabs and answered their question. "As far as I know, she won't be at the house. It's pretty much just for adults."

"Probably past her bedtime," said Larry.

Mark snickered.

"Assholes," I said.

"And we're all yours," quipped Larry.

"I'm so lucky."

"So you should be," said Mark.

We moseyed over to the punch bowl again and got some punch with sherbet, but only partially filled our cups. Larry sneaked a cup of spiked punch and poured a bit into Mark's and my cups, then the balance into his. "Bottom's up, boys."

On Tuesday when I went to Klages after school, and before my final rehearsal at the synagogue I checked the comic book racks, but there wasn't much out. *Detective*

#338 showed Batman with a super punch. Marvel's *Daredevil* #7 looked interesting. Paul would be happy to know the new issues of *Action* and *Adventure* were in. Action featured a story where Clark Kent was in prison.

As I was leaving, I discovered a copy of Ian Fleming's James Bond novel, *Goldfinger*, in the small magazine and paperback rack near the front door. The cover had Bond played by Connery holding a gun against a background of Shirley Eaton's golden, naked body. I snatched it up. Gifts had been good and I had the fifty cents to cover the paperback's cost. I figured that if the Rabbi's speech was too boring, I could bring something to read.

People started arriving on Thursday. Aunts, uncles, distant cousins of Dad's I'd never met came in by train and plane and were taken to the Sioux Apartment Hotel, a huge red brick building on 17th Street and Grandview. At one time it'd been an elegant place to stay. We'd even stayed their one night when we moved here, because the moving van wouldn't come until the next day. My parents ran a cab service. Dad was constantly schlepping from either the train station or the airport. A few congregants offered to help pick up guests, and dad took them up on it. My Aunt Rose and Uncle Herman, Grammy's kid sister and brother-in-law from Chicago booked in at one of the fancier hotels downtown. Grammy had offered them to stay with her, but her place was a bit small. I got relegated to a fold-a-bed in Morrie's room as Nana Esther and Grandpop took over my room. I knew my bedroom would reek of cigar smoke. It was just for the weekend, but I wasn't sure I'd survive.

At four o'clock on Friday, I got dressed in my suit. Dad put my tie on since I hadn't learned how to tie it yet. Dad had Morrie and I stand with Mom and he took a picture, then he gave me the camera, a Leica 35mm range finder he'd gotten second hand, and had me take a picture of Mom and him. I also took a picture of Shadow. After all, he was a family member too.

Before we left the house, I had my marked prayer book and I slipped the copy of *Goldfinger* into my suit jacket pocket. It fit perfectly. Nana and Grandpop were driving to shul. They'd take Grammy. Dad gave them directions. Hopefully Grandpop wouldn't get lost. One time he was going to a Shriner's convention in Atlantic City. He started out early in the morning. Three hours later Dad got a call from him. "Hey Duvidal, how the hell do I get out of the city and get on the interstate?" Dad ended up driving down to where he was and guiding him out.

Friday night we had Shabbat dinner in Kaplan Hall. Mom, and her sister Eileen did the candle lighting. Aunt Eileen had taken the train in from Chicago, but Uncle Rob and my cousins Naomi and Ruth couldn't come. I recited the Kiddush and Hamotzi. The Women's League had prepared dinner. We had chicken soup with kreplach—the Jewish version of wontons, but stuffed with beef. For the main course we had a roast chicken dinner with wild rice, and peas.

Rabbi Silverman and his wife and kids were seated next to us. Across from them were mom's parents. Grammy, Uncle Herman and Aunt Rose sat further down. It was smart to separate the grandparents. We didn't want a fight to start up.

The problem was partly old world prejudices. My dad's parentage was German. Mom's was Russian. According to Nana the problems with Germans were that they didn't have a sense of humor. But the real problem was that somehow Grammy never thought Mom was good enough for Dad. It was one of the reasons we moved from Chicago. I remember hearing my parents talking. Mom told Dad that if he wanted their marriage to last, they needed to get away from Chicago. Mom was tired of Grammy bugging her and dropping in unannounced.

After dinner I followed Dad to his office on the right side of the bimah. I went to the bathroom, then Dad reviewed the few parts I was leading.

At two minutes of eight, the Rabbi buzzed Dad's office and with impeccable timing, we entered onto the bimah from the hidden doors. I looked out. The place was packed tighter than a fat lady in a girdle. People were even sitting behind the choir in the balcony. The first several rows on my right were filled with family. I took my seat on the other side of the door. Pulpit chairs are the most uncomfortable chairs anywhere. They look swell, but they're either too hard so it's like sitting on cement, or too soft, as in this case, and my ass sank in. I sat back. Dad and Rabbi walked to their lecterns. The chattering dropped off and the choir began with Ma Tovu. We sang or read in English unison several of the psalms. Dad and the choir did *L'cha Dodi*, and *Tov L'hodot*, Psalm 92. And then we were into the main evening service. Everything went smoothly. I glanced out and saw Larry and his family sitting in their seats midway from the bimah. We stood and silently recited the Amidah. Afterwards, Dad sat down and Rabbi Silverman began his sermon. I checked to see if anyone was looking, and slid the copy of *Goldfinger* out of my suit jacket pocket and began to read.

Rabbi Silverman was talking about his recent trip to Mississippi. "As you know, I have returned from a recent trip to Mississippi to observe and experience the struggle of Negroes in the south, and the prejudices they face, which is similar to those we faced down through the centuries. There is no question as to the injustice, the gross injustice in not permitting a segment of our citizenry to vote. The question I pose is, would we behave differently if we were thrust in such an environment of injustice, or would we, too, try to rationalize our guilt away? I have to report that I was not well received by the Jewish community of thirty-five families or so in Hattiesburg. In fact, the president of the shul told me, in no uncertain terms that I was an embarrassment to the Jewish community there. It hurt me, as I tried to understand this feeling, as part of the white community's feeling of disgust for any white man who sleeps in the poor Negro section of town. However when I went to the shul the older members received me quite cordially. These are men who are closer to our tradition. Who still speak a little Yiddish. Who understood the words in the Siddur; who told me in private that they were proud of Rabbis who come down to do the work of their consciences..."

Rabbi Silverman droned on. I sort of half paid attention. Given the topic, I probably should've paid more attention. In fact, it would probably have been better if I had paid full attention, but not because of his message. I tend to shut down when I'm reading. I'm oblivious to my surroundings. One time in fifth grade I was reading this mystery novel and didn't even hear the lunch buzzer go. Miss Hamilton had to give me a shake. Turns out I had missed ten minutes of my lunch hour.

"...Shabbat Shalom, and now we'll continue with the Kiddush on page 28 of our prayer books."

Silence.

"Ahem," grunted the Rabbi.

I felt something tap me on the shoulder. I shook myself, startled, and looked up. Rabbi Silverman was giving me his serious look. Oops. I saw Dad staring at me, raising an eyebrow. Shit, caught in the act. I jammed the paperback in my pocket and got up.

I walked across the bimah to Dad's lectern. I took the silver cover off the silver Kiddush cup and lifted it with my right hand. I began to chant, "Baruch atah adonai..."

I was definitely going to get a lecture when I got home. But let's face it, Rabbi's sermon versus James Bond? Who would you choose?

At the end of the service I walked down the middle aisle with the Rabbi and Dad to greet people. Mom joined us. Grammy took Morrie into the social hall. I shook hands until I thought my arm would fall off. And even though it was Shabbat, I ended up having both pockets on my jacket, as well as my inside pocket stuffed with envelopes. Maybe they should put larger pockets in suit jackets.

"I hope you're going to pay more attention tomorrow Jeff," whispered Rabbi Silverman.

"Yes, sir. Definitely."

"Good."

Dad gave me a gentle whack in the back of the head. "No book tomorrow."

The reception line ended and I could escape into the Oneg. I managed to squeeze my way to the table with the coffee, tea and punch. Larry, Mark, and Mainard were there.

"So what happened up there? You fall asleep?" asked Mainard.

"Sort of tuned out."

"Uh huh-daydreaming as usual?" asked Mark.

"Something like that."

Larry looked at me suspiciously. He then eyed the bulge in my jacket pocket.

"What? Come on, let's get some punch," I said.

"We want the good stuff. Today you are a man, so therefore we should be allowed," said Larry.

We trooped over to the table and started ladling some punch from the adult bowl.

"I don't think so," came a voice from behind. We turned and looked. Mark's dad was standing there. He was a tall bear of a man. He looked at the disappointment on our faces. It didn't change his mind. "When you're older."

"But I'm an adult by Jewish standards," I said.

"Yes, but not by Iowa legal standards. Good try though," he chuckled.

Parents have a nasty sense of humor.

We wandered over to the pastry table and I snatched a chocolate chip cookie.

"Didn't know you could have that," said Mainard.

"It's my Bar Mitzvah." I stuck my tongue out.

Suddenly the cookie was snatched away. I turned and saw Larry take a bite out of it.

"We wouldn't want you to fall off the wagon." He grinned devilishly.

More people came over and shook my hand. Then the relatives found me. Pinched cheeks, kisses and hearty handshakes besieged me. When I looked around, my fellow musketeers had vanished into the sea of people.

By the time we got home it was ten-thirty and I was exhausted. I remembered to hang my suit up so it wouldn't wrinkle and crawled into the rollaway bed. I slept like a corpse.

Saturday morning after a light breakfast of toast with cream cheese and jam and a cup of coffee, I went to shul early with Dad. I left my copy of *Goldfinger* at home. Mom and Morrie would walk with Nana, Grandpop, and Grammy. I was glad I wasn't walking in that procession.

At the synagogue I sat in Dad's office and went over my stuff while he prepared. I had my siddur, Haftorah book, and my speech. I also had a Tallit (prayer shawl) that my Grandfather in Israel had sent me. He and my grandmother had divorced when Dad was five. After that, Grandfather Yehuda emigrated to Israel. Later he remarried. Dad had a couple of stepsisters there. The collar of the Tallit had my name on it in silver thread. I said the blessing and put on the Tallit.

The service started promptly at nine o'clock with Mr. Nussaman doing the preliminary service and ending every sentence with an oy, oy. By nine thirty Dad took his lectern and began to chant the prayers leading to Shacharit, the morning service, in his deep baritone voice, "Shocane ad marom v'Kadosh shemo…" (He abides in eternity, exalted and holy.)

By ten o'clock when we started the Service for Taking Out the Torah, the synagogue was jammed. All our relatives and family friends were sitting on both sides of the aisle down in front. I saw the Katzmans sitting behind my Mom and Morrie, who were sitting in the front row. My grandparents were sitting on opposite sides of the center aisle. Further back I could see Larry sitting with his mom and brothers. Mr. Shaeffer, as president was sitting on the bima next to the Rabbi. Further back I thought I saw Mark and his family and behind them April and her family. Sunlight streamed in through the stained glass windows and lit the sanctuary up in an array of rainbow colors.

Rabbi Silverman signaled me and we stood before the ark. Dad sang "Ein Kamocha va-Elim Adonai" (None is compared to you Lord our God).

Nana and Grandpop opened it. I knew Uncle Herman and Aunt Rose would be doing the opening and closing when we returned it. Rabbi handed me the Torah. We then turned around and my Dad began to sing "Shema Yisrael Adonai Eloheinu, Adonai Ehad" (Hear Oh Israel, the Lord is our God, the Lord is One.)

When we returned to the bimah after the Torah procession I sat down and Rabbi Silverman called up my father for the Cohen aliyot. As Cohanim, descendants of the high priests, we could only have the first or seventh aliyah. Then, Dad went to the side and followed as the Rabbi read the section from the Torah. Mr. Schaffer was acting as one of the shomerim, the guardians to follow along and ensure the Rabbi didn't make any mistakes in chanting the Torah. Half way through I knew Dad and Rabbi would switch as Shomerim as Dad read the second half of the reading. Thankfully, our synagogue had adapted the triennial reading style so that we read only one third of the weekly portion instead of the complete portion. It cut the service down by at least fifteen to twenty minutes.

Finally it was my turn. I heard my Rabbi call me by my Hebrew name.

"Yamod: Shlomo Ari ben He-Hazzan Dovid ha-Cohen, Maftir. Hazak (strength)."

I stepped up and touched the Torah with the fringes of my tallit, then kissed it. I began chanting the blessing, "Barchu et Adonai Hamvorach" (Blessed are you Lord, the one who is to be blessed). I followed along after the blessing as Dad chanted the section of Torah. I recited the blessing after.

The Torah was lifted and taken away. Dr. Katzman, Hagbah, the person who lifted the scroll to show the sections that had been read sat down with the Torah. David Katzman, honored with Gelilah, put the dressings on. A hush settled over the congregation.

I stood at the Torah table, my red covered Haftorah book in front of me. I remember what Dad had told me. You don't need to look at anyone. Just concentrate on the text. I felt butterflies in my stomach, and I was thankful I only had a light breakfast. It would have been embarrassing to puke on the bimah. I took a deep breath. I stared at the page and began to chant the Blessing before the Haftorah: "Boruch atah, adonai, eloheinu melech ha-olam, asher bachar…"

I don't remember much. The words flowed and a feeling of warmth washed over me. I could hear my voice but it didn't seem to be coming from me. I finished the recitation of my haftorah, words from the prophet Malachi. "Hinei ahnochi, sholach lachem et Eliyahoo Hanavi lif-nai bo yom Adonai ha-gadol v' ha-no-rah" (Behold I will send you Elijah the Prophet before the coming of the great and dreadful day of the Lord).

Not the most uplifting message to end on I thought. I looked up. Mom was wiping her eyes with her handkerchief.

Next came my speech that went flawlessly. I hadn't bothered to revise it from when the Rabbi gave his approval. Afterwards he came over to me and sort of addressed me and the congregation.

"Jeff, we're all proud of you today. I know your parents are particularly proud, and you share a unique honor in being the first Cantor's son ever to have a Bar Mitzvah in this synagogue. This Shabbat, Shabbat ha-Gadol, the great Sabbath before the Israelites exited Egypt, was the first step the Israelites took towards their becoming B'nei Mitzvah, children of the commandments. They too were filled with trepidation about what that would mean. About what the future would hold for them, as no doubt you do. But their faith in Moses and in God to show them the way, gave them strength. You've had good teachers along the way too, especially your father who trained you for this day. And I know you will continue your studies. This is only the first step of becoming a Jewish adult, of taking responsibility for the many mitzvoth we're commanded to follow and do. Jewish education is life long, Jeff. We look forward to your continuing participation and leadership in this congregation now that you're on the path to adulthood.

"In the Torah portion today, Metzorah, we learned about health laws in relation to communicable diseases such as leprosy. The priests examined such people, who were suspected of having such diseases. If the diagnosis was positive, the person was required to bath regularly, his belongings and clothing cleaned or burned depending on the disease and the time it took for the individual to regain their health. Periods of reassessment were done.

"In ancient times disease was thought to have its origins not just in hygienic terms, but religious as well. Persons with such diseases as leprosy were assumed to have sinned in some way and sacrifices were prescribed accordingly. While we might find some humor in this rather superstitious approach to illness and medicine, it is interesting to note that because of the kashrut laws about personal hygiene, Jewish communities were seldom inflicted by epidemics and plagues, even in later times such as the middle ages when the black plague scoured Europe. Given our understanding of disease, it's interesting to speculate how such diseases would have been interpreted and dealt with back in ancient times.

"Unfortunately, not all diseases are physical in nature. Today the disease of racial hatred and anti-Semitism is still at epidemic proportions. We see how our brethren are treated in the Soviet Union and other parts of Europe and the Middle East. We've seen countries like Nazi Germany incite hatred and mistrust in Mid-eastern and European countries. This type of mental disease cannot be easily rectified; we cannot isolate these groups and individuals as priests did with lepers. And so the disease of hatred spreads. It threatens not only our well-being but those of other religious and racial backgrounds. Our history is filled with wars or intervention by God who wiped out our enemies. But times have changed. We have learned that hatred breeds hatred; violence breeds violence. Today's medicine is education. We must build bridges of understanding between cultures, religions and races. That is one of the reasons I went down South. To show support for our Negro brethren, and help ensure that they have the same rights as the rest of our great country.

"Education and dialogue is the only way to wipe out the disease of hate. Each of you can do your part, to improve understanding and tolerance in our daily dealings with the wider community.

"The prophet Isaiah proclaimed that we should be a 'Light to the nations'. This means to lead by example in doing the mitzvoth of T'kun Olam, of repairing the world. By teaching tolerance and understanding, by dealing fairly with all, let us join with others to lead the way away from hatred and intolerance and thereby hasten the coming of the messianic era. And now it is time, with your father's help, to invoke the three fold benediction upon you."

Dad came over. He chanted the priestly blessing in Hebrew and the Rabbi translated it into English: May the Lord Bless you and Keep you. May the Lord let his countenance shine upon you and be gracious to you. May the Lord show you kindness and bless you with peace."

The Rabbi then turned to the congregation. "We will continue with the Musaf service. Hazzan Jeffery Reimer will lead us." Rabbi Silverman winked at me.

A murmur of approval rumbled through the crowd.

I recited the Musaf amidah, and my mental blockage vanished. I pronounced *titsavim* correctly. I glanced over and saw my Dad give huge a sigh of relief and a nod of approval. I continued to chant the service, lost in the prayers and feeling amazing energy course through me. A kaleidoscope of emotions washed over me as I led the congregation in singing *Sim Shalom*, Grant Peace.

After the service a sea of people washed over me shaking my hand, stuffing envelopes in my pocket, pinching my cheeks, and slobbering kisses, none of which were more important to me than April Blackman. I saw her in line next to her mom. Mrs. Blackman with her beehive hairdo and bright yellow dress looked like she'd swallowed a whole turkey as she waddled up the line. When April, wearing a white dress and her patent leather shoes, came up to me, I extended my hand to shake hers. She had other plans, and pushed my hand aside and gave me a tight hug, her arms around my neck were so tight I could barely breathe. A long hard kiss on the lips followed. "You were great," she whispered in my ear.

I glanced over and saw my mom with eyebrows raised and my father grinning. Mrs. Blackman looked flabbergasted. God, I'd never hear the end of this.

More people came through the reception line greeting us as they made their way into the social hall.

"He's got a voice like an angel," said Mikayla Israelson, one of my dad's choir members said.

"He did a great job, you should be proud of him," said another congregant.

"You should become a Cantor like your father," said Mr. Weinberg. (Like that was ever gonna happen I thought.)

Mrs. Lipshitz shook my hand and pinched my cheek. "Mazel Tov, you did very well."

She then ignored my mother and shook hands with my dad. Mrs. Lipshitz had a bit of a problem with mom. When we first got here, my parents were introduced to like two hundred and fifty people that first Shabbat. And, they all expected them to remember all their names. The following Shabbat Mrs. Lipshitz came up to my mom and asked her, "Do you remember me?"

Mom was a bit flustered and replied, "Yes, you're Mrs. Shitlips."

Several Yom Kippurs have come and gone, but Mrs. Lipschitz has yet to forgive Mom.

Uncle Herman pinched my cheek and ruffled my hair. "A fine job Jeffery."

"And if you hadn't fallen asleep," said Aunt Rose, giving Uncle Herman a bit of a glare, "you would've heard his speech. Such a mensch!" Aunt Rose leaned down and kissed me on the cheek. I just about gagged from the scent of her perfume. She wore red lipstick and I knew there'd be a mark. There always was.

Uncle Herman shrugged, and shook my hand in a crushing grip. For an old guy, he was really strong.

Other cousins and aunts paraded by giving me handshakes and hugs. I thought my arm was going to fall off, I was so tired of shaking hands. But with each handshake, another envelope was thrust into my pocket. I figured I still had a few handshakes left in me.

The head table was set up in front of the stage. A bottle of Heinz Ketchup sat in front of my setting, along with a cup of wine and a Challah. My parents and grandparents sat on either side of me. Rabbi Silverman and his family sat on the end to my right. When everyone was seated, Dad led the Kiddush and Hamotzi. A low din of conversation rumbled off the concrete walls of the social hall. Ladies from Women's League served lunch, doing us first. The brisket was delicious, and as requested, I got the end pieces which were a bit better done.

As I was shoveling in a forkful of brisket, Aunt Rose came from behind and gave me another kiss on the cheek, and whispered, "Who was that nice looking girl who gave you a kiss?"

"Just a friend," I muttered.

"Really," replied Aunt Rose and went back to her seat. I saw her nudge Uncle Herman and give him a wink.

"I think April really likes you," said Mom.

I rolled my eyes and dunked another piece of brisket into the glob of ketchup on my plate. I jammed the forkful into my mouth.

A few more people came up to wish me Mazel Tov, the Jewish version of congratulations and proffered some envelopes. I said thank you and looked around for Mom's purse. My pockets were overflowing.

After I ate, I managed to excuse myself and headed for the bathroom. At least there was one place I might get a modicum of privacy. However my buddies, Larry, Mark, Mainard, Paul, and Tim caught up with me in the hall.

"Wow! That was impressive. I didn't know you could sing," said Tim.

"Don't over do it, it might go to his head," said Mark.

"It's ok. Nice job, Slim," said Larry. "By the way, I stood up for you last week."

"Oh really?" I looked at him suspiciously.

"Yeah, someone said you weren't fit to eat with the pigs. I said you were."

Paul burst out laughing.

I looked at Tim. "See what I have to put up with?"

But he didn't hear me. He and the others were laughing too hard.

"Your dad ream you out for reading during the Rabbi's sermon last night?" asked Mainard.

I shook my head. "I apologized to Rabbi Silverman. I told him reading helps me relax."

"What did he say?" asked Mark.

I straightened up and lowered my voice, trying to mimic. "That it was all very well and good, but not during services, and not trashy novels. Now, if I'd been reading Talmud, or Rashi, that might be a different story."

"Guess I'd better not try it," said Larry. "Good thing you weren't reading a comic book."

"No kidding," I said. I remembered the run-in I'd had on one of my Hebrew lessons with Dad the year before. Rabbi Silverman stopped by and poked his head in to say hello. I looked up and the new issue of *Batman* fell out of my binder. He just about went ballistic. If I hadn't been meeting Dad, I'm sure he would have confiscated it. Of course he didn't know that Dad usually read my comics while I did written Hebrew work.

"Now, if you'll excuse me, I gotta take a leak." I waved off and bustled down the hall. I went into one of the stalls in the Men's room and took a deep breath. I peed. Washed my hands and stood there staring into the mirror.

I'd done it. Today I was a man-well sorta, maybe, not really. But all the studying and cramming had paid off. I'd done perfectly. I took another deep breath. I was tired. Drained. Bereft of energy. I needed dessert.

When I re-entered the social hall Dr. Katzman and David came over and shook my hand. "You did alright young man," said Dr. Katzman.

"Good job," said David. "Guess you can breathe easy. And, when you have time you can come over and I'll teach you a couple more judo moves. "

"That'd be great," I said.

"Anyway, we'll see you tonight," said Dr. Katzman.

I saw the gaggle of girls from the B'nai Mitzvah class huddling together near the stage. Janet, Cindy, Susan, Molly, and Beth looked at me and giggled. I nodded and grinned at them. It was nice to be acknowledged.

I headed for the dessert table. In the center was my Bar Mitzvah cake. It was a rectangular chocolate with chocolate icing and white trim. A little figure of a young boy in a black suit standing at a lectern was at the top of this icing created book. The 'pages' were white and yellow trim surrounded it. On the left side was my name and the date. On the right it said Mazel Tov in blue icing with a yellow Star of David beneath it. Mrs. Greenspan was cutting the cake. She saw me and gave me a corner piece. I thanked her and grabbed a chocolate chip cookie off one of the pastry trays and headed back to my seat.

Morrie had gotten his cake. The evidence was smeared on the corners of his mouth.

"Can I go now? I'm done," he said to Mom.

"I guess, but stay in this room. Don't go out and don't get your clothes messy."

Great advice but I knew my brother. His shirt-tails would be flying out in no time. He left the table and looked for his friend Jacob Sherman. The two were thick as thieves and made Dennis the Menace look like a choirboy.

Last year Morrie decided he was going to freeze bugs and bring them back to life by warming them over the stove. Mom went to the freezer and she found a dozen Dixie cups covered with wax paper. In each cup was a frozen bug. After getting over her shock, she promptly collected them and turfed them into the garbage.

Another time, Morrie's friend Dennis Littleton got mad at his parents and dumped all the food out of the fridge and rolled it down the alley. Morrie was there and didn't stop him. Dad grounded him. Morrie complained, "I didn't do anything,"

Dad replied, "You should have. Do you know how much food costs? You should've stopped Dennis."

And then there was the time, well I was maybe partly to blame, we used the cord from the vacuum cleaner so Morrie could rappel down the laundry chute to the basement. We were playing Flash Gordon and Morrie had to escape from a crashing spaceship. Unfortunately Mom was down there doing laundry and when she looked up, she saw Morrie's dangling legs and let out a shriek. And then there were the dirty clothes bombardments when Mom went to get clothes out of the basket below the chute and Morrie or I would dump more dirty clothes down on her, as we pretended to destroy Ming's evil forces.

After services we headed home. A couple of ladies from Women's League would bring the leftover pastry along with some more stuff to the house for tonight. It was a sunny day. It felt good to be done, and free from studying. I couldn't wait to get home and get out of my suit and into some jeans and a t-shirt.

The family, relatives and our close family friends the Katzmans, came for dinner. Dad had gotten cold cuts: corned beef, pastrami, roasted chicken, along with potato salad, potato chips, coleslaw, and pickles. He'd gone to the bakery and gotten some good caraway rye and some pumpernickel. The platters were picked cleaner than vultures eating a cow carcass. Afterwards my grandparents, and Aunt Eileen, my mom's older sister, helped clean up. Uncle Herman, Uncle Robert and Dad hauled up cases of liquor and pop from the basement and set up a small bar area in the living room.

People started coming over at eight o'clock. Larry and Mark showed up and we grabbed some pop and a plate full of hors d'oeuvres and pastry and headed into my temporary bedroom. Morrie was in there playing with his army figures. There was a battle going on. He mussed up a blanket into a hill and had men planted in them. Down below tanks were surrounding it. He looked at our plates. "I want some."

"So, go and scavenge," I said. "Aunt Eileen or Nana will set you up."

"But I'm tired of getting my cheeks pinched."

"That's because you're so cute," I said.

Morrie stuck his tongue out at me and left the room. "Peace at last."

"At least he doesn't run around naked," said Larry.

"That could be a good thing, especially tonight," agreed Mark.

"So where's your girlfriend, Slim?" asked Larry as he shoveled a mini-bagel with lox into his mouth. "Despite what you said earlier, I thought you'd change your mind."

"Huh?"

"April Blackman," said Mark. He turned to Larry. "He's getting senile now that he's a Bar Mitzvah." He turned back to me and said with an evil grin, "I saw the smooch she planted on you."

I turned slightly red. "She's just a good friend."

Mark turned to Larry. They looked at each other and nodded. "Uh huh."

"Her parents will be here tonight. She won't. Kids aren't invited."

"Uh huh," said Larry. "Anyway you're going to be getting an invitation to a dance next month. My aunt and uncle along with the Glass and the Davidson families are hosting a Bat Mitzvah party for Beth, Cindy and Susan. It's going to be at the Holiday Inn and they're hiring a live band."

"Cool. Only one problem. I can't dance."

Mark smirked. "Maybe April can teach you."

"Piss off."

"My brother showed me some moves. It's easy," said Larry.

I looked doubtfully at him. But Marshall was a couple of years older. He went to lots of socials and dances. Maybe he did pick something up. "Something to look forward to," I said.

We went out and scarfed some chips and pastries. Relatives assaulted me with hugs, kisses, cheek pinches, and iron handshakes. It was twenty minutes before I escaped back to my room where Mark and Larry were sitting. They had the radio on. Gerry and the Pacemakers were singing *Ferry Across the Mersey*, to the land where I belong—"

I don't know when the party died down. People streamed through the house like a river. Mark and Larry's parents left with them around eleven o'clock. I went to bed. Morrie was already asleep. He'd eaten a lot of food. I hoped he wouldn't puke on me.

The next morning I found Mom in the kitchen slicing bagels. There were platters of sliced tomatoes and cucumber, lox, and Challah buns and bagels on the dining room table. I could smell the coffee brewing.

I turned around at the sound of footsteps coming down the stairs and Grandpop and Nana were there. "Good morning boychick," said Grandpop. He was a short bald man with glasses. This morning he wore a pair of gray slacks and a white shirt with the collar button undone.

I smiled. "Good morning."

"Anything I can do to help?" asked Nana Esther.

My mom shrugged. "Most of it I have done. David just went to pick up fresh cinnamon buns from the bakery."

"What time are people coming over?"

"Probably in an hour."

"I don't have to go to Sunday school?" I asked.

"Not today. You get to rest. But before you disappear, go and grab a towel. There's some dishes on the drain board."

I groaned. So soon, it's over. The services flew by and everything seemed like a dream. It was over. The ordeal was actually over. I could sit back and relax. I was the ganza macher now. I grinned.

"Is Morrie still asleep?" asked Grandpop.

"Yes, he was exhausted. He can sleep for another half an hour."

"Well just don't stand there Lou, grab a towel and help out."

Grandpop ignored Nana Esther. "You get a paper around here?" He looked like a convict waiting to escape.

Mom shook her head. "It's in the living room."

Within seconds he disappeared. No doubt he was sitting in the white leather armchair reading the paper. If the TV hadn't been in my parent's bedroom no doubt that'd be on too.

After brunch Dad pulled out his camera and got pictures of the Katzmans, our cousins from Minneapolis, my Aunt and Uncle from Chicago, my grandparents, and an older couple, the Deutchmans, who had known my mom's family when they'd lived in Philadelphia. It was a bright sunny day. The temperature was in the mid-sixties. Dad handed his camera to Uncle Herman who took a couple of family shots. We stood on our front lawn, Dad with his arm around Morrie. My mom was on his right, and me next to Mom. Then Uncle Herman took another picture of my parents, Grandpop Nana, Cousin Minnie and my cousin Beth. I bent down on one knee in front of them. Morrie wasn't in the picture. He had to run into the house to pee. That was ok with me.

Sunday night we lay around like zombies. Mom and Dad were exhausted. Dad with the help of Mr. Shaeffer and Dr. Katzman had helped schlep our relatives to the airport and train station. A few who had driven from Chicago had left after brunch. For dinner we had leftover coleslaw, and cold cuts. Mom and Dad had potato salad, but Morrie and I wouldn't touch the stuff. Monday I had school. And that reminded me I had some reading to do for homework. But at least I'd have my room back. Mom had the sheets in the dryer.

After dinner, we cleaned up and I went upstairs. I lay on my unmade bed and it was strange. I didn't feel any different. I thought I would've. After all, I was a Jewish adult according to our tradition. But other than counting in a minyan, nothing else had changed. I was still a kid in seventh grade that had school, homework, and no driver's license. I guess I should've felt proud of my accomplishments. I'd chanted my Haftorah, led part of the service, dispensed a few, very few, words of wisdom about my Torah portion; and yet, every Jewish boy went through this. I was no different than those who had come before me. This was not the transformational event of a lifetime. I'd reached a goal. But there were more goals on my path to adulthood. At least I wouldn't have all that extra studying to do once my homework was completed.

On Monday, I sat in Miss Anderson's English class. We were studying the short story, and reading a story from Ray Bradbury, *The Fog Horn*. It was about a sea monster attracted to this lighthouse because of its foghorn. I loved reading Bradbury. He was the only writer I thought who wrote poetry in prose form. They'd made a movie based on the story. I'd seen it in Chicago on Sci-Fi Theatre on WGN. I hoped we'd get to see the film in class.

At lunch, I sat with Mark and Tim.

"Thanks again for inviting me to your Bar Mitzvah," said Tim. "That was quite something." Tim unwrapped a ham and cheese sandwich. I didn't understand what this obsession with goyim was for ham and eating meat and dairy together.

"Just wait until his voice changes," said Mark. He took a bite out of his salami sandwich.

"You're just jealous. My voice is changing, just more gradually than yours." I put down my corned beef on rye with brown mustard.

Josie Bresler walked by. Josie had been in my Hebrew school classes at the JCC. Her parents were members of Temple. Her Aunt had taught us in Hebrew school. She had short blonde hair and a willowy figure. She stopped at our table. "Nice job Jeff."

"Thanks."

Josie smiled at us then joined a group of girls.

"Guess chicks dig Bar Mitzvah boys," said Tim.

"Right," I muttered. But inside, I was smiling.

Passover started on the following Shabbat. Mom and Dad had worked all of Thursday changing dishes, washing cupboards, countertops and dishes. Passover dishes and pots and pans were hauled up from the basement. Oilcloth covered the kitchen counters. Carpets were vacuumed and linoleum floors washed. I helped Dad haul the regular dishes to the basement. The little bit of chametz, foods with leavening, were boxed and put into the basement storage room. Out of sight, out of mind.

Friday when I got home from school the house was filled with the smells of chicken soup, carrot tzimmes, and brisket. The Seder would begin when Dad got home from evening services. The Blackmans were invited for the first Passover Seder.

Mom was making up the Seder plate: parsley representing Spring and renewal, roasted egg, a symbol of life, and a roasted chicken bone to represent the Passover offering, salt water to represent the tears of our ancestor's suffering, horse-radish to represent the bitterness our ancestors suffered as slaves, and charoset, a mixture of apples, honey, wine, cinnamon and nuts, representing the mortar that the Israelites used to make bricks for Pharaoh's building projects. I loved the charoset. Even better was making a Hillel sandwich, a mix of horseradish and charoset on matzoh. Mom also had hard-boiled eggs in saltwater, boiled potato (in Europe green vegetables were hard to come by, so many Jews used potatoes), and plates of matzah.

Passover celebrates the exodus from Egypt. When the Israelites fled from Pharaoh, they didn't have enough time for their bread to rise, so they ate unleavened bread. According to the Torah, we were commanded to remember this event and eat matzah, unleavened bread, for seven days. The Talmud expanded that. We also couldn't have any food with leavening agents in it; or anything that expanded when cooked like: rice, corn, and beans. And of course anything used to cook or serve on during the year, couldn't be used for Passover either. Hence the changing of the guard.

The Seder is a meal centered around a service. We use the Haggadah, a book that is a collection of excerpts from the Torah, the Talmud and other sources that tell the story of the exodus and the miracles God performed for us. There are prayers we had to recite. During the Seder we're supposed to have four glasses of wine. We kids got kosher grape juice; but because I was Bar Mitzvah, I could have wine like the adults. Usually the first Seder, Dad had a lot of us participate either in Hebrew or English. The second night when it was just us, he rattled through it in Hebrew like a racecar driver in the Indy 500.

Thankfully Morrie was old enough to do the Four Questions, which start the response for the telling of the Passover story. Dad had told me I'd do the Festival Kiddush that I had learned by listening to him over the years.

"Go up and change," said Mom when I walked in the door. She had her apron on and was using the carpet sweeper in the living room.

"Do I have to wear a tie?" I hated ties, probably, because I didn't know how to tie them.

"No, just a pair of dress pants and a white shirt."

"No jacket?"

Mom looked at me with a somewhat exasperated expression. "NO jacket. Now go clean up and change. The Blackmans will be here shortly."

I walked swiftly down the hall and pounded upstairs.

I was lying on my bed reading an issue of *Green Lantern* when April came in. The comic had a great cover of Green Lantern apparently having been changed into a robot. I looked up. She strode over, leaned over and planted a kiss on my forehead. I put the comic down and she kissed me on the lips.

"Hi."

"Hi," I had a big shitfaced grin on my face. It was very hard to remain cool and aloof when April was with me. I pushed myself up into a sitting position and swung my legs over the side of the bed. April sat down next to me. She wore a white blouse, red skirt and white knee high socks. She had black patent leather shoes on. She smelled clean and fresh. I put my hand over hers.

"Getting over the big weekend?" she asked.

"Yeah, but it went so fast. All that work and it was over in a blink of an eye." I looked at her. "If it weren't for the presents, I wonder if it'd be worth it."

"It's part of our tradition that goes way back."

"Well to sometime in the middle ages. It's actually a combination of Ashkenazi and Sephardi traditions. Back in Moses' time, kids our age would be getting married."

"Ewwww, like I have to put up with creepy guys now. Well, except for you." April smiled.

"The thank you notes are gonna take me forever."

"You have to show appreciation," said April. For being younger than me, there were times she was definitely smarter. And that scared me.

"I'm having a birthday party in a couple of weeks." April's birthday was on the nineteenth. She dug into her purse and pulled out a small white envelope. "This is an invitation. It's going to be on Sunday afternoon on the twenty-third."

"Ok. Am I going to be the only guy there?"

"Pretty much. I think Scott Kuperman may come. He's in my class at school."

I nodded. Kuperman was a nerdy, thin red-headed kid with black horned rimmed glasses. He and his family lived two blocks from the synagogue.

"I couldn't think of having a party without my boyfriend there," said April. Her eyes flashed. I blushed. She leaned close and kissed me on the lips again. I closed my eyes and melted. Oy, a girl's party. Word was going to spread fast.

"Dad's home. We're going to start the Seder!" Mom yelled up the stairs. We came downstairs. Mrs. Blackman was humongous. Bigger than a few days ago. It looked like she had a boulder under her pale green dress. Her boobs were pressing against the fabric and I tried not to stare at them. I wondered how she could walk without tipping over. Mr. Blackman smiled at me and proffered a hand. He reminded me of Dennis the Menace's father with his brushed back black hair and black horned-rimmed glasses. He was tall and lean and was wearing a gray suit.

We sat around the dining room table, Dad, wearing his grandfather's white kittel at one end, my mom with Grammy on her right at the other end. Mr. and Mrs. Blackman and Susie sat to Dad's left, while Morrie, me and April sat on the right. Considering I was left-handed, sitting in the middle was not strategically smart; but I know Dad wanted Morrie next to him for the Four Questions. April was quite happy to sit next to me.

Dad didn't drag the Seder out. We were eating within a half an hour. I passed on the gefilte fish, but enjoyed the Charoset on matzah. Mom, with Grammy helping, brought in bowls of chicken soup with matzah balls. The box of Mandelen, soup nuts, made the rounds too. For the main course there was brisket, kugel, carrot tzimmes and string beans. Mom believed in green vegetables. As the adults had dessert - coffee, mandelbroit, and sponge cake (Grammy's was great) we kids searched for the afikomen.

The word 'afikomen' is Greek and means dessert. It's a piece of matzah that's hidden at the beginning of the Seder. Part of the tradition is for the kids to search for the hidden matzah and bargain for returning it. The meal can't be completed until the afikomen is shared. Dad didn't bargain. He had prize for all of us. Morrie and Susie got some Bartmans chocolate rocket pops. April got an Archie comic and I got the new issue of *Batman*. Definitely, better than candy.

Mrs. Blackman had the baby the next day. It was another girl. They named her Jessica at a naming ceremony a month later.

Chapter Twelve

It was a rainy Sunday afternoon when Dad dropped me off at the Blackmans. Mom had bought April's gift. I had no idea what it was. It was wrapped in pink and white wrapping paper with a pink bow. She had smiled at me when I left and said, "Have a good time."

Being at a kid's birthday party, especially a girl's birthday party and being like the only guy, was embarrassing. But April had invited me. I didn't want to hurt her feelings. I did like her. I just was uncomfortable about the whole boyfriend thing.

"Come in Jeff," said Mrs. Blackman. In her arms, swaddled in blankets a small pink face with a few wisps of dark hair peeked out at me. "You can hang your coat in the closet here. As you can see, my hands are full." She smiled one of those knowing adult smiles. "The kids are downstairs in the recreation room. Go on down."

I walked out of the entranceway. There was a staircase off the hall. I went downstairs. I could hear some music. The recreation room was large. A folding table had been set up with folding chairs in the middle. A white tablecloth covered the table and eight places were set. Along one wall was a soda fountain. Mr. Blackman was making ice cream cones, floats and milkshakes. He looked up when I came in. "Hi Jeff. What'll you have?"

"Jeff!" April wearing a white chiffon dress came over and hugged me. "Thanks for coming."

I smiled and handed her the gift. I assumed mom had gone out and gotten some nice blouse or something. She had handed me the wrapped gift as I was leaving.

"Thank you." She took it from me and set it on a card table against the wall. Other gifts had been piled up there.

"Name your poison, Jeff!" boomed Mr. Blackman. "Milkshake? Sundae?"

Mr. Blackman wore a white apron over a striped dress shirt and gray slacks. There were four girls sitting at stools of the fountain counter. They turned and looked me over. One of them, a small girl with dark brown hair nodded to April. I guess I got the seal of approval or something.

"I'll just have a cone," I said to Mr. Blackman.

"What kind of ice cream?" he asked.

"What have you got?"

"Vanilla, chocolate, strawberry, Neapolitan, and orange sherbet."

"I'll have the sherbet." I was still trying to lose weight and felt more self-conscious about it whenever I was with April.

Mr. Blackman put a generous scoop on a sugar cone and handed it to me.

"Thanks."

I could hear the door bell ringing upstairs. A few minutes later two more girls came down. They were blonde haired twins. Following them was Scott Kuperman. He wore brown slacks, a yellow shirt, and gray vest. He looked at me as April greeted him.

"I didn't expect to see you here," he said.

"Nice to see you too," I replied. Was he jealous? Did he secretly like April? The thought struck me like static shock. I had never considered that other guys might like April.

The party was sort of boring. The girls huddled and spoke silently among themselves, occasionally stealing glances at Scott and myself. Scott and I didn't have a lot in common. He was a bit of an egg-head compared to me. So we sort of stood around with our fingers up our ass. We played Pin the Tail on the Donkey and darts. I was pretty good at darts. We had gotten a dartboard for Chanukah the year before, and Morrie and I practiced and played in the basement. I discovered I had pretty good natural aim. I beat Scott who was not happy about it. Too bad for him.

We ate cake. It was chocolate with a white and pink frosting. Candy flowers decorated the corners. We had another crack at having sundaes, floats or milkshakes, and then April opened her gifts. She got some bubble bath and shampoo, a couple of board games, a diary, and some books. She saved my gift for last. It was a green and yellow plaid knit sweater. And she loved it. She came over and gave me a hug and kiss on the cheek. The girls giggled hysterically. Scott looked as if he'd loved to have skewered me with a few of those darts. I noticed Mrs. Blackman nudging her husband when April had hugged me. This was going to get back to my folks. I was doomed.

***

July 2012: Thursday

Billy Greenberg, present owner of the Indian Head Hotel just off the interstate, led the Thursday morning minyan. Well, except for the short weekday Torah reading which I did. He chanted Shacarit at warp five. Afterward a couple of the old guys, Hal Blackstein, the former JCC director, and Abe Feigelbaum, invited me for breakfast. We drove caravan style down Jackson Street through downtown and then turned down 4th and pulled up at the Little Chicago Deli. It was a diner. We took a booth. A dark-haired young waitress brought us coffee and menus.

"So you see the JCC is now a Boys and Girls club?" asked Hal. Hal must've been in his early or mid-eighties. He'd served in Korea. He was still trim, his silver hair cut short.

"Yeah, Monday I did sort of a nostalgia drive around," I said. "Things have changed." I had also noticed that my former Northside Junior High had been torn down to make room for some senior residences.

"As you said kiddo, things change," said Abe. "The city was in the dumps when a lot of the slaughtering houses closed down in the eighties. And then Gateway came in and it provided jobs and a real boost to the community. But that didn't last. Everything got shipped and outsourced. After Gateway pulled out the Stockyards revived; but now we have a bunch of damn Mexicans here. They bring their gangs and drugs. Shit, this use to be a safe place to live."

I rolled my eyes. Why is it the most persecuted people in history can be the most intolerant at times? River City was more ethnic and diverse than when I was growing up there. To me, it added to the tapestry of the city in a positive way. Obviously Abe didn't see it that way. Old attitudes are hard to change. But having been involved with interfaith in my other congregations, I intended to make it one of my priorities here too.

"But we got some great Mexican food now," said Hal.

"Yeah and all it does is give me gas and the shits," muttered Abe.

The door opened and Jack Bernstein came in. Abe waved to him and he came over. Jack Bernstein was the grandfather of the Bar Mitzvah bocher. He was in his late seventies, a husky balding guy with a beak of a nose. His rheumy eyes seemed enlarged behind thick lenses in Aviator frames. He wore a brown jacket and a tweed cap on his head. He squeezed in next to Abe, who was no small guy either. Abe had a couple of gas stations and a bait store. The bait store was on the edge of the stockyard's area. He also sold beer and spirits. Everything an angler needed.

"So Rabbi, is my Stan ready?" asked Jack.

"I won't know until I meet with him. We're supposed to rehearse on Friday, though I would've liked to see him before. Apparently he's very busy."

"I'll talk to Shirley. You know we're helping to pay for this shindig. My daughter-in- law is a mid-western JAP. You'd think this was the inaugural dinner for the President, shit!"

"It's her first Bar Mitzvah. A lot of parents go meshuga," said Hal.

"Remember Lois Blackman? Elegant lovely lady, but my God, she took her girls to Chicago for their dresses because she said there was nothing decent here. We have stores. Hell, Omaha has stores. But no, they weren't good enough for her," ranted Abe.

"One shouldn't speak ill of the dead," said Hal.

Abe looked questioningly at me.

"I got a call last night. She passed away. I'm meeting with Jake later this morning," I said.

"When's the funeral?" asked Jack.

"Sunday. Normally it should be on Friday, but one of the daughters is in Israel and can't get back in time, so I told the Chevra we'd do the funeral on Sunday."

"Poor Jacob. This is gonna be tough on him. His brother passed away young," said Abe.

"I know. You didn't have a Rabbi or a Cantor then. Dad came up to do the funeral. Stan was barely forty if I remember," I said.

"Yeah, he died in like 1972 or something," said Hal.

"They had three daughters, right?" asked Jack.

"Yes, April, Susie and Jessica. Jessica is a bit younger than the other girls. She must be in her forties now," I said.

"Where are they now?" asked Abe.

"Well the oldest, April married some corporate lawyer out in California, and the other one, Susie, I thought was working for NASA out in Florida. Jessica, lives in Denver, Colorado," said Hal.

"Jessica is in Israel. She was on vacation. That's who were waiting for," I said.

"Nice girls. Pretty girls as I remember. In fact," said Hal, eyeing me carefully, "if I remember correctly you took April Blackman out."

"We left here in 1968. I didn't have my license until after we moved. I never took April Blackman out."

"I remember you dancing with her," he said. "And I'm not senile."

Chapter Thirteen

May 1965

The space race was heating up with the Russia, Luna 5 crashing on the Moon. A U.S. air force base was bombed in Bien Hoa South Vietnam. Cambodia dropped diplomatic relations with us. Seventeen thousand people were killed in a windstorm in Bangladesh. Israel and West Germany began diplomatic relations, and several Arab countries broke off relations with Germany because of it. Lucky Debonair won the Kentucky Derby. Meanwhile school continued and I received the invitation to a Bat Mitzvah party at the Holiday Inn as predicted. It was on Saturday, May 22nd.

The second week in May Dad took me downtown to Mort Smith's pawnshop and had me pick out an electric guitar and a small amp. Mort's place was next to the Century Cinema. He also owned a small confectionary shop that sold penny candies, ice cream bars, pop, cigarettes, cigars and some magazines. In the back of the store was a pinball machine. A lot of the older Jewish teen guys hung out there. Along the right wall was a door and through there, was the pawnshop. Mort's brother Daniel ran it. Daniel was a long, lanky man with a droopy mustache, just like the Frito Bandito. His graying hair was slicked back and shone under the fluorescent lighting.

"I figured you should start with a second hand instrument, to see if you really like it," said Dad.

Dan Smith took me over to a far wall. On pegs hung a variety of guitars. Some had nylon strings, some had metal, and then there were the electric guitars, flatter, more colorful than the stained wooden ones. I saw a black and silver Silvertone electric and pointed to it. "How about that one?" I asked.

Dan reached up and took it down. He handed it to me.

"It's a good starter. Silvertone is a Sears brand. Let me get a cord and a small amplifier." He went to another section and brought out a small amp with a Fishman label and a black cord with quarter inch plugs on either end. He plugged one end into the guitar and the other into the amp. "Give me a sec," He took an extension cord and plugged the amp in. "Go ahead."

I held the guitar and ran my fingers over the strings.

"Hang on, let's turn it on." Dan reached over and turned a knob on the body of the guitar. I strummed again and the room rocked with unharmonized sounds.

"It needs to be tuned," said Dan. "But it works."

"How much?" asked Dad.

"Give you the whole kit and caboodle for thirty-five bucks."

"Sold." He looked at me. "Guess it's guitar lessons for you."

I cracked a broad smile. This was going to be swell.

Two days later I dropped piano and started guitar lessons after school. There was a music store down from the synagogue on Pierce. My teacher was a bit of a shock. She was an old crone of a lady with frizzy gray hair, loose skin and big blue eyes that peered at him from behind thick glass frames.

"I'm Liz," she said. "So you want to play guitar. Do you read music?"

"I'm in the school orchestra. I've played violin for five years and I've taken two years of piano."

She nodded with approval. "And now you want to take guitar so you can have your own band, I bet."

"Yeah, I guess."

"Ok, well you know you need discipline to practice, but obviously you have that. Next you'll need patience. You'll need to learn where the notes are located and how to pick and chord. Like this." She hooked up my guitar to an amp and sat down with the instrument across her bony knees. Suddenly the music exploded. I recognized it as a song called *Johnny Be Good*. Her left hand fingers flew up and down the neck of the guitar while her right forefinger and thumb held a pick that seemed to move with a rapidity of a machine gun that amazed me.

"Wow," I said when she finished.

"Thanks." She grinned. "You'll play like this too, eventually."

I was ready for my first lesson.

***

The week before the party I had a sleepover at Larry's. Larry was interested in photography and actually had a darkroom set up in a storage closet in the basement. But it was also his sanctuary. He had managed to squeeze an old sofa in there, along with a table and a portable record player. More importantly, he installed a latch on the door so his pain in the ass little brother couldn't breach it.

"You get the invitation?" asked Larry.

"Yeah, it came earlier in the week."

"It'll be fun. Lots of girls. Live band."

"Yeah, but I don't know how to dance," I said.

"I'll show you the moves Marshall taught me. Easy."

I gave Larry a rather skeptical look.

"You gotta trust me Slim."

"Uh huh."

"Here, look." Larry got up and put a record on, it was *I'm Telling You Now* by Freddie and the Dreamers. I watched Larry's feet. He sort of did a box move to the rhythm of the beat. Step one foot forward. Move the other one parallel, one step back, then slide the other foot back. It was dancing in a small square or rectangle. "now move your arms," he finished. "Sort of like watching a boxer punch low. See? Easy. Try it."

I got up and mimicked his moves. He was right; it was stupidly easy. Larry put on another record: *"Woolly Bully"* by Sam the Sham and the Pharoahs. By the end of the song, I had the moves down pretty well.

"So, are you going to ask Janet to dance?"

"Yeah, that's the plan. Hopefully I'll have a chance to ask her."

Larry sighed. "You're problem is your Dad's the Cantor. The kids think you're a goody two-shoes."

"I'm just a normal kid."

"What's true and what they think are two different things. And by the way, I don't think there's anything normal about you."

"Kish mir en tuchas." Telling him to kiss my ass in Yiddish, I flipped him the bird.

"Not even if you bent over." Larry laughed.

***

That week Coach Pittman took us outside and we started running around the outside of the playing field. Three times around was a mile. We then did sprinting the fifty-yard dash, which was one block. We were timed. We were to have physical fitness exams in three weeks. I was going to die. Inside the gym, we did one hundred sit-ups, (well some of us). My stomach was so tight I could barely stand up straight afterwards. He had us climbing the ropes. I couldn't climb to save myself even if I'd been on a sinking clipper ship. I was a Jew. I sucked at sports. Mark tripped and skinned his knee. Lucky bastard got out of gym for two days that week. Tim fared little better than I did, but then, he weighed less.

On Wednesday at dinner, Dad asked if I sent a Thank You card to the Nussenbaums. I looked in my notebook and showed him that their name was checked off.

"Well, they never received it. It may have been lost in the mail. Send them another one."

"But I did mail them one. I'm not responsible if it doesn't get there," I said.

Dad sighed. "Look, they're upset that they didn't get a thank you card. Now while you aren't responsible for the mail, it's important that they receive one from you. It'll take you five minutes and they'll feel better. And, I don't need any problems while my next contract is being negotiated. You like living here? You have friends? Just write the note."

"Ok, I'll do it after dinner."

"Good." Dad returned his attention to the chicken fried steak mom had made for dinner. It was one of Morrie's and my favorites.

On Thursday after school, Dad sent me to get a haircut. Apparently he had problems with the long shaggy look I was cultivating. I told Bill I didn't want it cut too short, but he gave me the standard Princeton cut anyway. I'd have to talk with Dad. I wanted to wear my hair longer, like the Beatles or the Rolling Stones.

Friday night we went to services. Larry and his folks were there. We talked after services during the Oneg.

"So, how formal is this dance?" I asked. "It didn't say on the invitation."

"Tie and jacket. Susie and the girls want to dress up."

"Girls tend to like to do that, I've heard." I thought of April always dressing up for services or like when the Blackmans were there for the Seder. She looked pretty good.

"You look like you need your pants taken in. You've lost more weight," said Larry. He pointed to the material bunched up on the sides.

"No time to do that before Saturday night."

"Maybe we can take you down to the store tomorrow afternoon and do them. I'll talk to my dad."

"It'll have to be on the q.t. given it's Shabbos."

"Yeah, we can hide you in the trunk. That's where we usually stash the dead bodies." Larry was such a kidder.

I didn't have to hide in the trunk as it turned out. I took a change of clothes and after services we went to Schaffer's Men's Wear and I got my pants taken in. Turned out Mr. Schaffer would take us to the party and my dad would pick us up.

The Holiday Inn was downtown near I-29 North. Mr. Schaeffer pulled up in front of the motel in his 1964 tan colored Chevy Bel-Air. Larry and I got out and went in. There was a sign in the lobby directing us to the ballroom, but it was pretty easy to find. All you had to do was follow the music. Outside, the parents were standing around smoking. We nodded hello and walked in. The lights had been dimmed. We took a moment and looked around while our eyes adjusted. On a small stage a five-piece band was playing *I'm into Something Good*. Streamers and balloons had been taped to the walls. Along the right wall, near the door, were a small bar and a long table with bowls of snacks: potato chips, popcorn, pretzels, and a huge punch bowl with a block of sherbet floating in it, but obviously no booze. Along the left wall were chairs. Several tables were set up and people were sitting in the shadows.

Larry and I moseyed over to the bar and each got a coke. We looked around for Mark but couldn't see him. As usual most of the guys were hanging out by the food and the girls were sitting on the other side of the room. I saw a number of guys I knew from Hebrew school and Young Judea, a youth group for upper elementary students.

Leonard Rosenfeld grunted a hello. Rosenfeld's parents were big machers, bigshots, at the Temple and well off financially. Leo was a fat, loud-mouthed bully who had picked on Josie Bresler relentlessly He'd gotten me in trouble numerous times at Hebrew school. He kept bugging me or joking around and when I responded, I got sent out to the hall for talking. I remember one time he got sent out and high tailed it for the bathroom thinking it'd be safe; but Mrs. Bresden marched right into the Men's room and hauled his ass out. His shadow, Stuart Goldberg went to the same school as Larry. He was into sports and had a bit of an attitude. Arnie Rosenthal, and Louis Rissman, both of whom had been at Hebrew school with me, were there too. There were a few older guys there like Max Weiss, Alan Dishkoff, Gary Shindler and David Fishman. They were sophomores in High school like Larry's brother Marshall. And they were on the dance floor. I saw Alan dancing with Janet as their gyrating bodies passed by. Damn.

The band finished their song and started with a rendition of the Kinks' *You Really Got Me*.

"Let's go and ask a couple of girls to dance, Slim," said Larry.

My feet felt like two slabs of concrete, but I obediently clomped after him. We found a table where Debbie Stein, Molly Weiner, Beth Levine, Debbie Fine, Cindy Greene, Susan Glass, and Marilyn Sheckter were sitting. The girls looked nice in their dresses. I noticed Debbie and Susan were wearing heels.

Larry, the schmoozer, said hi and asked Cindy to dance. She nodded and stood up. Shit, I couldn't stand around looking lost. Marilyn Scheckter was sitting next to me. I looked down and tapped her on the shoulder. "Uh, want to dance?"

Marilyn hesitated a moment and seemed to look at the other girls for approval. She stood up. "Ok." She was an inch taller than I was, but thankfully she was wearing flats.

Marilyn had on a rose colored dress with lighter red flowers on it. Her black hair was parted in the middle and swept her shoulders. She was actually quite cute. I put my drink down on the table, and I took her hand, which was soft and dry and we headed out to the dance floor.

The band started their rendition of *I Feel Fine*. I watched Marilyn. She was gyrating and moving her feet in some complicated pattern. I tried to remember the steps Larry had shown me. I found the rhythm and moved in that box step. I bent my arms and moved them back and forth like a boxer hitting low punches. I probably looked like a battery operated toy robot. The music reverberated throughout the room. Marilyn smiled at me and mouthed, "Thank you."

We stayed on the dance floor for two more numbers: *Do Wah Diddy* and *Can't Buy Me Love*.

The band announced they were going to take a short break. The lights came up slightly. Marilyn thanked me again and drifted back to her friends. I stood there catching my breath. My shirt was sweaty and stuck to my back. I reached up and loosened my tie. I needed a drink.

I saw Larry talking to Mark near the punch bowl. Debbie Stein was standing next to Mark. Despite his denials, it was obvious they were a couple. I went over and helped myself to a cup of punch. It was Hawaiian Punch mixed with 7-Up.

"Saw you out on the dance floor," said Mark.

"That was nice of you to ask Marilyn," said Debbie. "She's still new here and very shy."

"Figured I had a better chance of her accepting," I said.

"You looked nice out there," said Debbie.

I blushed.

"Slim is so humble," said Larry.

"He did a nice thing," said Debbie. She gave Larry the arched eyebrow look. "Come on Mark."

"See you later," said Mark as Debbie led him off to join her friends.

"So young and in chains already," commented Larry.

I nodded in sympathy, but thought to myself, what a lucky bastard.

"I want to go over and look at the band's instruments," I said.

"How's the guitar lessons coming?" asked Larry.

"I've had three so far but since I read music, I'm moving along. I know where the notes are located already. But strumming technique takes time."

"I was thinking maybe I should take up drums," said Larry.

I looked at him.

"Girls dig musicians," he said.

"Stick to photography," I replied. Larry's voice was changing, as was Marks'. Mark's was starting to get very deep. Larry's voice was sort of like static on the radio.

As we were walking over to the stage, a familiar figure flashed by. I turned. It looked like April, but what was she doing at a Bat Mitzvah party? She was a bit young for this group. I excused myself from Larry and turned and followed her. I caught up to her as she passed the bar, obviously heading for the door.

"April!"

She turned. I could see she had been crying. Her eyes glistened. "Hey, what are you doing here?" I asked.

"I was invited, as were my parents. They're friends of the Stein's and Levine's."

"Oh. Why didn't you tell me you were coming?"

"Well, we haven't been over to your place, have we? And, it's not like, you've called me, or anything. It's been two weeks." Her lower lip trembled. Her eyes flashed. "You're such a fucking asshole."

My mouth dropped. "April!"

"What, you don't think I know swear words?" April shook her head and rolled her eyes.

"I'm sorry. Been busy with school and guitar lessons."

"Oh. Well, you could've called. You should have called. I thought you said you liked me."

"Yeah I do, but if I had called, then your mom would be giving you the third degree or I would've had to answer a lot of stupid questions just to get to talk to you. And to be fair, you haven't been at services where we could talk." Suddenly I got the feeling I was wandering in a minefield and no matter where I stepped, I was going to get my ass blown off. I sighed. "Look, you know how I feel about you, but I wish you would've told me you were coming."

"Why? Would you have danced with that girl then? I saw you on the dance floor. You seemed to be having a good time."

She was hurt and jealous. I felt a bucket of Jewish guilt spill over me. She was right, I was a bit of an idiot. I did like her, but I also noticed a lot of other girls. But that wasn't important now. April was special to me and I'd let her down. I wanted to say something, but didn't know what. Part of me said keep your mouth shut. Don't say anything. Tread carefully. The fact was Marilyn was sort of cute. And, she was my age. I looked at April. She wore a green dress that looked nice against her dark brown hair. I also noticed she was wearing a bit of makeup.

"You're wearing makeup," I said.

The quivering lip grinned a crack. "Mom let me. Said this was a formal party and that young ladies were allowed to wear makeup. She knew the other girls would."

"Oh. Well, uh, you look nice. Really nice."

"Thank you."

"So you're staying?" I shuffled my feet. I could feel my heart racing.

"Are you going to ask me to dance?" Her eyes zeroed in on mine.

The band was starting up again. I could hear one of the guys tuning his guitar.

"Yes."

"You're not embarrassed to be SEEN with me?"

"Of course not. And, you know I do like you. You know that. I already feel like a heel."

"Good. Now you can make it up with me."

"Make out with you?" I joked.

April smiled. "You need to *really* make it up to me if you want that. Now, take me dancing."

The lights dimmed. The band began with a recent song by Freddie and the Dreamers, *I'm Telling You Now.*

April grabbed my hand and I followed April out onto the dance floor. I discovered April knew how to dance. Her moves were more complicated than Marilyn's. "Where'd you learn how to dance?"

"Gym class."

"They teach girls dancing in gym?" And here I was sweating my balls off running around like Nazi hoards were after me.

April looked down at my feet. A puzzled look appeared on her face-along with the crack of a smile. "What are you doing?"

"Dancing."

She giggled. "Ok, if you say so." She looked up at me and shook her head, and laughed again. "I'm going to have to teach you."

The song ended and band started singing *See You in September.* It was a slow song. I looked at April. I didn't know what to do. Larry hadn't said anything about slow songs.

She shook her head. Hopeless. "Follow my lead." She took my hands. My left hand she put on her hip, the other she held up and clasped mine. "Just slide and step like I do."

I stepped on her foot.

"Ouch."

"Sorry."

"It's ok," she said, sounding like an exasperated mother.

We started again. As I got into the rhythm, April moved closer to me. Her head leaned against my shoulder and we drifted around the dance floor. I could smell her hair and a hint of perfume. I started to get a boner. She leaned closer to me. I looked around and saw the floor was crowded; but April steered us through and I didn't step on her feet, and I didn't bump into anyone.

We danced through two more songs: *I Can't Get No Satisfaction* and *Silhouette,* one fast and another slow one. I definitely got a hard on. My shirt stuck to my back. April seemed quite comfortable dancing close. I held her a bit more tightly. And, I have to admit; it felt good. It felt natural.

The song ended. We held each other a moment longer, then separated. We looked at each other. I wanted to kiss her. But not in public.

"Let's get something to drink," April suggested. She took my hand and led me over to the bar. I ordered two Cokes.

"Well, well, didn't know you were babysitting, Reimer."

I turned around Leo Rosenfeld and Stuart Goldberg stood behind me.

"You got a problem Rosenfeld?"

"Guess you can't get a real girl who has tits," snickered Leo.

"You're an asshole," said April.

Leo Rosenfeld glared at April. I'd been intimidated by kids like him, and was afraid. But maybe it was because I'd lost weight, or maybe it was because David Katzman had taught me some moves. Or maybe it was because I didn't want to see April hurt, or maybe it was the guilt I felt for ignoring her; the bottom line was, I couldn't let this pass. My dad had always told me, "I don't want to hear about you starting any fights, but I expect you to finish them."

Leo started to shove April. I grabbed his hand and squeezed, giving him a nerve pinch. I did have strong hands and forearms from playing the violin, piano and guitar. I also knew where the nerves were thanks to David. I applied a touch of pressure. He yelped and backed off.

Stuart stepped forward. I shot a glance at Goldberg. "Stay out of this. Let the fat fuck fight his own battles."

A few kids had started gathering around. They couldn't help it since we were blocking the bar.

"Protecting your girlfriend, Reimer?" He leered at April.

"Go away, leave us alone," I said.

Leo looked around at his 'audience'. "Reimer's so hard up he has to dance with little kids."

April frowned. She was getting mad. "Yeah, but you like to hit girls."

Leo's attention shot back to us. "Better tell her to shut up Reimer."

"No one tells me what to do fat ass," snapped April.

I glared at April. Jeez, watch what you say I thought. But she did have a temper. And maybe it was the culmination of a lot of frustration being a kid at a teen party, or maybe she was still pissed at me. But I knew she wasn't going to shut up.

Leonard lunged for her. I grabbed his arm and did a hip toss like David and I had practiced. And, it actually worked. Rosenfeld flew past April and smacked on the ground. Out of the corner of my eye I saw Goldberg move. He threw a punch. I caught his wrist, swung around and twisted his arm behind him. I shoved him. He lost his balance and hit the table with the punch bowl. It tottered, slopping punch down the front of his pants and on his shirt. He caught himself and turned around, facing me.

Leo was picking himself up. I swiveled and kicked him in the stomach, knocking him back into the bar. I moved aside as Goldberg ran at me and stuck my foot out. He tripped and went down on Rosenfeld.

Suddenly Mr. Stein and Mr. Levine were there.

"What's going on?" bellowed Mr. Levine.

"Those two boys were picking on me. Leonard Rosenfeld shoved me," said April.

Mr. Stein helped the boys up. He took a look at Goldberg and said, "You better come with me."

"You did this?" asked Mr. Levine.

"He was protecting me," said April stepping around me. She put her arm around mine. She gave him the wide-eyed innocent hurt look.

Mr. Levine nodded to me and then announced to the small gathering crowd, "It's over. Go back to dancing and having fun."

Larry and Mark came over to us.

"Where'd you learn the moves?" asked Mark.

"David Katzman taught me some judo."

"You know, Slim, Leo's going to be gunning for you." Larry's eyes followed Stuart and Leo being escorted out by Mr. Levine.

"He's an asshole that needed to be taken down a peg. He shouldn't pick on girls." I said. Inside I was trembling. But it had felt good to stand up to Rosenfeld.

April grabbed my hand. "You can talk later. I like this song, and you owe me."

She dragged me out towards the dance floor. The band was playing *She's Not There*.

"Such a nice couple," I heard Larry chuckle.

The rest of the dance was uneventful; I did notice a number of people watching us on the dance floor. I also thought I saw Mr. and Mrs. Blackman poke their heads in while April and I were gliding around during a slow song; but with the mass of kids dancing and the dimness of the lights I doubt they could see us.

The party broke up at midnight, the pumpkin hour. April thanked me and gave me a quick kiss on the lips before she headed out to find her parents. Dad was in the lobby having a cigarette and talking to the Levines and Steins when Larry and I left the ballroom.

He saw us and waved us over. "Ready to call it a night?"

"Yeah, we're tired."

"Have fun?" he asked.

"It was the highpoint of the weekend," said Larry.

Dad nodded and led us out to the parking lot.

My parents had this uncanny intelligence network that seemed to know everything I did. Well, almost everything. Of course the next morning as Dad and I were driving to the synagogue, he had to comment.

"Heard you had a bit of a scrape last night," He tapped his cigarette on the half-opened window. It flew off into the distance.

"Leonard Rosenfeld was picking on April Blackman. He's a bully." I said.

"Well fighting doesn't solve anything, but I know Mr. Blackman is grateful. And from what I've heard, Leo Rosenfeld's a little momser."

"Yeah. He picked on Josie Bresler all the time in Hebrew school. He use to go over and punch her in the arm when she was having milk in the canteen."

Dad nodded as he stopped at red light on 18th Street and Douglas. "Mrs. Levine thought it was very nice that you danced with Marilyn Scheckter. Not easy being the new kid, as you know. But apparently April had a good time. She likes you, you know."

I didn't like where this conversation was headed. I merely grunted. What is it with parents?

The next morning, Sunday school class was small. A number of the kids had obviously been allowed to sleep late given the party last night. Unfortunately, I was not among the lucky ones. Mark and Larry showed up ten minutes late. The only girl who showed up was Julie Fine. Needless to say we didn't accomplish much. But we did have a good discussion on the current opening baseball season.

***

July 2012: Thursday Afternoon

Stanley Friedman was a short nervous kid with a shock of brown hair like Harpo Marx. A typical kid, he wore a baggy t-shirt, jeans and sneakers. His mother, Shirley, came into the office with him, a blue pinstriped suit on a hanger slung over her shoulder. She looked to be in her late thirties or early forties. A pleasant looking woman with short dark hair and dressed in a mauve blouse and black skirt. Her dark eyes zeroed in on me. "Rabbi Reimer?"

"Yes, pleased to finally put a face to the voice on the phone," I said.

We shook hands.

"I brought his suit. The photographer will be here shortly. I thought we could take a few pictures after the rehearsal."

"That would be fine," I replied. "Let's go into the sanctuary."

"If you like, you can have a seat and listen," I said. I turned to Stan and nodded for him to go up on the bimah.

The bimah was one step up from the floor. Rows of light colored wooden pews with red cushions angled towards the bimah. There was a modern looking glass Torah table and a light wooden lectern on the right side. Two typical high-backed uncomfortable straight chairs sat on either side of the Ark. The Ark itself was curtained, and I knew when opened was actually a small alcove with four Torahs supported upright on a shelf inside.

"We'll start with Friday night. What parts are you doing?" I asked.

Stanley hesitated and then squeaked out, "The Shema and the Kiddush."

"That's fine. You have your Siddur?"

He nodded affirmatively.

"Let's hear you do the Shema," I said. I sat down in the front pew. "Remember to project your voice. Don't rush the prayer."

Stanley opened his mouth. A cat's claws on glass doesn't even come close to the sound that screeched from his open maw. I've been in the business for thirty years, and I know from my own friends long ago that this is a dangerous age for boys. Voices begin to change. There's no control. It can go deeper than a bass fiddle or, in Stanley's case, an ear shattering, glass cracking high-pitched noise that would make a bat keel over. But I have to hand it to Stanley. He persevered. So did I. His pace was good. He actually enunciated the words clearly. I decided to wear my contact lenses on Shabbat. No use risking my glasses breaking.

And so it went. He did the Kiddush. He led the Torah service. Like all B'nai Mitzvah kids he was nervous, even a bit sweaty. He lacked self-confidence. As I listened and watched him, I remembered a bit of what I'd been like at this age; but while I'd been a bit nervous, confidence had swelled within me as I got into 'the groove'. It had felt right and natural. For Stanley, this was anything but natural.

Seeing him tottering as he held the Torah scroll, I decided that maybe his father would have the honor of carrying it for him during the hakafot. The guests would be very upset if he dropped it. According to tradition if you drop the Torah or witness it being dropped it's a forty day, daytime fast. The luncheon would definitely go to waste.

I opened the Torah and he squeaked out his Maftir portion. He practically shouted out his Haftorah. (I'd turn the mic down on the Torah table) He delivered his speech with all the emotion of a robot. His eyes were glued to the words. I suggested, after looking over his D'var Torah that maybe he could look up once in a while.

"Just pick a spot on the back wall above the people's heads. From this angle they'll think you're looking directly at them." I made a few pencil arrow marks on his pages to indicate where to do so.

"My dad told me to picture the people naked."

I looked at Stanley. "Do you really want to imagine that? I mean, I don't know how you'd keep from laughing."

Stanley laughed.

We finished up the rehearsal. The Bernstein's photographer popped his head in. I told him it was fine. It was a good thing Stanley wasn't Superman. Lois Lane would've been run over by the freight train before he managed to change and come out. His mother adjusted his clip-on tie. I waited until the standard shots of the Bar Mitzvah kid 'reading Torah' were taken; then wrapped and dressed the Torah. The photographer took the standard pose of the kid holding the Torah in front of the Ark. I hovered nearby just in case Stanley started tottering. The Torah weighed about thirty-five to forty pounds. After the pictures had been taken, I put it back in the Ark.

Since the Friedman's were Reform, there'd be no additional Musaf service Saturday morning and that meant the service would be about twenty minutes shorter. It would give the congregants some time for their hearing to return to normal before lunch. I checked my watch; just enough time to do a bit of work on my charge to Stan before I headed for the airport.

The airport lay seven miles outside the city. As I drove onto the interstate, I remembered hot summer evenings, the air so thick it must've been like breathing in the rainforest, when we'd drive to the airport and watch the planes take off. There was also a small SAC base there and occasionally we'd see the fighter jets go out on maneuvers. There always seemed to be a breeze on the highway, even when it was hot and sultry in July and August. Occasionally we could persuade my dad to stop at Dairy Queen or A&W root beer on the way home. Back then an ice cream cone was fifteen cents, and an icy mug of root beer, a dime.

There was little traffic. I had tuned into a local FM station and the sound of The Association singing *"Cherish"* filled the car. It brought back a lot of memories of BBYO dances. I turned off the air conditioning and rolled down the window letting the breeze ruffle my hair. There was a faint smell of manure. I took the airport exit and drove down the short road to the airport. The air force base had been closed years before, and the homes and barracks converted into civilian housing.

I parked the car and walked into the low one story terminal. There was a small café to my right and then rows of banded vinyl chairs. Through the clear glass partitions I could see security with its detectors and conveyor belts and X-ray machines. I checked the arrival schedule. I had at least twenty minutes. I took out my iPhone, opened my Kindle app and opened up the Nero Wolfe mystery I was re-reading and sat down to wait.

It was hard to concentrate. I'd left River City in August of 1968. We moved to Oklahoma City where dad shared a pulpit with mom's cousin Michael who was the Rabbi there. It was there I met Fred, a fellow comic book collector and bookaholic, and his skeletal sidekick Bucky, who ended up deliberately flunking English so he wouldn't graduate and get drafted; Bob the Hobbit, who introduced me to the Lord of the Rings saga which I wolfed down in ten days during study halls, and Jerry Samuels my singing partner. All of us were from out-of-state; transplants in the redneck Bible belt.

I met Jerry in art class. He was a dark-haired guy, taller than I and leaner. He wore bellbottom jeans and a paisley shirt. Jerry definitely wasn't an Okie. (Standard Okie high school dress was a white t-shirt, blue jeans and pigskin cowboy boots. Hat was optional.) There was just something that drew me to him, a kindred spirit. It turned out he was Jewish and played guitar. His parents belonged to the Temple. They'd moved here from Flint, Michigan. His dad was in retail management at Arlen's and they'd been transferred to Oklahoma City. He had a sister Susan who was four years younger than us, and a brother Stanley six years younger.

We ended up forming a folk-rock duo called Double J's and did the coffee house scene, parties and busked on Paseo Street, a three block stretch between Walker and Dewey filled with head shops, small cafes, a tobacconist that sold the 'good stuff' under the table, and a couple of clubs. Our dream was to find a record deal. I was young, brash and invincible.

In 1970 after graduating high school, Jerry and I took a road trip up to River City. We crashed at the Fishmans, friends of my parents, for a week. Larry Shaeffer was going to take some publicity photos for us. I called April. It was great to see her. She'd filled out a bit and definitely had a more feminine figure. Seeing her after three years, we'd written to each other but the letters sort of diminished after the first year I was away, sent waves of emotion through me. But I was also a self-conceited ass, trying to impress her for God knows what reason.

Larry got some of the old crew together. There were AZA members and girls I hadn't seen or talked to in three years. It would be the last time I saw many of them. A few of the guys were drafted. Others were leaving for college out of state, and never came back. Everyone's lives had moved on. Tim was out in California now. His daughters married. He and his wife were grandparents. Paul was doing public relations in Omaha. The rest of his family scattered across the fifty states.

Anyway, at that visit, Jerry and I performed with April doing some harmonies on a couple of songs. After the gig, April and I slipped away. On the pretense of taking her home we parked, made out and lost our virginity.

I remember pulling off on a side road that led to some farm. There were still farms out on Country Club Blvd. back then. We found a break in the barbed wire fence and went out to this open field. We lay on the grass and looked up at the night sky. A myriad of stars filled it. It almost gave me vertigo. And under a moonlight sky we kissed and explored and got naked. Even to this day I remember the coolness of her skin, which turned damp and sweaty as we progressed to having sex. Thankfully I had a rubber in my wallet-one must always be prepared. But the fact is that I'd had that rubber in my wallet for months. John attracted girls like a flower to bees. Me, not so much. In fact I'd not even gotten to first base before April, and well, that night with April was a homerun. And I'm not saying it was great sex, it wasn't. We were awkward; we were excited, and I didn't have the control that comes with experience; but we did satisfy each other. Afterward we lay in each other's arms feeling the warmth that comes when two bodies are intertwined. I took April home. We promised we'd write to each other. But of course I never did.

In the fall, Jerry and I studied music and art at a local college. At that point I was unsure as to whether I'd continue my dream to be a comic book illustrator, or embark on my path as an entertainer. Unfortunately taking art classes in high school did not really prepare me for the sort of portfolio Art colleges were looking for, and the tuition was astronomical. We did the coffeehouse and club scene getting our act more polished. Most of the material we used we composed, though we did throw in some Paul Simon, Beatles, Dylan and John Denver.

And then Jerry met this girl Kathy. She got pregnant. They got married and John settled down. I performed a bit as a solo act but it wasn't the same.

Two years later our family went up to River City for April's uncle's funeral. April and I went out for a drink. We talked in a dimly lit bar that April went to when she was in town. But in the end, the flame flickered and blew out as we moved on, and life overtook our childhood dreams. Whatever romantic feelings we'd had for each other were in the past. We had different destinies.

A new board came. Mom's cousin Michael resigned as Rabbi. Dad's contract didn't get renewed and the family was moving to Galveston. I had a decision to make. I had my BFA. I'd been active at the synagogue teaching Sunday school, supervising the youth group and singing in Dad's High Holiday choir. As much as I wanted to run away from the "family" business like sort of a modern day Job, I finally had to admit that synagogue life was in my blood. I made the plunge and applied to Hebrew Union College's School of Sacred Music. I could've just as well gone to the Cantor's Institute at the Jewish Theological Seminary in New York, the conservative movement's training ground; but I'd have more creative opportunity in the Reform movement where musical instruments were used. Dad had gone to HUC for the first two years of his cantorial training before dropping out by my unexpected arrival, and didn't go back to his studies until four years later-at the Cantor's Institute that was originally in Chicago.

My dad was thrilled that I wanted to follow in his footsteps, and understood my reasons for taking a more liberal path. He made a few phone calls and arranged for the applications and booked an interview for me. The end of that summer Jerry was being trained in retail management in Detroit. I moved to New York. The Double J's were no more, though we did try to write some new pieces via long distance.

Part way through my program I came home one summer for a bit of vacation, and my parents set me up on a blind date. There was a family in Galveston, the Weinsteins, who had a daughter studying Journalism at Columbia in New York. Her name was Debbie. She was a vivacious willowy blonde with soft brown eyes and a prominent patrician nose. I took her out and we seemed to hit it off. Being both in New York made it easy to see each other. She came to my student pulpits for the High Holy Days. One thing led to another, and now we were coming to celebrate our thirty-fourth anniversary.

I checked my watch, and then the board. Her flight was arriving from Minneapolis. Little did I know there'd be another surprise on that flight.

Part III: The Summer of '65

Chapter Fourteen

June 1965

A coalmine explosion in Japan killed 236 people. Gemini 4 launched carrying McDivitt and White into space for 62 orbits. The Yankees thrashed the White Sox 12-0. U.S. troops were on the offensive in Vietnam. And I couldn't wait for school to end, which it did in mid-June.

All I wanted was freedom to goof off. It'd been a grueling year going to school and preparing for my Bar Mitzvah. My guitar lessons would end at the end of June for the summer. I bought a music book containing a collection of Beatles' songs from *A Hard Day's Night*, and was practicing trying to sing and chord at the same time. Every night after I finished my homework, rather than drawing and making comic books, I worked on chord progressions. I had nicely callused fingertips on my left hand.

Larry came home with us after services the Saturday after school ended. We pretty much hung out in my room talking about summer plans and another Bat Mitzvah party.

"My Dad's taking me on a buying trip to New York next month," said Larry.

"Wow, that's nice of him."

"Well it's pretty evident that Marshal wants to be a lawyer, but Dad's hoping that I'll help run the store after I finish college. Other than that, I'm working at the store part time over the summer, but we'll still have time to get together." Larry was sitting in the chair at my desk drinking a bottle of Coke.

"Yeah, Mark is working for his dad too. I think though that they're going to go to some resort in the

Wisconsin Dells for a couple of weeks," I said. I was laying on my bed, my arms behind me, propping up my head. "We're going to Miami to visit my grandparents next month. It'll take us around four days or so to drive down, but we're also stopping off in Chicago to visit family. I'm hoping we get to go to the Field Museum of Natural History. The mummy section is really cool."

"When are you leaving?" asked Larry.

"After the fourth, so we can have that sleepover. I'm planning on getting a bunch of firecrackers and sparklers."

Larry's eyes lit up. There was nothing better than fire and explosions.

"And of course you and Mark still have studying to do for your Bar Mitzvahs," I gloated. Mark's was the end of August, and Larry's in October.

"Yeah, don't remind me."

"Well, you'll have a few weeks off while we're away," I said.

"Not really. I'm meeting with Rabbi to fine tune my speech before we go to New York," said Larry.

"It's over in a flash," I said. "I couldn't believe how quickly the services went."

"Not from where I was sitting."

"Tough shit." I changed the subject. "You going to study with Rabbi Silverman next fall?" I asked. Dad had told me that the Rabbi was going to start a Modern Hebrew class twice a week, and a class on Rashi before Mincha on Saturday afternoon. Dad also told me I was attending. This was not an option. I protested a bit about the Saturday afternoon, but I was interested even though it'd cut into my goofing off time. It just wasn't cool to let Dad know.

"Yeah, Dad's insisting and apparently Mark will be there too."

"The Three Musketeers," I said. "One for all and..."

"Everyman for the pop machine," finished Larry. "By the way, you scored brownie points at that party last month with the girls. Asking Marilyn to dance was good. I heard she had a good time. And, apparently, they thought it was SWEET of you to dance with April Blackman, seeing how she's younger. I didn't mention you two had the hots for each other."

I glared at Larry. "Asshole."

Larry merely laughed. "You know it's true. Look, you got the girls taking notice of you. You're not just the Cantor's goody-two-shoes kid, especially after nailing Lee. Speaking of which, Stuart warned me that Leo might be looking to get even. You really pissed him off, not, that he didn't have it coming. I told Stuart to stay clear and let that asshole fight his own battles. Hopefully he'll listen."

I didn't want to think of Rosenfeld, and I sure as hell wasn't going to mention that April was coming over tomorrow. "Let's go up to the park," I suggested.

"You taking Shadow?"

"Sure, there's lots of bushes for him to pish on."

The next afternoon the Blackmans came over. It was hot and sunny. We had squirt gun fights outside, April and me against Morrie and Susie. We determined that refills on the outside faucet was a safe zone, and you couldn't hit anyone when they were refilling. Morrie, the little bastard, turned the hose on me when he noticed me watching him refill. I ran after him, and would've gotten him except Grammy spotted me and went for the broom in the back porch. I strategically retreated.

Finally, dirty, our clothes spotted with water, we trooped inside. Mom sent the kids down to the basement to clean off at the sink. She provided towels to dry off with. I went upstairs to my room to change and dry off.

In the bathroom I stripped off my socks, t-shirt and shorts, and I wrung them out in the shower stall. I pulled out the retractable line and hooked it up in the stall and hung my stuff up. I was about to head into my bedroom when I heard a footstep and a little gasp. I turned around to find April standing in the bathroom doorway.

"Oh."

I stood like a deer waiting in the headlights of a Mac truck waiting to get pulverized. "I'm—uh—changing."

"Uh huh." She didn't move. But she was giving me the once over.

"I need to get some clothes on."

"Ok." She stood aside and let me pass. I noticed she had shut the door. Last thing I needed was Susie and Morrie, or worse yet, my mom barging in.

She followed me into the room and sat down on the bed, watching while I pulled out another t-shirt and a pair of cut-off jeans from my dresser drawers. April didn't close her eyes or turn away. She was observing me closely. Thankfully I didn't have a hard on.

"You know, normally when someone's changing you give them some privacy."

April giggled. "Sorry."

"But not really, right?" I pulled on my t-shirt.

She sat there with a broad smile across her face. "Doesn't bother me. I've seen my dad in his boxers."

"I'm not your father. Nor do I wear boxers." I balanced on one leg and started putting on my cut-offs.

April smiled. "Nope, you're my boyfriend." She got up, came over to me, put her arms around my neck and kissed me. My cut-offs dropped to my ankles.

"I should get dressed. If someone walked in…"

"I locked the door," whispered April.

I was nervous and excited and had no idea where any of this was going. Hormones were pouring through me. April was more assertive than I'd ever seen. She was cool and collected, while I was a wreck. Given that I was older, it should've been the other way around.

199 • The Cantor's Son

"I want to thank you again for being so gallant at the party last month. It meant a lot to me." She kissed me again on the lips.

When I came up for air and we parted, I said, "Rosenfeld is a bully. He's intimidated me before, not to mention gotten me into trouble for talking in class. I spent a lot of time at Hebrew school in the hall because of that bastard."

"I think you got him back," said April.

She was still very close. I could feel myself getting hard, and that made me nervous. "I really do need to get dressed."

She glanced down. "Don't have to on my account."

I shook my head and removed her arms from around my neck. She stepped back. I pulled my cut-offs up and snapped and zipped them on.

"You're not that shy little girl," I said. "You go for what you want."

April smiled. "Yeah, I am, but not with you. According to my horoscope, it's part of my personality."

"I'm an Aries too," I said.

"That's why we're perfect for one another."

Time to change the subject. I nodded and pulled out my guitar. "Care to sing? I got a whole book of Beatles songs."

"I'm getting a guitar this summer. We'll be able to practice together."

We spent the rest of the afternoon singing. And a bit of smooching as well.

***

Summer took on a different feel. Being older, I could now use the power lawn mower. Usually it didn't start unless you cursed while you pulled the cord. I had to mow the lawn once a week. Dad trimmed the bushes on the weekend. When Mark and Larry had a day off or two, I schlepped my sixteen pound bowling ball down to Sunset Shopping Centre to meet with them and Mainard. Bowling was thirty cents a game, so, for a buck ten we could play three games and have a coke. Sometimes Paul and I, with Robin and Morrie in tow would bike up to the Ericson pool and swim. The change room smelled of chlorine, piss and B.O. The cement floor was wet and slimy and disgusting. The circular shaped pool had a fenced off deep section in the middle along with low and high dive boards. I was afraid I'd skewer myself on the wrought iron fence if I jumped off the board. I remember when I took swimming lessons the summer I was nine. The lessons were at eight o'clock in the morning and water was cold enough to form ice cubes around your balls for the rest of the day.

In the evenings, I hung out with the kids in the neighborhood. We'd meet at Robby Cramer's house. The group consisted of his sister whom I've mentioned before, the very cute Janice, a slim, tall brunette, who was five years older than me; the Chilton girls, of whom the youngest, Nan, went to Northside Jr. High, her sister Barb, a curvy dark-haired busty girl; and the Thompson girls: Tina Thompson a blonde tomboy, and her sister Shelley, a statuesque blonde. Mark Patterson, who lived across the street from us, was also part of the neighborhood gang. Mark was a bit of a nerd who could always be heard practicing piano, sort of like Schroder in the Peanuts comic strip, and, Mike Saunders the dark-haired newcomer to the neighborhood. Usually we played tetherball and listened to music on a portable record player. Occasionally, though, Robbie would bring his drum set out and Mike and I would have our guitars and we'd jam a bit. Sometimes we'd have neighborhood water gun fights. We'd race around, down alleys, through yards. We'd refill at anyone's spigot and of course that'd be a safe zone. Usually I teamed up with Paul Anderson and Tina. We'd played cowboys and army when we were kids, so we knew how to cover each other's backs.

201 • The Cantor's Son

But some nights we hung out at Chilton's because of Mr. Cramer.

Mr. Cramer was an abusive drunk mechanic. One time he hit Robby so hard that Robby flew out the back screen door, off the back stoop and landed flat on his ass in the worn out lawn. And it was all because his Dad had a bad day. We tended to keep it down when his Dad was around.

I also spent my time riding my bike and working with the weight set I had gotten as a Bar Mitzvah gift. I slimmed down more, gained some height, though still shorter than dad, and got stronger.

One night Robby Cramer and I had a sleep over on our back porch. And, it turned out there was a girl's sleepover at the Chilton's. The Chilton's house sat on the corner, and had a screen enclosed front porch. The idea of the girls wearing nothing but nighties bombarded Robby's and my interest. At eleven thirty we left the confines of my back porch, slipped through the back yard next door, and clambered over the short retaining wall. Like the old cowboy scouts we crept silently along the side of the Chilton's brown frame and brick home until we reached the front porch. We could hear the music blasting the Dave Clark Five. There was a small open vent along one wall of the porch. Bobby and I peeked in. The girls were showing a lot of leg and a fair bit of form in the skimpy pajamas and nighties. Robby and I glanced at each other and grinned.

Robby whispered, "Want to have some fun?"

"What do you mean?"

He pointed to the hose that was wound up on the side of the house. "Bring it over here."

I unwound some hose. Robby took the spray end and adjusted the sprayer. He shoved it through the opening. The girls were dancing to the music. We looked again and got rewarded with some nicely rounded bottoms and long bare legs.

Robby nodded and I went over and turned on the water. The next minute there were screams drowning out the music. We laughed so hard we had tears trailing down our cheeks. My sides ached.

"What the hell is going on?" yelled a male voice.

Robby and I looked at each other. Oh shit, Mr. Chilton was up. We leaped off the retaining wall and into the yard next door. We tucked and rolled, clumsily got to our feet and made a hasty retreat back to my porch.

The screams faded. Too bad we couldn't have stuck around long enough to see the girls run out in their wet nighties. But all in all it was a successful raid.

Later Robby went out to take a leak by our cherry tree. And I heard a girl's voice, "Well that's pretty pitiful." There was a sound of female laughter as a humiliated Robby ran back to the porch. Touché'.

Chapter Fifteen

July 1965

As planned since we weren't leaving on vacation until after the 4th, I arranged for Larry to stay overnight. Dad didn't like driving on the highway on holidays. He said there were too many assholes on the road.

Dad believed in celebrating the 4th in style and had purchased gobs of smoke bombs, bottle rockets, snakes, and a fair number of Butterfinger and Black Cat firecrackers. Though the fourth was tomorrow, Dad just had to test a few of the items he had bought. And it wasn't like he was the only one doing it either. In the alley, Dad fired off bottle rockets until the people living in the Belleview apartments complained about the noise. On our front walk Larry, Paul and I lit snakes, small black capsules that expanded in to curly, black smoky things that, well, looked like snakes. Dark gray stains dotted the sidewalk. We took Butterfinger firecrackers and shoved them down anthills, Paul Anderson had tons of them on his yard, and we stuffed them all, then lit them. The lawn was peppered with small blasts and gobs of dirt and dead ants exploding into the air. Morrie and Robin stuffed two firecrackers down one ant hole and blew a nice divot on the front lawn, one that would not amuse Mr. Anderson, who was a foul tempered man.

A bit later, after my folks went inside, dragging a whiny over-tired Morrie. Larry, Paul and I then got the brilliant idea of taking some of the rotten apples off the lawn and shoving the slightly larger black cat firecracker into them. We lit the fuse then hurled them down the alley. They exploded spreading applesauce and bits all over. However, there's always some adult to spoil the fun. One such person was Mrs. Goldblatt who lived in the Belleview. She stuck her head out of her window and yelled down, "What the hell are you little momsers doing? I'll call the police! You stop that this instant!"

We decided that valor was overrated and made a beeline out of the alley.

It was getting dark and Paul headed for home. Larry and I went back to my place. Upstairs we started getting ready for bed, though by no means were we planning to go to sleep. We'd taken the rollaway out of the closet and set it up under the window.

"The girls have been talking about you, Slim."

"Oh? You know something you're not telling me?"

"Yeah, apparently Marilyn Scheckter really likes you. Look, I know you probably still have a thing for Janet too, but truth is she likes Scott Miller." Larry leaned back on the rollaway and put his head on the pillow. "But of course that might pose a problem for you. Keeping two girls on the line is dangerous, Slim."

"What's that supposed to mean?" I asked.

"You got April," said Larry, ticking off one finger, and now you got Marilyn." He stuck up a second finger. "You'll have chain on each of your balls," chuckled Larry.

"Look, April is my special friend, but it's not like we're going steady or anything."

"I don't think that's the way she sees it, Slim. And, you do make such a sweet couple." Larry made a kissing noise. "God, just really admit you like April. There's nothing wrong with it."

I hurled my pillow at him and nailed him in the nuts. He groaned. "You bastard!"

I laughed. "You know, we still have some firecrackers left."

"Well we won't have time to blow them off tomorrow. My dad's picking me up at nine. I'm working at the store."

"We could get rid of them now." I glanced at the window above Larry's head.

I went over, and standing on the rollaway opened the window as wide as I could. "We have to be careful to throw over the roof to the entrance."

I lit a firecracker and hurled it. It went out over the front law and exploded. Firecrackers were still going off around the neighborhood even though it was ten thirty at night. Larry lit one and threw it. It exploded on the front walk. Larry lit another one and hurled it. It exploded at the edge of the front lawn.

I lit another and didn't quite clear the roof. It bounced off it and went to the right and exploded. Shit! Almost got the bush in front of my parents' bedroom window.

The next thing we heard was the sound of thunder, and it wasn't from any fireworks. My parent's bedroom window shot up and I heard my dad, "WHAT THE HELL DO YOU THINK YOU'RE DOING? YOU ALMOST LIT THE HOUSE ON FIRE! GO TO BED!"

Larry and I looked at each other. We slammed my bedroom window shut. I shot across the room and turned off the lights. We lay down in bed and threw our covers. My heart was pounding. It reminded me of a saying one of my Cub Scout leaders used to say: Do not poke an angry bear with a stick.

In July, there were border clashes between Israel and Jordan. President Johnson signed The Medicare Bill into law and tobacco manufacturers had to add health warnings on cigarette packages. Civil rights protests and unrest rippled continuously through the south in the heat of summer. And it was a real eye opener for me.

When I'd gone to elementary school in Chicago, my class was filled with kids of all races and backgrounds. It was like being in a mini-United Nations. My second grade teacher, Mrs. Jacobson, ensured we respected each other's beliefs and cultures. She made it a point to have kids explain their culture or religious holidays. It was fun to learn about our differences. So when I saw the riots going on in the news, we talked about it at the dinner table. I remember my mom telling me about visiting cousins in Richmond, Virginia and her Aunt reminding her not to use the Negro washrooms or drinking fountains when she disembarked the train. I had a hard time understanding that.

The drive down to Miami was a long hot grueling one. Going through Tennessee I saw shacks that looked worse than the crumbling neighborhoods on the other side of Broadway in Chicago. There were roadside stills advertising Peach cider. We joked we could probably put it in the car and use it as gas.

The miles rolled by. We stayed at small motels that were cheaper than the larger chains, and of course had no swimming pool. Some had air conditioning units in the windows. Morrie and I had loaded up on comic books. I had picked up a *Batman* 80-page Giant that featured Batman and Robin on strange alien worlds. I'd also picked up the new copy of Daredevil and Detective comics, along with The Atom. Morrie had a *Dennis the Menace* eighty-page annual. I had also borrowed two Matt Helm books from Mainard, along with a Man From U.N.C.L.E. adventure by Michael Avallone, and a copy of Ian Fleming's *Live and Let Die*. I had enough to read when I got bored.

After spending the night in Chattanooga, we crossed into Georgia early one morning. The sun was barely a slash across the morning sky. Low laying mist made the orchards look like rows of skeletons. The road curved through gently rolling farmland. I could make out houses and barns when they were situated close to the road. We stopped at a small restaurant, Dad and his truckers' stops, on the outskirts of Atlanta. We walked into the small café and heads turned. There were a lot of fat truckers. A few farmers wore overalls. We sat down at a table. A thin red-haired waitress who looked older than Nana came over with menus. Dad as usual ordered his scrambled eggs in butter with toast and coffee. Mom ordered a small order of hot cakes for Morrie. I had cold cereal: *Frosted Flakes*. The only time we could get sugar-coated cereal was on vacation; though sometimes we could nag mom into buying *some Alpha-Bits* or *Sugar Pops*. The waitress brought the food shortly, and I noticed on everyone's plate was a clump of hot white meal. It reminded me of cream of wheat. Well, Morrie took one look at it and boomed in his ever big voice, "What's this crap?"

You could hear a dime drop on the floor. The other customers turned and stared at us.

"It's called Grits. It's like cream of wheat. If you don't want it, I'll take it off your plate," said Mom, speaking softly to my brother. She glanced at Dad. Dad glowered and gave us the 'shut up' look. I wondered if Dad had his gun with him. Were we going to have to shoot it out?

I don't know if Mom knew, but Dad showed me a .25 Beretta automatic, just like James Bond had in the beginning of *Dr. No*. He said it was for protection. I hadn't understood fully then, but I did now. We ate quickly and left.

Not to be outdone by breakfast, my dear brother Morrie caused another kerfuffle an hour or so later. Morrie had an official Popeye the Sailor captain's hat made of molded blue plastic that he insisted on wearing. While he walked in front of my parents when we stopped, I stayed back a few feet not wanting to be associated with him. Anyway Dad was smoking while driving so Morrie and I rolled down the back windows to get fresh air. Well, a whip of wind and Popeye's hat blew off Morrie's stupid head. The kid screamed as if someone was attacking him with a machete. Dad pulled onto the shoulder and screeched to a halt. He half-turned in his seat and looked at us, his eyes burned into me accusingly.

"I didn't do anything to the little cretin. I've been sittin' here reading. He's upset because his stupid captain's hat blew out the window."

Dad zeroed in on Morrie who was making with puppy dog eyes and flowing tears. "I want my hat! I gotta have my hat!"

Mom looked pleadingly at Dad. Dad blew smoke out both nostrils, muttered something unintelligible out of his mouth, and got out of the car. He started scanning the side of the road, walking along this wooden fence. I got out to help him. Morrie dashed out too.

"Morrie! Get back here!" yelled Mom.

But of course, Morrie, being Morrie, ignored her. He ran after dad. Dad turned to him. "Get back in the car. I'm looking for your hat."

Suddenly Morrie stopped and pointed. "There it is, Dad!"

We stopped and followed Morrie's finger. I looked through the fence and saw a spot of blue. "It's in that field," I said.

Dad looked at the fence. He turned and looked at Morrie, who now had an expression of utter joy and hope on his little face. Dad muttered something under his breath. I'm pretty sure it wasn't something he wanted us to hear. He put both hands on the top rail. The fence was only five feet high. He put his lower foot on the lower rail and was about to swing over when he stopped. I don't blame him for stopping. There was a humungous bull strutting towards us. He sort of side glanced the hat and then looked at us. Challenging us. You want the hat, come and get it. Heh. Heh. Heh.

No way Dad was going to fight a bull over a stupid plastic hat. He got down off the fence, scooped Morrie up, and strode back to the car with me in his wake. Morrie screamed his head off

"I WANT MY HAT!" cried Morrie. .

"SHUT UP!" yelled Dad.

We arrived back at the car and he ordered Morrie back into the car.

Mom looked at Dad.

"I'm not getting stomped by a fuckin' bull over that stupid hat! JEZUZCHRIST ALMIGHTY!" Dad shook his head and got back in the car.

Morrie continued to cry as we pulled out and headed back down the highway.

It seemed that there were miles of tattered shacks leading into Atlanta. We'd seen similar sights as we drove south. On the front porches were usually a couch or chair with an old Negro sitting in it. No matter how dilapidated the houses were, most had TV antennas sticking up on the roofs. We hit a detour that took us off the interstate and through part of the city. Traffic was jammed. We'd hit Atlanta during the morning rush hour. I saw a mean faced cop directing traffic. We stopped. The car in front of us had Illinois license plates. The cop took one look at the car and spit on it. The glob hit the windshield and oozed down. Mom looked at Dad.

"Don't say anything," said Mom.

We drove down I-95 to Miami along the coast, passing through pastel colored towns and glimpses of ocean. We drove by Cape Kennedy. Traffic was heavy and the last day seemed to drag forever. Dad pushed the Ford Station wagon. It overheated and we had to stop. We sat on the tail-gate, drinking Orange Crushes as the car cooled down and Dad only seemed to heat up. Obviously relaxing on vacation was something that would take time for him.

Chapter Sixteen

Miami, Florida

Nana and Grandpop lived in a three-bedroom bungalow with a screened in porch in a new residential area of North Miami. There were palm trees in the yard. Small lizards scampered everywhere it seemed, but Morrie and I thought it was kind of cool. Morrie and I were going to sleep on cots on the porch. Nana said it was cooler there. Mom and Dad got the guest bedroom. The other bedroom had been turned into a TV room for Grandpop where he smoked stinky cigars, listened to ballgames on his transistor radio and watched reruns of Perry Mason, all simultaneously. And God help it if you thought he was asleep and tried to change the channel.

What I couldn't get over was the suffocating heat in Miami. It seemed all I did there was sweat. One day we drove out along this bridge or causeway to Parrot Island. They had a nice beach, but we were told we couldn't go out in water deeper than our waist because of sharks. They actually had two guys in a rowboat further out looking for them.

A lot of the time we spent visiting Mom's cousins who, like cockroaches, seemed be all over the place. One of them, Sam, was a coin dealer and gave Morrie and me a whole box of foreign coins, mostly from the Caribbean and South America. They were really neat. We even got a book on coin collecting. The collection was to be shared, but Morrie seemed to be hoarding certain plastic sets. I guess some of the coins reminded him of Pirate Doubloons.

Another evening we went to this diner called Wolfie's off Collins Avenue that is sort of like the main drag where the big hotels like The Fountainbleau were.

They had a great deli, and the portions were humongous. Morrie and I shared a piece of Lemon Meringue pie for dessert. Mom and Dad went there a few times with some other couples while we were down there.

Nana also introduced us to some kids in the neighborhood who were around our age. There was a sandy haired kid named Kevin, and skinny blonde haired boy named Harold. Hal had a younger sister named Molly who was a year younger than Morrie. Mostly we sat around and talked and tried to catch lizards. One afternoon I was in desperate need of comic books, so Kevin said we should go walk up to the mall. It was a newer neighborhood without a lot of large trees, or shade over the sidewalk. It was very hot. But that didn't stop the six of us walking about a mile to the strip mall that had this huge store like Woolworths or Kresges. Thankfully the place was air-conditioned. We bought frozen pops in the snack section. Among the paperbacks and magazines I found some comics, but they had weird titles like *Dollman*, sort of an Atom rip-off, and some other heroes I didn't recognize, but it was better than nothing.

The Rabbi, from the Temple that my grandparents belonged to, came over one afternoon. He was really nice and had five kids, all younger than me. He and dad talked shop. But from that, I got set up on this sort of blind date, thanks to Nana.

Her name was June Moskovitz and she was built like Wonder Woman but with light brown hair instead of black. My eyes came up just above her boobs, which were like big round cantaloupes. She hung around with these two brothers, Jake and Daniel. I think they were twins. Both were about five-nine, skinny with narrow faces and curly dark brown hair. They wore white t-shirts with the JCC logo and blue jeans. They were three years older and had their driver's licenses. They picked me up in this boxy silver Mercedes and we went to a bowling alley.

We played three games and I managed to average a score of 180. Dan and Jake were impressed. June gave me a tiny kiss for each strike I made. When it was her turn, all three of us guys were glued to her ass. Very round. Very firm. She wore a pair of tight khaki colored shorts and a yellow Hawaiian shirt that pulled across her chest. It was hard to concentrate.

Afterwards we went back to June's house. It was a Spanish-styled two story white stucco furnished with dark mahogany furniture. June's parents worked. They were lawyers. June had an older sister, but she was at the beach with friends. So, it turned out, we had the place to ourselves.

June's house had a sunken living room with white shag carpeting, an L-shaped brown leather couch, and two armchairs. In the center of the furniture was a glass coffee table. We sat around it, drinking ice tea and chatting about school and life in Miami.

"We should play a game," suggested Dan.

The two brothers looked at each other. June smiled. "I know what you want."

Jake got up and went into the kitchen and came back with an empty 7-Up bottle. He put it on the coffee table.

"This is a variation of spin the bottle," said Dan. "Each of us spins the bottle and whoever it points to gets to go into the front hall closet with June."

I nodded. I wasn't quite sure what we were going to do in the closet, but I could take an educated guess. June seemed quite enthusiastic about it.

Dan went first and spun the bottle. It pointed to Jake. Jake got up, took June's hand and they disappeared into the hall.

"So how are you liking Miami?" asked Dan.

"It's ok, a bit boring at times. I like my grandparents, but there's not a lot to do. We've seen a few things, but Mom and Dad tend to go off a bit and leave us."

"Well I guess they need time together. Our folks tend to go out of town on business a lot. Sometimes together, and sometimes separately."

"Yeah, but you guys can drive. You're not stuck at home."

"Well we're both working part-time over the summer. I'm doing some retails sales, and Jake is doing some lawn care. Our parents think it's good for us to earn our own money."

"I've shoveled walks in the winter, raked leaves in the fall, and will probably do some lawn mowing when we get back."

June and Jake came back in. We sat down and Jake spun the bottle. This time it pointed to Dan. Dan grinned and he and June went off down the hall.

"You're a pretty good bowler," said Jake.

"I got my own ball as a Bar Mitzvah present and have been several times. Dad gave me some pointers. He used to bowl a lot when he was in high school and college. My friends and I go to this bowling lane not too far away. And, it's air-conditioned which is a plus."

Third time lucky. The bottle pointed to me. I went with June down the front hall and into the closet that was rather deep and spacious. Cracks of light came through the doorframe. We stood there, I wasn't quite sure what to do.

"Do you want to feel me up? Or kiss me?" she asked.

"To be honest, I've never played this game. What did the other guys do?"

"Usually cop a feel, take a peek or kiss."

"You enjoy that?" I asked.

"Well, it works both ways," said June. In the dim light I detected a slight smile.

This game was certainly a few notches up from the spy game April and I played with all bets open. I have to admit I was curious to touch and feel, but then of course that worked the other way too. I could feel June's warm breath on me. Our bodies were close. But for some reason I wasn't as horny as I thought I'd be; a bit nervous, a bit scared, but not horny. I didn't have a hard on, and it's not because she wasn't a good-looking girl. She was hot. But for some reason I started thinking about April. Now April certainly didn't have a body like June did, though potential was there a couple of years in the future. Was I in love with April? I didn't think so, but at the same time I felt guilty about being with June. I had to admit it; I missed April. What a fucking dilemma this was. Opportunity in front of me, and I stood frozen like a Catholic priest in a whorehouse.

"You know, we don't have to do anything. You don't seem too comfortable with this."

"Thanks."

She kissed me briefly on the lips and we went out to join Jake and Dan. I didn't see June or the twins again.

The rest of the holiday was uneventful. A week later we headed back up north with a pair of lizards in a glass cage that Nana Esther had given us, and a set of bongo drums Morrie traded a couple of small toy cars for. Driving back through Alabama Morrie was pounding on his bongos singing Yankee Doodle. Not a bright move, given the social unrest and Southerner's attitudes towards Northerners. Anyway, Morrie had been singing for quite some time. Suddenly Dad pulled over and stopped the car. He got out and went around to the back. He snatched the drums out of Morrie's hands and put his fist through the larger bongo drum, and handed it back to Morrie. The rest of the day was blissfully silent.

Tragedy struck the lizards, named Bud and Abbott, in Indiana. We stopped overnight at a Holiday Inn. Dad lugged the suitcases in. Morrie, inadvertently put the lizard tank on top of the air conditioning unit. We went for a swim, and then quickly came up and changed for dinner. Morrie saved some salad for them, and fed them when we got back in, but they seemed a bit sluggish. The next morning they became lizard pops. Morrie reached in and tried to wake them up, but they were stiffer than an English butler at a hootenanny. Sadly, and with some tears, we gave them a formal burial at sea by flushing them down the toilet.

Driving across Iowa a foul mildew smell permeated the car.

"What the hell is going on?" wondered Dad.

Mom turned to him. "I don't know, but maybe you should pull over and we'll check."

We pulled over onto the shoulder near Parkersburg on highway 20. Dad and Mom took all the stuff out of the car and couldn't find the origin of the smell. Dad then opened the trunk and started sniffing the suitcases. The smell emanated from Morrie's bag. No surprise there. Mom carefully opened it and as she started lifting layers, her hand felt something squishy. She shrieked. Dad investigated. Turns out my dopey brother had a couple of ocean sponges he'd picked up at the beach. He'd wrapped them in wax paper and stuffed them into the suitcase after mom had packed it. The smell was disgusting. Worse than rotten fish. Worse than the dead bat Paul Andersen and I had found in his back yard. Worse than the skinned ducks a neighbor Mr. Pierce had been cleaning out by the alley. And of course Mom would have to wash all of Morrie's stuff when we got home.

"What the hell were you thinking?" Dad exploded.

Morrie stood there with a quivering lip.

"Relax. It's ok. No harm done," said Mom.

"The trunk is going to reek for weeks. I don't know if I'll ever get that smell out." Dad stomped off and paced for a bit, while Mom threw the sponges in a paper bag with some other garbage.

Mom intervened, "He didn't do it intentionally. He didn't know better."

"For Christsake, who the hell takes stuff like that?" Dad was still ranting as he put the luggage back in the car. "We'll pull into Parkersburg and I'll get some rope. I'm putting that suitcase on the roof."

Mom rolled her eyes. There was no use arguing. But Morrie was the big loser. No bongos. No lizards. Though likelihood was he would've frozen the reptiles at home and then tried to resuscitate them over the stove. He still tried it with bees, wasps and spiders with no success. They tended to go snap, crackle and pop when you held them over a gas flame. Mom continually found little Dixie cups with insects in them, covered in wax paper in the freezer. She was not amused.

July 2012: Thursday Evening

Debby was one of the first ones off the plane. She wore a white blouse, blue jeans and a light denim jacket. Her blonde hair was pulled back in a ponytail. She pulled a small red carry-on behind her. I took her in my arms and kissed her.

"I'm all sweaty," she whispered.

"I'll make you sweat more." I grinned.

"You're incorrigible."

I wiggled my eyebrows. "You like my youthful exuberance."

"Or something after all these years."

"Jeff! Is that you?" The voice sounded familiar. I turned and looked. There was April! I hadn't seen her in almost forty years, but I'd recognize her anywhere.

April reminded me of that actress, Wendie Malick, with a slightly upturned nose. Her hair was just off her shoulders. Her breasts were more prominent now, and her hips had widened a bit, but she was still relatively slim and beautiful. She wore a black pants suit with a light blue blouse. Next to her was the man I assumed was her husband. He was taller than me, at least six feet compared with my five-nine. He had a sharp jawline, brown eyes, his salt and pepper hair was brushed back. He wore an Armani suit and a Rolex watch on his left wrist. He flashed a smile. I bet he was a real shark in the courtroom.

"April! Hi. I'm sorry to meet you under the circumstances. Our condolences. I wish I had known you were coming in on this flight." God this was awkward. We hadn't seen or talked together in decades. But here she was. And here I was. And she needed me. And she seemed happy to see me.

"It's ok. The important thing is, we've made it." She walked towards us.

We hugged; it was somewhat awkward. I could feel the emotional strings tug at me. It had been such a long time. I still felt guilty when I thought back of how I had treated her, and how she had deserved to be treated. But the past is past. You can't erase it. All you can do is remember and learn from it.

I took a slight step back. "It's good to see you. You look great."

April cracked grin and we made introductions. She gave Debby the once over. Women tend to do that so I've been informed. Her husband was named Irwin. He seemed to give Debbie the once over too. I grinned inwardly. I think we were both lucky stiffs having the women we did in our lives. I hoped he was good to April. I hoped she was happy.

"I'm glad you're officiating at the funeral. My sisters are basket cases. Dad's a wreck."

"I know. I phoned him when I got in. We're meeting tomorrow morning at your home to discuss the service and shiva."

Irwin looked around the airport. "So this is River City. How quaint."

I don't know if he was being polite or condescending but I hated him already. Debbie gave me the look, after appraising April. So this is your old flame? Debbie had seen that picture I had of April and her sister taken right before we moved in August, 1968. I took it in our backyard under the elm tree. In that picture April was a tall skinny kid in a sleeveless top and khaki shorts. But that was a long time ago. I never told Debbie about April's and my one night tryst in 1970, nor was I about to bring it up anytime soon.

"We were going to grab a bite, care to join us?" I asked.

"We're famished. It's been a hectic day. We're staying with dad. Let me give him a call. Dinner would be nice." April whipped her cellphone out and stepped a few feet away to make the call. Irwin smiled at us and looked around at the passengers making their way out of the terminal. Awkward moment.

Chapter Seventeen

August, 1965

As the Lovin' Spoonful song goes, "Hot town, summer in the city..." Riots broke out in Watts when two cops tried arresting a drunk Negro man. It ended with thirty-four people dead, over a thousand injured, and millions of dollars in property damage. Race riots also broke out in Chicago. The Vietnam War was raging and the anti-war protests were growing. These were not the dog days of summer. I was not as naïve as I was the year before. Watching the news every evening gave me things to think about other than girls and the latest Beatle's hit. I was still a kid in many ways. But the world was bigger now.

Things I'd seen in our travels south, the poverty, the feeling of desperation, the hatred had been burned into my consciousness. I loved my country, but there were things wrong with it. It was not the land of freedom and liberty I thought it was. There wasn't much I could do now, but when I got older I promised myself to do what I could to make the world a better place.

Coming back, I rejoined the group of us neighborhood kids meeting almost every night at Robby's to listen to records, play tetherball and hang out. One night I brought my guitar, and Robby hauled his drum set out of his house, and Mike brought his electric guitar. We tried some songs like *I Feel Fine*, *Little Old Lady from Pasadena* and *Wipeout*. When it got dark we sat on the Chilton's retaining wall in the front yard and told ghost stories and dirty jokes. I was a little sad, Paul and I didn't hang out as much anymore. Turns out, the Andersens were moving. Paul's parents were getting a divorce. His mom was going back to school to study art and get her teaching degree at Morningside College on the Southside. The neighborhood was changing. I was changing, and I still wanted to cling, in some way, to what was and not what was to be. But change is inevitable.

Another B'nai Mitzvah party, sponsored by the June Bar and Bat Mitzvahs: Weiners, Polikoffs and Greenstone's, was held on Saturday August 7, the second weekend we were back from vacation. And thankfully I didn't have to get dressed up for it. Jeans and a short-sleeve madras sports shirt were fine.

Stone Park covered sixteen hundred acres and sat along the bluffs and ravines of the Big Sioux River on the edge of the Loess Hills. Thick Oak forest covered most of it. We turned off Hamilton Boulevard onto Stone Park Boulevard. Dad's headlights bounced in front of us. I was riding shotgun with Larry, Mark and Mainard in the back of the Ford.

"Where's the party again?" Dad asked as he peered into the darkness.

"Cabin Four," I said.

I saw a sign pointing to the campground. Dad took a sharp turn and wound his way up the hill.

Because we had to wait for Shabbos to end, we were the last ones to get there. A lot of the older kids were there too. I could hear the music pouring out of the cabin as Dad pulled up. The adults were out in the parking lot smoking and schmoozing. We piled out of the car. Mark's Dad would give me a ride home.

I saw Dad pull up and park. He got out and joined the group of parents.

We headed inside. The cabin wasn't as big as I expected. It was wall-to-wall people. Max Weiss was acting as DJ and spinning the records on a portable stereo system. A couple of lanterns gave dim light to the shadowy bodies bouncing to the beat of The Beach Boys' latest release, *Help Me Rhonda*. A table on my right held bowls of potato chips and pretzels. Bottles of pop and paper cups and a bowl of melted ice were on the far end.

The group of girls from our class was huddled on the other side of the room by the window. We snaked our way over. Mark of course paired off with Debbie Stein. Les asked Molly Weiner to dance. I looked around. I felt like a heel asking someone else to dance. I wished April were here. But she wasn't, nor would she be. I saw Barb Zeffman talking to Debby Galinsky. I willed my feet to move.

"Uh, excuse me," I said. The girls stopped and looked at me. I smiled at Debbie, then asked Barb to dance.

She looked at me for a moment, and nodded to Debbie. "Sure."

Max put on Herman Hermit's *Mrs. Brown You Have a Lovely Daughter*, and we wedged our way onto the dance floor. We danced two dances. The second was to the Temptation's *My Girl.* I danced a polite slow dance. Barb was good looking with those sexy sloe-eyes. After the music ended, she thanked me and went back to her friends. Pam Zellman had now joined the group of Temple girls.

I wandered over to the snack table and poured myself a cup of 7-Up. Suddenly I saw Marilyn Scheckter standing next to me. She was looking wistfully at the dancers.

I put my drink down. Well, if I was gonna be a ladies' man tonight, might as well get with it. I tapped her on the shoulder. She jumped and spun around.

"Sorry, just wanted to know if you wanted to dance," I half shouted. Max had the music turned up.

"Sure," she shouted back.

Do Wah Diddy Diddy blasted in the room. I remembered some of the moves April had shown me. At least I didn't step on Marilyn's toes.

Max put on Bobby Vinton's *Earth Angel*. The room smelled of perfume and sweat...and a bit of sour gas. I took

Marilyn's hands and we danced. The room crowded as it was pushed us together. I could feel her breasts touching me and could see her shiny dark eyes watching me.

"Thank you for asking me to dance, Jeff."

I smiled.

She leaned forward and kissed me gently on the lips. Oh oh, this was trouble.

The song ended and we went back to the snack table.

"What do you want to drink?" I asked.

"Coke is fine."

I took a paper cup and poured her a drink. As I was about to hand it to her, someone bumped my arm and the drink went up. Suddenly my face and hair were awash in Coke; I blinked and took off my glasses. Marilyn looked upset and rightly so, the front of her white blouse was wet and dark, revealing her brassiere.

"Sorry," said a familiar voice. "Didn't mean to get you all wet."

I put my glasses on and turned my head. Leonard Rosenfeld with Stuart Goldberg in tow continued to plow through.

"Asshole," I muttered. I turned to Marilyn. "Come on, let's get you dried off." My shirt was wet too, but it'd dry.

Marilyn looked down at her wet blouse and blushed. She was visibly upset and I didn't blame her.

Cindy Davidson came over. "Come on Marilyn, we'll get you cleaned up."

Arnie Rosenthal handed me some napkins. "He should've looked where he was going."

"That's the trouble," I replied, "I think he did."

The rest of the evening was uneventful. I managed to snag one dance with Janet Greenstone, and another with Barb Zeffman. The last dance was with Marilyn, looking a bit drier and wearing a sweater from one of the parents.

The following Saturday, the Blackmans came over after services. Mr. Blackman dropped them off on his way to the store. I hadn't seen April since June. I had called her when I came back, and we talked about going swimming at Lief Ericson pool, but for some reason it never materialized. Thinking about her, I felt a little apprehensive, and a little horny. Come to think of it, I was always horny when April came over.

The girls used Morrie's bedroom to change. Mrs. Blackman had brought shorts and shirts for them. It obviously wouldn't do to play in dresses. She had hangers for their clothes.

I went upstairs. I put on jeans and a blue t-shirt. I hung my clothes up carefully. Dad got mad if my stuff was lying around. "That's not the way you treat good clothes," he'd say.

When I came down, the table was set for lunch. Mom served chicken salad sandwiches made from leftover challah and roasted chicken. There was a plate of carrot and celery sticks on the table.

"Why don't you kids eat on the porch? It's cooler there," suggested Mom.

Dad nodded and set up the card table and folding chairs. I helped him.

Morrie and Susie glared at each other across the table.

"Do you like SEE FOOD?" he laughed and opened his mouth to show his half-chewed bite.

"Ick! You're so rude!" said Susie.

I rolled my eyes and looked at April. I sat back, took a chomp of my sandwich and stretched my legs. And encountered April's foot.

"Sorry," I mumbled. She was wearing flip-flop sandals and with my sneakers I could've smashed her.

"It's ok." April smiled and ran her foot up and down my calf. I could feel her toes kneading my leg. I stared at her.

"How was your trip?" she asked.

"I'll tell you about it later." I cocked my head towards our siblings. April nodded.

My parents and Mrs. Blackman, along with the baby, came outside to sit in the back. The trees on the north side of the yard gave a fair bit of shade, and Morrie and Susie were running around shooting up the alley. April and I slipped back into the house, carrying our dirty dishes to put in the sink. We made a beeline to my bedroom upstairs.

I shut the door behind us. "So what do you want to do?" I asked.

"I don't know," she said coyly. She stared deep into my eyes. I could feel my heart speeding up.

"I have a few pictures of our trip if you care to see them," I said.

"Ok." There was a bit of disappointment in her reply. She moved closer to me and I could feel her breath. I closed my eyes for a moment. I wanted to kiss her. What was stopping me? Why was I acting like such an idiot?

I took the packet I'd gotten back from Klages a few days ago. I sat on my knees and spread the prints out on my bed. "Here's my grandparent's house. That's them by the front door." I pointed to the picture. April leaned over next to me. I could feel the warmth of her skin next to me. She liked the beach at Parrot Island. I had a picture of two of the brightly colored birds.

"They had guys looking for sharks there," I told her.

I had pictures at Wolfie's, along Collins Avenue that I'd shot from the car. I had a neat picture of a lizard. And I had gotten one of the cop spitting on the car in front of us going through Atlanta. April leaned closer. I could smell the scent of the shampoo in her hair. I had the urge to kiss her neck. What was it about her that drove me crazy?

And why didn't I just swoop her up and kiss her? I really wanted to. It's not like we hadn't kissed before.

I rolled off the bed and got my guitar. I didn't plug it into the amplifier, but picked *All my Loving* while sitting on the floor. April lay across the bed and peered at me. Our eyes locked.

She rolled over onto her back and looked at me upside down. "We went to the country club almost every day. It was ok, but I wish we could've gone somewhere exciting like you did. I missed you Jeff. Did you miss me?"

"Yeah, I did." It was the first time I'd admitted it to myself. Then I told April about the afternoon with June. I didn't spare any details. She listened. She appeared a bit apprehensive when I told her about the spin the bottle game. "Thing is, I do like you, I really do; but I sometimes find myself thinking about other girls in general, too."

"But you didn't kiss that girl June or do anything," said April.

"No. I wanted to, I think. But I just froze. I thought about you. I didn't want to hurt you."

"Hmmmm. You could not have told me anything about it."

"Yeah, I guess, but it wouldn't have been right. You deserve to know what happened, or didn't happen. I do care about you. You're the only girl I can really talk to about stuff. You're the only girl I've ever kissed." Marilyn kissing me didn't count because I hadn't initiated it. Besides, this confession was bad enough.

"So I'm not your girlfriend?" asked April.

"I don't know. I don't know if I can make a commitment to one girl right now; but you're very special to me. I realize that. And, I do have feelings for you, though I know I've been hesitant to really admit that to you. I'm just fucking confused."

"I'm sorry. I know I'm sorta forward." She paused, and went on, "Well, I do know I like you. You're the only boy I've ever kissed. The only boy I've ever danced with," she said. She giggled. "And the only boy I've ever seen in his underwear." She reached out, put her arms around my neck and kissed my cheek.

I turned my face to her and kissed her gently on the lips. "So what are we then?"

April rolled off the bed and sat next to me. "Who cares? We'll figure it out I guess; but we're together and that's all that really matters I guess." She leaned her head on my shoulder and I took her hand and held it tightly.

Part IV: What the Future Holds

July 2012: Thursday Evening

We pulled into the parking lot of the Green Gables Restaurant on the corner of 18th and Pierce. The restaurant was still a landmark in River City. Three generations of family ownership went back to 1929. The restaurant was white stucco in sort of a Tudor style with green-shaded stained glass windows. Out in front was the infamous Hot Fudge Hound, a wooden cutout of a dog wearing a hot fudge sundae on his head with a cherry on top. Irwin glanced at it and rolled his eyes.

"How quaint," he muttered.

I realized that compared to L.A. River City was a hick town. We had felt a bit the same way when we'd first moved here in the 60's; but of all the places I've lived, River City was always home. We didn't have the fancy restaurants or burger joints he was used to; but then again, he was a conceited prig.

We walked inside and a middle-aged woman wearing a black apron over her green knit dress, at the reservation booth looked up. "For four?" she asked.

"A table for four will work," I replied.

She nodded and pulled out four menus and showed us to a table in the center of the room. She gave us the menus and returned with a pitcher to fill the water glasses. The tables were old-fashioned laminate with wooden captain chairs. There were booths along three walls, with a break in the far wall where the kitchen doors were. Tables for two or four people were scattered in the center. The place hadn't changed in forty years. Pictures of some old pop artists were in hanging frames over the booths.

The Gables was still owned by one of the Temple members. We used to go there for the odd week night dinner. They always had fish on the menu. I remembered they made a mean tuna melt on rye too. When I was in my early teens, it was also the place we hung out after dances at the Jewish Community Center which used to be three blocks down. Apple pie a' la mode, root beer floats, bowls of French fries. It was teen heaven. And they had pay phones so you could call your parents to pick you up, essential for those of us who didn't drive yet.

While we'd moved from River City when I was sixteen, I had stayed in close touch with Mark and Larry over the years, but there were many I didn't. Sitting at the table I wondered what had happened to the group that had been in my religious school class, and some of those I'd gone to elementary and junior high school with. How many had gotten married, divorced, had kids, or were even still alive? I'd reconnected with Tim on Facebook, along with other high school classmates of mine in Oklahoma City. I still kept in touch with Jerry and Fred. Bob the Hobbit had passed away from a heart attack ten years earlier.

My thoughts shifted. Dad's last pulpit had been in Nashville. But by then I had a pulpit of my own in the Boston area. There were a few congregants of mine I had kept in touch with, but people seemed to sail in and out of my life.

"Decided what you're having?" asked Debbie.

"Toss up between the tuna melt and the fish and chips."

"I'm going try the burger," she said.

"They're good, but my favorite is the hot corned beef on rye," said April. She looked around. "It's been ages since I've been here. It never changes." She looked at Irwin.

"What would you recommend?" he asked. He held the menu at arm's length.

"The Reuben's are good here, or the steak sandwich. Iowa is known for its beef," said April, "Or, order what I'm having, hot corned beef sandwich on rye."

"So, I guess I don't have to ask-Where's the Beef?"
Irwin chuckled at his cliché joke.

The waitress came and took our orders. There was
an awkward silence after she left.

"I'm meeting with your Dad around eleven to
discuss the funeral service," I said.

"We'll be there. We're staying with him."

"I'm surprised your parents didn't move into
something smaller after you girls left," I said.

"It was Mom's dream house. She couldn't leave.
And up until a few years ago, they still did a fair bit of
entertaining."

"A lot of the old crowd retired to Arizona," I said.

"Is your mom still in Nashville?" asked April.

"Yeah, she was working up until around three years
ago," I replied. "Her friends are there. She's got this
musician boyfriend who at eighty-five is still doing club
gigs. They even go line-dancing."

April giggled. "Good for her."

"How old is your mother?" asked Irwin.

"She turned eighty in March," I said.

"But she's in good health and quite active," said
Debbie. "I should have her energy when I'm her age."

"You look like you're in good health," said Irwin.

Debbie blushed slightly. "I work out. Fitness and
eating healthy, well most of the time," She glanced down at
her plate. "Pays off in the long run."

Looking at me, Irwin asked, "When did your father
pass away?"

"He died from a heart attack in 1986. He'd come to
see us and then headed to Seattle to do David's Bris. They
got back to Nashville. Mom was out shopping. He had a
heart attack. She found him in the study. The ambulance
came, but it was too late."

"I'm sorry to hear that," said Irwin.

"Well diabetes and heart disease are known in the family. He'd been told to change his diet, stop smoking and reduce stress, the latter being the hardest in this business. He used to say that being a Cantor you had one foot in the door and the other on a banana peel."

Irwin chuckled. "So I take it you watch your stress levels."

"I swim, walk, do Tai Chi. I also never smoked and thanks to Deb, watch what I eat-though tonight being a bit of an exception."

"I play golf and tennis," said Irwin.

"My brother golfs. So does my ex-singing partner Jerry. But I could never get into it. I did play tennis, but I screwed my ankle once too often doing martial arts so I have to take things a bit less intense exercise-wise."

April finished chewing a bite of her corned beef sandwich and took a swig of Diet coke. "I'm glad you're here to do the funeral," said April.

"So am I," I replied.

I learned that April had met Irwin when she'd worked for the Los Angeles Times and covered a trial that Irwin was working on. He'd been impressed with her assertiveness and quick wit, not to mention that she was gorgeous. He asked her out and dating turned serious. They'd been married eighteen years and had no kids, but three dogs: Max, Moira, and Beau. Max and Moira were Scottish terriers. Beau was a golden lab.

April had left the Times to do freelance which allowed her to spend more time doing volunteer work for the SPCA, and was on the board for a couple of animal rights groups. She eventually carved out a niche doing marketing and public relations for them.

Debbie told them how we'd met and spent a lot of time talking about our kids: Marissa, twenty-eight married and with a two-year old son Joseph who was a natural

'Dennis the Menace'. They lived in Seattle. Her husband Brad worked for Google. Our son David was twenty-five, still single (as far as we knew), and was working as a police officer in Chicago. It did not please his mother, but he tended to do what he wanted.

"You still do clubs?" asked Irwin.

"Not in a while, but in Chicago there was a folk club I use to perform at."

"Jeff and I use to practice together when I first got my guitar," said April. "We had fun." April winked at me. Yep, memory like a computer.

Irwin raised an eyebrow and glanced from April to me. "Did you now?"

"That was a long time ago," I said.

"Still be nice to do it again, maybe after shiva," said April.

"Are you going to be here for the full week?" I asked.

"Maybe a bit longer. We'll need to get dad settled and figure things out. He's going to have a hard time coping without Mom," said April.

"My dad went through the same thing when my mother passed away three years ago," said Debbie.

"I'm sorry to hear that," said April. "Is he coping?"

"Yes, he's got himself a lady friend. They love cruising."

The waitress came with our meals. Little was said as we scarfed down our food. The Tuna melt tasted as it always had. Debbie reached over and took one of my fries. She'd ordered a salad instead. I should've been wiser about that too, but once in a while it's ok to treat yourself.

"This steak is perfect. Melts in your mouth," said Irwin.

April just grinned and took a bite out of her sandwich. Like Debby, she'd ordered a side salad too. She looked at me, "May I?"

I nodded and her hand shot out and snagged a fry.

"He's good about sharing," said Debby.

"Yes he is," agreed April.

We parted company around nine. The restaurant was closing. April and Irwin were driving the rental car, a Lincoln coupe, which made sense since she knew her way around. We got into my Silver Corolla XRS and headed home.

"That was very nice," said Debbie.

"I thought it went well," I agreed.

"So anything you care to tell me regarding your first love, Dear?"

I stopped at a red light on 16th and Jackson. I glanced over at her.

"It was obvious you two have history. I don't think you've told me everything."

"Probably not something you want to hear too much about," I said. "Besides, it was a very long time ago."

"Hmm..." Debby turned and looked out the window as I pressed on the accelerator.

July 2012: Friday

I made it back to the synagogue by one. My stomach growled, but I had no time for lunch. The meeting with Jacob Blackman had been difficult. As April had said, they still lived in the dream home they had built almost fifty years ago. The living room furniture was still covered with plastic, only to be taken off for company. The place was spotless.

Susie opened the door. She looked at me curiously then turned and said with a raised voice, "Jeff is here."

April and Irwin were sitting in the livingroom with Jacob. He sat in his bulky comfortable armchair, and me on the edge of the sofa. April was sitting on the arm, her left arm around her dad's shoulders. She looked up and smiled. Irwin was leaning against the sill of the big picture window looking out at the street.

I opened my briefcase and took out a handout that explained traditional mourning practices, as well as some of the traditions about the funeral. I handed copies to April.

"Do you want some coffee or tea?" asked April.

"I'm fine, thanks."

Susie sat down on the other end of the couch. Her face was calm, but hard. I suspected she was not a happy individual at the best of times. She seemed to watch me with dagger eyes.

I walked them through the service. Jacob would sit the full seven days for Shiva though he doubted the girls would stay. "It's the right thing, the traditional thing to do, isn't it?" he asked.

"Yes it is, but there are options. While we honor the deceased, shiva the first week is for intense mourning. Saying Kaddish is more for the Mourner than it is for the deceased. We need time to grieve, though some find the services comforting, others would rather mourn and remember in their own way. Typically people will sit for three days or seven days. The Chevra will bring a seven-day candle of remembrance for you. You should have a stand outside the door with a bowl and pitcher of water so people can wash before they enter when returning from the cemetery."

"We were married a long time," said Jacob. "She was a Montreal girl. I met her at a BBYO convention. She was my princess."

I nodded sympathetically. At times like these, it was best for the Mourner-to-be to lead the discussion.

"I don't know if the girls will want to speak at the funeral," he said.

"They can if they wish." I looked at April and turned to Susie, "There's no hard and fast rules for the eulogy. If it's too difficult, I will do it. Otherwise I'll do a short introduction and then they can speak at that section of the service. So, during Shiva obviously you don't work. It's traditional to stay home. People will come to visit. They'll bring food so you don't have to cook. It's a good time to find comfort in remembering. It's traditional to cover the mirror, though there's no halachich reason for it. In mourning, one shouldn't be concerned with vanity of appearance."

"Are we allowed to bathe? Shower?" asked April.

"Well during Shiva, the Ultra-Orthodox or more traditional Jews probably wouldn't except for hygiene purposes. I don't have a problem, nor do most people today. The fact is that ultimately everyone mourns differently. Do what brings you comfort while you grieve."

"What happens after Shiva?" asked Susie.

"You move into a period time called Sheloshim, which refers to the first thirty days. During Sheloshim you do go back to work and start to slowly go back into the process of living. It's customary for some not to listen to music or go to party or the theatre. Judaism is very logical.

We realize the importance of grieving but life is important and one must return to it. But again, this mourning period is for you. You have to do what works for you."

"What about the headstone?" asked Irwin.

"Not something you have to worry about now. Traditionally we mourn for eleven to twelve months depending whether you're Conservative or Reform. The stone and unveiling is usually done before the first yahrzeit. Halachically speaking though, it can be done any time after Sheloshim."

Jacob nodded. He looked weary and drawn. Mind you, he was probably pushing eighty-five. But the humor in his eyes had died. The feeling of energy surrounding him had diminished. He looked thin and frail, not the robust dark-haired man I had remembered from my youth.

"I'd like to say a few words," said Susie.

"That's fine." I noticed April's look of concern. "Did you want to say something too?"

"Maybe. I'll work it out with Susie," she said.

"That's ok. We can meet briefly Sunday morning if necessary. I think the funeral is scheduled for eleven o'clock."

I glanced at my watch. I had to prepare for Shabbat and services, but I didn't want to rush. "If there's nothing else, then I will see you Sunday." I stood up.

Jacob got up. "I'll see you to the door."

"I can do that Dad," said April. Irwin went to his wife and put his hand on her shoulder.

"No, it's okay. I've been sitting too long anyway."

I followed Jacob to the door. As he opened it, he looked at me. "We always liked you. April always liked you. At one time we thought that maybe you and her…" his voice trailed off.

I nodded. "That was a long time ago. Life took us down different paths."

I put my hand on his shoulder as I stood up. "Do you need anything?"

"My wife," he whispered. "I really need Lois here." He stared at the floor and wept.

The smell of roasted chicken wafted through the house as I walked in the side door that led to a small laundry room. Coming through the other end put me in the kitchen. Debbie was busy making salad.

"Little early for dinner prep?" I asked.

"Figured you'd want to eat early, considering there's a Bar Mitzvah this weekend."

I gave her a hug and a kiss on the cheek.

"How'd the meeting with the Blackmans go?" she asked. Satisfied that everything was under control, we sat down at the kitchen table.

"As expected, Jacob is taking it very hard. The girls don't seem particularly upset, but it might be the shock of it all. Lois went very suddenly. Heart attack I believe. I don't think Susie was particularly close to her mother. April is more pragmatic. Haven't met the little sister yet. She doesn't get here until tomorrow."

We ate an early dinner at 4:30pm. My food would have plenty of time to digest before I had to sing. After dinner we went to change. I hated wearing ties, but given that it was a Bar Mitzvah, I would have to look more formal. Debby put on a lemon colored dress and white heels. She watched me staring at my closet.

"The gray suit with a navy blue shirt. Gold tie."

"Yes, Dear."

At the synagogue, I vocalized for five minutes, and hauled out my Acoustic guitar. The songs for Kabbalat Shabbat always sounded better with accompaniment. I sat at my desk and reviewed my sermon, then sat back and stared out the window. The sun was lower now. I took a deep breath and cleared my mind.

I glanced at my watch. It was a quarter to eight and no sign of the Bar Mitzvah kid or his family. Great. Five minutes passed and no sign of them. I made it a rule to tell the B'nei Mitzvah families to be at shul at least fifteen minutes prior to the service. It gave people a chance to get organized, and for the kid to go to the bathroom before services. I also suggested they limit the amount of water they drink on the bimah. In my last congregation, I had a kid who must've chugged two bottles of water. When the time came to be called up for his Maftir, he grabbed his crotch and ran down the center aisle of the sanctuary yelling, "I gotta go; but I'll be back!"

I put on my tallit and entered the sanctuary. I placed my guitar on the guitar stand next to my lectern and went to schmooze with the congregants for a few minutes. Most of the B'nai Mitzvah family's relatives were seated in the front three rows. It was eight oh-three. Time to start. Hopefully they'd show up.

I went to the Bimah, picked up my guitar and began a rendition of Jeff Klepper's *Ma Tovu*. The congregation quieted down and I could hear voices singing along as people opened their prayer books. Shirley Bernstein's mother Mrs. Kotzmann came up and did the candle lighting. I then welcomed everyone and explained how our prayer books went from right to left-for the non-Jewish guests. We went through the Kabbalat Shabbat singing *Yedid Nefesh*-Hearts delight, Source of Mercy...; Taubman's *Rommamu* at the end of Psalm 99; for the older congregants I did a traditional Lewandowski *L'cha Dodi*-Greeting the Shabbat Bride; and Janowski's rendition of *Tov L'hodot*, the Sabbath Psalm 92. I sprinkled three English readings of Psalms in between. Where the hell were they?

I announced the page for the Hatzi Kaddish, a short prayer of praise that divides minor sections of the service and asked the congregation to rise. Suddenly I noticed a slight commotion in back and looked up to see Allan Bernstein hustling his son down the left side aisle to the saved seats in the front row. He grabbed Stanley's sleeve and brought him to a halt. Shirley Bernstein dabbed her eyes with her handkerchief and stood next to her husband.

I turned and faced the Ark chanting the words of the Borachu, the formal invitation for congregational prayer: "Barchu et Adonai ham-ma-vo-rach" (Praise Adonai the One whom is to be praised). The congregation responded, "Boruch Adonai hamvorach, l'olam va-ed." (Praise Adonai the one who is to be praised forever and ever.) I asked the congregation to be seated and sang Ma'ariv Arvim. A prayer that acknowledged God's creation of the moon and stars.

Stanley, wearing a brown pin-striped suit and black loafers, came up when it was time to do the Shema and V'ahavtah, a prayer that recognizes God as the one God, and reminds us to do all the mitzvot and to pass our traditions down to future generations. Stanley's voice squeaked but he did fine. I let him go and sit with his parents until I called him up for Kiddush, the blessing over wine at the end of the service.

Services ended at nine. The Bernstein's waited until most of the congregation had cleared to the social hall for the Oneg, before approaching me.

"We have to apologize," said Allen. He was a husky guy in his early forties wearing a pinstripe gray suit. His brown hair was starting to thin in front.

"I was getting concerned. I wondered whether something serious had happened."

"Stanley got nervous and locked himself in the bathroom. I hammered on the door. Shirley was beside herself. She pleaded with him. In the end, I got a screwdriver from the garage and popped the lock and hauled him out."

"Let me talk to him for a minute or two. Go in with your guests."

I waited until the Bernsteins had left the sanctuary, then asked Stanley to sit down. The kid was trembling.

I sat next to him. "Nu? You were nervous so you locked yourself in the bathroom?"

"I was really scared. I was afraid I'd make a fool of myself."

"I see. Now tell me, do you know your material?"

"Yes. I even got the Haftorah melody humming in my brain."

"So, you know your stuff. And you should know, that if I didn't think you were ready, I'd postpone your Bar Mitzvah. I mean, you'd have to learn a different parshat and all, but..." I let my voice trail off.

"And I started thinking about all the people here. All the people watching me."

I looked Stanley square in the eyes. "Son, let me tell you the truth. The truth is half the people are dozing off and the other half are glued to their siddurs. On top of that, there's only one thing going through their minds."

"What's that?" asked Stanley jumping to the bait.

"They're thinking, thank God it's not me up there having to do that."

Stanley chuckled.

"Look, I'm not going to let you make a fool of yourself. I'm your safety net. Got that?"

He stared down at his hands for a moment, and then looked up. "I got it."

"Good." I stood up. "Now, let's stop wasting time and go in and nosh at the oneg."

Several congregants greeted me when I entered the social hall. Most of the people I knew were seniors, some remembered my parents; and I tried to remember the names of the younger members who introduced themselves to me.

The social hall had white stucco walls. To my right was a theatrical stage, its curtains drawn. I knew the religious school used it for the Chanukah concerts, and Purim spiel. Four long tables, cafeteria style with chairs filled the center of the room. Along the left wall was a table laden with a fruit tray, pastry tray and two urns, one for hot water and the other for decaf coffee. At the end of the table were several bottles of pop: root beer, Diet Coke, and Orange Crush. Plastic and Styrofoam cups, paper plate, napkins and plastic cutlery were at the end. Not quite as elegant as Beth Zion's Onegs of my youth, but certainly less mess to clean up.

Dr. Katzman, using a cane to support himself, tottered up to me. He wasn't the robust doctor I remembered of my youth; instead, before me was a shrunken man. "You did good boychik. Your father would be proud, and your voice is pretty good too."

"Thanks. Where's Netta?" I asked referring to his wife.

"At home. She was a bit under the weather."

"You didn't drive did you?" I asked.

"I'm ninety-two. I haven't driven in three years. Mr. Horowitz gave me a lift." Dr. Katzman nodded to a tall weed of a man in a brown suit.

"So how's it feel to be back here, permanently?" he asked.

"It feels good. It feels like home."

He squeezed my right arm. "I think I'll go and get a glass of tea."

Mikayla Israelson, a former member of my Dad's choir came up to me. Mikayla was about five years older than me. But you couldn't tell that by her hair color. It was blonde with a streak of red. Mikayla was in the insurance business. But unlike many who dressed conservatively, she tended to go for a very modern look. She took my hand. "Nicely done, but of course I expected no less. You have a different style than your Dad."

"I know, but it is as it should be. I'm not him. There are some pieces of his though that I do."

"We should talk about putting together a holiday choir."

"That'd be nice. Give me a call on Tuesday. I'm taking Mondays off."

"Smart man. Working twenty-four/seven will drive you nuts."

Audrey Shaeffer came up. She'd cut her long dark hair. It was now off her shoulder. She wore a dark blue dress and pumps. Audrey gave me a brief hug and kiss on the cheek. "It's great to have you back. You and Deb have to come to the house for a swim one afternoon."

"How are the girls?"

"Michelle is here. She's working as a life-guard at Lief Ericson pool. She goes back to school in Chicago end of August. Lori got an internship at the Pentagon. And, she has a boyfriend. He's kind of Orthodox though."

"And? Serious?"

"I don't know. She's not saying much."

"Weddings are a good thing."

"I'm glad you're here."

"So am I."

Beth Zion had been without a Rabbi for a time. I trained Lori for her Bat Mitzvah via tapes and phone calls, then came down to officiate. I trained Michelle doing lessons via Yahoo Messenger and co-officiated with the Rabbi at the time.

Audrey turned as Debbie broke through the crowd and came over to me. "Good Shabbos."

We kissed briefly.

"Hi Audrey," said Deb. She turned to me. "Good sermon."

"You're my star critic." I leaned over and whispered in her ear. "I think perhaps a Shabbos mitzvah is in order."

"I do believe it is," she replied and winked at me. Hot damn, I was going to get lucky tonight.

The ladies hugged briefly. Audrey said," Welcome to River City. Guess this is quite a change for you. I told Jeff, you'll have to come over for a swim. We can kibbitz then.

Deb took my arm. "I'd love that, but I doubt this weekend. This is a busy weekend. Are the Bernstein's having a party Saturday night?"

"Yes, at the Marina Inn across the river on the South side. I have the invitation in my office. We'll have to go," I said.

"I got invited too," said Audrey.

"That's great, at least there'll be one person there I know. And, of course I'll meet more people whose names I won't remember." She grinned. "And then we have the funeral. What time is it on Sunday?"

"Two o'clock at the cemetery."

"Good, then after services Sunday morning, you're taking me to breakfast."

"Any place in particular?"

"I'll let you know what I feel like having Sunday morning. And now it's time for some dessert."

"The chocolate covered strawberries are to die for," said Audrey.

She winked at me and sauntered off following Audrey towards the desserts.

July 2012: Saturday Morning

It was a beautiful summer morning. The sky was deep blue and the green of the trees lining Court Street contrasted like a painter's canvas. The street was quiet as I drove to shul. Deb would join me a bit later. Audrey had offered to pick her up. For me, I loved the early morning. It gave me time to clear my mind, center myself spiritually, and prepare for what I had to do.

I got a cup of coffee from the kitchen. Our maintenance guy Bob always made a pot when he opened up. I took the cup back to my office. A lot of voice teachers tell you that you need to watch how much coffee or caffeinated drinks you have, as it tends to dry out the vocal cords. For me, it tended to help dry out my sinuses and get rid of extra phlegm. I did a few vocal exercises, then grabbed my sermon and music and went to the sanctuary and got my lectern arranged. Afterwards I went to the bathroom. Always go before a service; because once it starts, you got no place to go.

A few of the older members, Mr. Katzman among them came in. I didn't expect the majority of the congregation to come until around ten o'clock. Mr. Katzman came over. We hugged. He was like an adopted uncle to me. Before Grammy had moved to River City, Morrie and I had stayed there weekends when my parents were taking the USY kids to convention or weekend conclaves.

"So where are David and Naomi now?" I asked.

"David and his wife are still in Phoenix, both teaching at university. Naomi's in San Francisco doing her painting and lecturing and teaching."

"She was here visiting you several years ago when I did Lori Shaeffer's Bat Mitzvah."

245 • The Cantor's Son

"Yep, and now my grandson is in university. At Berkeley."

"What's he taking?"

"Who knows? Something with computers," said Dr. Katzman.

Mr. Smith came over. "Nu, so are you going to shmooze all day or are we gonna have a service?"

I looked around. I had nine crotchety alter kackers (Yiddish for old farts) in the pews. I noticed the last two rows in the sanctuary were crammed with non-Jewish friends who'd been invited. Non-Jews always come on time. It's too bad we couldn't take a lesson from them.

"I thought I'd give the Bar Mitzvah family a few minutes." I checked my watch. It was nine twenty-five. Where the hell were they? I could feel my stomach churning. "Let's give them five minutes, then I'll start."

"Okay, but we better be through before noon. I got a twelve-thirty T-time.," said Abe Feigenbaum.

At nine-thirty I started chanting Ma-Tovu to a Danny Maseng melody. Still no sign of the family. Fifteen minutes later I finished the preliminary service and in marched the Bernsteins. I nodded to Stanley who slipped up and sat in the chair behind me. Mr. Bernstein and his wife sat in the front row. Mr. Bernstein looked thoroughly pissed. His wife ignored him. A couple of minutes later the grandparents came in and sat quietly in the second row. By the time I hit the Amidah, a section of silent prayer, and asked the people to rise, the rest of the family got there. The pews were filling up.

Stanley led the opening paragraphs of the prayer section. I tried valiantly to sort of keep him on tune, or at least the rest of the congregation.

When we were about to start Torah service, I called up Stanley's parents, who with forced smiles presented him with his Tallit. I then began leading the congregation in "Ki Mitziyon…"

Shirley's parents opened the ark and I stepped in and took a Torah. I gave it to Stanley's dad. The ark was closed. We turned and I began singing "Shema Yisrael Adonai Eloheinu, Adonai Echad (Hear Israel, Adonai is our God, Adonai is One)."

We did a hakafat, taking the Torah into the pews and around the congregation then returning to the bimah. Stanley's dad put the Torah on the larger lectern we used for reading and helped undress it. I announced the page the reading would begin on. We used a triennial system so, I was reading from the middle of the portion. Mr. Feigenbaum and Mr. Lansky acted as gabbais. Mr. Feigenbaum called up the first person for an aliyah. It was one of Stanley's uncles, a medium well-dressed man with graying hair. I showed him where to touch the Torah with his tzitzit and kiss it. He chanted the first part of the Torah blessing. I focused on the text and began to chant.

People came and went. We stopped after the fourth aliyah so I could do a Mi Sheberach prayer for those who were ill. Finally it was Stanley's turn. Mr. Feigenbaum's voice boomed," Ya-mod Tvi ben Shlomo ha Bar Mitzvah Maftir. Hazak!"

Stanley came up, his tallit draped over his shoulder's like Batman's cape. He began reciting the Torah blessing. "Barchu et Adonai hamvorach..." (Blessed are you Adonai, the one who is to be blessed)

Stanley finished the blessing and I showed him where his portion was. There was a look of terror on his face. "Just focus on the text. It will come. You know it." Stanley took a deep breath and began. In the end, he chanted it perfectly.

Mr. Feigenbaum called up Shirley Bernstein's brother as Hagbah, the person honored with lifting the Torah. Tradition was that you showed part of the section that was read to the congregation. I'd been taught to show at least three columns of text.

"Use the edge of the table for leverage and bend from the knees when you lift," I said.

Uncle Dan nodded. He did as I had instructed but his wrists were wobbly. Mr. Feigenbaum leaped to the rescue and righted the Torah and assisted Uncle Dan to the chair where his daughter Shaina who'd been called up as Goleilah, the one who dresses the Torah, put the belt on the scrolls and draped the mantle cover over it.

"Get comfortable," I told him. "You'll sit here through Stanley's haftorah."

Stanley was at the Torah lectern, his haftorah book open before him. I leaned over and whispered," Just concentrate on the text. You know this."

"Baruch atah adonai eloheinu melech ha-olam..." he began chanting the Blessing before the Haftorah.

I sat down in my chair to the left of the ark. I opened the Chumash and followed along. He chanted for twelve minutes then concluded with the Blessings After. He seemed to rush so I hissed at him to slow down.

When he finished, he took out his speech and began talking. Overall my predecessor had done a good job. Often parents or even Rabbis want to write the speech for the candidate. But it's important for the kids to write their own speech. I tend to guide them through it with a series of questions that helps them research the portion, as well as, find suitable Talmudic references or Midrashim. I do a final edit; but in the end it's the kid's words, not mine.

Stanley's speech was three minutes. When he finished I congratulated him and addressed him and the congregation.

"Stanley, your teachings about the Shema and V'ahavatah were excellent. I often refer to the Shema as the Jewish pledge of allegiance. Hopefully you will allow that prayer to guide you in remembering and doing the mitzvoth. It's a major undertaking to become a Jewish adult. The Shema and V'ahavatah have become the watchwords of the Jewish faith. It's one of the cornerstones of our liturgy. When we proclaim the Shema, we acknowledge God's sovereignty not only over us, but over the entire universe. According to our sages, when we say "V'ahavatha et Adonai Elochecha b'kol l'va-ve-chat.--And you shall love the Lord your God with all your heart." It refers to both our good and evil inclinations. "Ooh v'kol naf she cha,--with all your soul" means that you should be willing to sacrifice your life, and "ooh v'kol muh-oh-deh-cha,--with all your might" refers to our material wealth. Our rabbis believed that if wealth is at stake when we continue to observe our faith, then we are willing to sacrifice our material belongings to preserve our spiritual life. We are further commanded, as you noted, to pass on God's teachings and traditions to you, our future generation. Today you become a Bar Mitzvah, a son of the commandments and by doing so accept all the religious obligations that entails. I hope this won't be the last time we see you at services, or participating in services. Remember your heritage. Be proud of it. And remember we do mitzvoth, not because of any reward or punishment; but because it's the right thing to do. And by doing so, you become a better human being. Now I ask your parents to rise as we recite the Sheyheyanu, the prayer we say on reaching a once in a lifetime moment. Following that I will invoke the three-fold priestly benediction that dates back to Temple times."

We put the Torah back and chanted the concluding prayers, and asked people to wait until we'd recited Kiddush and Ha-motzi before the feeding frenzy began. I had Stanley and his parents leave first so that they could greet their guests and congregants as people entered the social hall for the Kiddush lunch. The service ended and the congregation rushed out like a herd of buffalo heading for the watering hole.

I took off my tallit. Deb came up and kissed me as she wished me a Good Shabbos. "Nice service."

I smiled. "You're a bit biased."

"True."

Audrey Shaeffer came up and wished me Shabbat Shalom. Dr. Katzman had hung back as well.

"You better get in there Jeff. I think the people are a might eager to chow down."

I laughed.

Shabbat afternoon we sat in the August heat in the shade of our screened porch. I looked out at the hills peppered with homes and remembered a time when it was all farmland and forest. Nothing stays the same. Progress is everywhere, even here in River City. I looked at Deb wearing a pair of ivory shorts and a yellow top. She had her Kindle on her lap reading some, as I called them, hysterical romance novel.

I had an old Saint mystery novel by Leslie Charteris on my lap. I enjoyed re-reading them. But I had a hard time concentrating. It was like a dream to be back here. I thought about seeing April again at her mom's funeral that I'd officiate at tomorrow. After that she'd be out of my life again. Our lives are on threads, on paths that changed and interweaved depending on the decisions we made. What would it have been like if we had married? If it had been possible to look at the other times we met after I moved away to reconnect in a more permanent way? If we had kept communicating, sharing and loving; what would our lives had been like? I remembered the hot passion we'd had when we'd gotten together after I graduated high school, and then a couple of years later after I'd been doing gigs on the road, and was finishing my undergraduate degree, and had started to really grow up. We'd both changed by then. We weren't the hormonal crazy teenagers that we had been. April was very career orientated and while spiritually aware, was not as observant as me.

I never regreted marrying Debbie. I loved her dearly. She was great. She'd been right for me. I was a lucky man and I knew it. We'd raised two great kids and had lots of life adventures. But sometimes I couldn't help wondering what life would have been like if I hadn't taken the path that I had, not that I had too many regrets. I'd been incredibly fortunate, despite some of the crazy congregations I'd worked for, or the roller coaster relationship I'd had with my brother, or grieving over family and friends who had passed away. If anything I learned to be thankful for the blessings in my life. I'd learned that life was short and that you couldn't hold grudges, because that hatred ate you up inside and it was never too late to say you're sorry, or to change. We had to value the people in our lives, though some entered for only a short time. We were all connected. Judaism believes that if we have the will, if we truly change who we are, it's never too late to repent, to change our lives to be more meaningful. I wasn't the wild guy who had been the entertainer, nor as full of confidence and certainty in things that I had been when I had been young and stupid. I had changed. But still, now in the middle years I realized that I still had that Lone Ranger mentality of riding in, doing what I could to help and riding off into the sunset until I was needed again. And that was rewarding. Who says you can't learn something from comics?

July 2012: Saturday Night

I grudgingly put on my navy blue suit and zipped up Deb's black cocktail dress. I really didn't feel like going to the Bar Mitzvah party. I'd been happy just reading and daydreaming the rest of Shabbat away. But duty called. It was important for the Rabbi to be seen at functions.

The party was at the Marina Inn and Convention Center in South River City on the Nebraska side. The building, a modern mixture of concrete and glass, was spread over rich green grounds along the river. We went over the bridge, entered the State of Nebraska and I turned left on East 4th.

"One of the last times I was over here was in 1970," I told Deb. "Jerry and I took Tim to a porno film."

"You did what?" She turned and looked at me.

"Well, Tim Shaunessy had never seen an X-rated movie and we felt it our duty to educate him," I replied.

"You did, did you? And you were such experts?"

"Well, not really. We'd been to a burlesque show at the Oklahoma State Fair, and we'd seen "I Am Curious Yellow" when it came out."

"They actually allowed that to be shown in Oklahoma City?"

"Yeah, I know. I thought the Baptists would be out there picketing or burning the theater down. Anyway you had to be twenty-one to see it; but they didn't even bother checking Jerry's or my driver's license."

"And how was it?"

"Boring. I mean it was very controversial because it had frontal nudity; but Swedish drama is boring. I was half-asleep by the time the good parts came on."

Debbie shook her head and laughed. "So what happened with Tim?"

"Well the Southside had looser film restrictions, so they had this X-rated movie house. We took Tim. I remember there were two films. The first was in color and had this lady doing stuff with fruit and vegetables that had never occurred to me. The second movie was in black and white and horribly shot. You could see the shadow of the boom mic and the cameraman. It was the usual father seducing the babysitter storyline."

"Uh huh. And how did Tim enjoy it?"

"We had to pry his clenched fingers from the chair and carried him out. He was in porn overload."

"You certainly had some experiences," said Deb. She shook her head. "Men will be boys, or maybe in that case, boys will pretend to be men."

"You forget my dear, that men have a Peter Pan complex. We never grow up. Besides, you love my youthful exuberance."

Deb rolled her eyes and shook her head. We both laughed.

I pulled into the parking lot. We got out. I locked the car and arm in arm we walked towards the building.

I could hear the pulsating beat of rock music as we entered the center and were directed to a main ballroom. We entered and were greeted by the Bernstein's. Balloons hung from the ceiling. I heard squawking and turned to see that all the tables had a cage with a budgie in it. What the hell kind of centerpiece was this? It sort of marred the elegantly laid tables.

Debbie picked up our place card and it turned out we were sitting with my coffee crony Abe Bernstein and his wife. We were at one of the alter kacker tables, but then given our age and generation, I shouldn't have been surprised.

The DJ played the typical Jewish Bar Mitzvah CD with Hava Nagilah, Mayim and a few other Jewish party favorites. We danced the Hora. Stanley was raised up on a chair and paraded around. I looked up. Stanley seemed three sheets to the wind, and I hoped, I prayed, he wouldn't puke on his guests.

Dinner selection was fish or chicken. The Bernstein's had been good about avoiding shellfish, pork, and mixing dairy and meat. Naturally Deb and I had fish. It was broiled trout on a rice pilaf with mixed vegetables. Most of the people had the chicken that was marinated in teriyaki sauce.

During dessert, apple strudel with fake whipped cream and some berries, the Bernsteins got up and thanked all their friends for helping out and their relatives for schlepping here from points east and west. And then, out came Stanley, rolled out on a small stage sitting in the middle of a drum set. He then began banging away. Apparently Stanley envisioned himself as another Ringo Starr. Who knew?

July 2012: Sunday

After morning minyan I drove back home. Entering the house I walked through the living room and into the hall. I could hear water running. Deb was in the shower. I went downstairs to my study and gathered my notes and Rabbi's manual and packed them in a small leather bag. I carried it back upstairs and put it on the kitchen table. I went outside and sat in chaise lounge on the back porch. I stared out at the deep green grass carpet and the rolling hills dotted with homes. Inside each of those houses breakfasts were being prepared, perhaps couples were making love, or some people were getting ready for Church. Each unit was a living breathing organism wrapped up in its own universe, aware but not aware of the one next to it. I remembered thinking these same thoughts one year in my late teens when I was working in a warehouse. There I had looked out from the second story window at all the homes and thought about all the lives, all the people going about their business. Lives touching, interacting totally caught up with their own problems and situations. Each individual experiences life on individual terms. There was a whole world of people, an entire planet and yet nothing more than a microcosm in the universe. It was then I realized how truly insignificant we were in relationship to all the universes in space. How many other planets were there out there with people going on with the task of living in a variety of circumstances? Yet there was an order to the universe. To the way the planets moved, to the life that existed. It was then I beheld the true power of God.

Sometimes I wondered if, when you died, if you didn't go back and relive your life and have the chance to make different decisions. Sometimes I visualized that life was a spider web of possibilities and you had numerous strands to travel that would allow for different outcomes. The Hasidim believe in reincarnation. An individual is born with a lesson to learn or a task to perform and his soul will keep returning as the individual lives to complete that task or learn that particular lesson. As I got older I recognized my own mortality. I'd seen too much of death and grieving. Truly, life was a gift. I didn't want to die. But that fate would be inevitable at some point. And in the end, material things really don't matter, though they certainly make life more enjoyable. But the important thing a person could do was to make the world a little bit better. The kind word, the helpful hand, giving to charity, each small positive thing a person did, makes the world a bit better. And that's what I tried to do.

"I thought I'd find you down in the Batcave," said Deb.

My basement office is a conglomeration of shelves housing Rabbinic reference books, volumes of Judaica, Talmud and Rashi. Several shelves crammed with volumes of music and books on nusach and trope. I also had a filing cabinet loaded with sheet music. There was a variety of old and new prayer books from all the major movements. One bookcase was heavily laden with hardcover collections of comic books and graphic novels. My desk is a double pedestal monster with a hutch, cabinets and a bookshelf.

"It's more inspiring outside. I turned my head. I caught my breath as I always did when I first saw her. "Just churning some thoughts."

"Well my stomach's churning for breakfast, so get up mister. You owe this lady a meal."

"Where do you want to go?" I asked.

"How about one of those trendy places down by the Stockyards."

"Not Green Gables?"

"No, not, Green Gables."

I got up from the lounge. "I am at your command."

We drove down Jackson Street and turned left onto 11th and continued until I hit Lewis Blvd. I turned right and continued until I saw Northern Auto Parts and made a left following a gravel road to the cemetery gate. There was not a lot of parking. I parked on the side of the road. Deb and I walked through the gates.

Mickey Rosenbaum called to me, "Over here, Rabbi."

Mickey was one of the Vice-Presidents of the Mount Sinai Cemetery Association. It had been started in 1884 on land donated by Godfrey Haftenback one of the first Jews in River City. Though the Chevra Kadisha society didn't have its own chapel or preparation facilities, it did rent space from the Meyer Funeral Chapel. The members of the society were volunteers who prepared the bodies and dug the graves. There was a men's and a women's group. In Judaism we don't believe in embalming, or dressing the deceased up in his or her finest clothes, or having their faces made up and hair done; Nor is the deceased buried in a big fancy coffin. Burial is swift, usually done within twenty-four hours. The body is washed and dressed in a Tachrichim, a white shroud. Men are typically buried with their tallit. The coffin is a plain pine box held together with wooden pegs and having rope handles. Everything must disintegrate back to the earth.

"You're out here early," said Mickey. He was around my age and height, with a round face, glasses and wispy salt and pepper hair. He wore black Dockers, a leather vest and a gray and white striped shirt.

"I don't believe the family should have to wait for me. Besides, I like to know where I'm going," I replied.

"This is really hard on Jake. He worshiped that woman."

"I know."

"Well, I know you'll do a good job. You know the families in this community. You have a history here."

"I've been away a long time," I replied.

"Yeah, but you're home now." He clapped me on the shoulder and went back out to the road to direct incoming traffic for the funeral. The Blackmans would be arriving in a rented limo furnished by the Funeral Chapel.

I checked my watch. People would probably be arriving soon. I took Deb's hand and we walked around the cemetery.

I'd lost family and my own dear friends in the intervening years. Life wasn't always for laughing. I thought about the people who I had known here and were no more. In fact, it was one of the reasons I was back here, in River City. Out of my friends here: Larry had died ten years ago from Scleroderma, an autoimmune disorder. Unfortunately I hadn't been able to make the funeral; but I'd officiated at his unveiling and his youngest daughter, Michelle's Bat Mitzvah. Mark had passed away in New York last year from a heart attack. He'd pre-deceased his parents, something that shouldn't happen. Mark left a wife and three daughters. The 'three musketeers' were no more. The fourth musketeer Mainard was alive, married and living in California. We occasionally kept in touch. Some of the others from that River City group I'd found on Facebook and made contact. I was curious to see how their lives had turned out. It was a long time ago since we were young. Life experience changes us. What we were, is not who we were now. I'd had my share of lumps and bumps too, been through my crucible of fire. I had regrets. I just didn't want any more now.

My mind too thought about the circle of life. Already here for a short time, I'd officiated at a Bar Mitzvah, I had a B'rit Milah, both lifecycle events for the young, and now officiating at a funeral. A life passes, another comes into being.

They'd set up an awning and some chairs by the gravesite. There was also a small portable podium and table for me to use. I knelt down and opened my briefcase and got my Rabbi's manual and music laid out. Debbie stood by and watched me.

People started arriving about twenty-five minutes before the ceremony. A lot of older members of the community were there as well as some of Mr. Blackmans employees. The limo came about fifteen minutes before the service was about to begin. Behind the limo was the hearse. The Chevra volunteers organized the assigned pallbearers and we walked the coffin to the gravesite, stopping seven times to symbolize that we are not in a rush to bury the deceased. We stopped.

The family went to the chairs underneath the awning and we did K'riah. In ancient times when one was in mourning, one would rent one's clothes and pour ashes on themselves. Today we skip the ashes, but we do tear something to show our grief. The orthodox men or women will wear old ties or suits or dresses, and make a small tear on the lapel. Now many use small black ribbons that are transferable to whatever one is wearing during the shiva.

Jessica, Susie and April supported their father as I put the ribbons on them and made a small cut that would help them make a larger tear. And then I had them repeat the traditional words acknowledging that God is supreme in matters of life and death: *"Baruch atah Adonai, Eloheinu Meleck Ha-Olam Dayan HaEmet. (Praised are you Sovereign God of the Universe, righteous judge). Adonai Na-tan, V'Adonai lachach, Y'hi shem Adonai M'-vorach."* (Adonai has given. Adonai has taken away. Praised be the name of Adonai.)

After K'riah I had the family sit down. I began with a reading from Proverbs: "A woman of valor, who can find? She is more precious than fine pearls". I sang two Psalms in Hebrew: The 23 Psalm (The Lord is my Shepard) and Esai Eni (Psalm 121-I lift up my eyes to the mountains). And then I added in a reading from Kohelet about how our eyes never have its fill of seeing. After that it was time for the eulogy.

I looked out and saw a couple of familiar faces: Julie Fine nee' Kalinsky and her high school sweetheart Aaron. They lived down in Omaha. Kevin Shamansky, a classmate of Susie's, and a close friend of Morrie's. Dr. Katzman was there. I know Mom regretted not being able to come in for this; but we'd just moved and it was just hectic enough as it was. I looked down at my notes and began:

"We die in the midst of living. No one really brings to completion all the goals towards which they strive. For when we reach one goal, there's always another we want. Life's satisfaction derives from struggle, adventure and purpose rather than one final moment of realization. And for most of us, life is something we don't want to give up, even when we acknowledge our own mortality. Today we come together to mourn the passing of Lois Blackman and share memories with each other. In the Torah there's a constant theme of reconciliation. We see it with Jacob and Esau. We see it with Joseph and his brothers. We see it with Moses, Aaron, and Miriam. Family relationships are always difficult at times. But life is too short and we should value the people whose lives we share, despite differences. Our years go too swiftly it seems. Lois Blackman lived a long good life. We must be thankful that though she was diagnosed with a terminal illness, her suffering was not long. We must remember that she lived a full life. She was a good wife, and she raised three daughters, whom she loved dearly. She always wanted the best for them. I now call upon April Blackman to share with us some of Lois' life."

I stepped aside and April came forward. She wore a black pants suit and a gray blouse. Her heels sunk a bit into the ground as she walked over the grass to the podium. In her right hand she clutched her notes.

April nodded to me and looked out at the surrounding crowd. "My mother was born in Toronto…"

Lois Blackman had wanted the best for her daughters. She'd wanted them to be classy women. She wanted them to be perfect ladies. She wanted them to be like her, the dutiful housewife. But times were changing. When the girls hit their teens there had been stormy times, and the era of the sixties didn't help as the counter-revolution changed values and lifestyles.

I remember the look Lois had given me back in 1970 when I showed up with Jerry to pick April up for the concert. She grimaced looking at me with my long hair, and hippy clothes. I was no longer 'the Cantor's son', that nice good clean-cut kid. But April grabbed my hand and led me out to Jerry's car.

The girls had been estranged from their mother for some time. And Lois had been disappointed that until Jessica got married, there'd been no grandchildren. As far as I knew Susie wasn't in any kind of serious relationship. April had married later and had no desire to be a parent.

Jake, despite working long hours, was a great dad. He understood that kids went through a rebellious period and that you needed to cut them some slack. He wasn't judgmental like Lois. But they did love each other dearly, and they loved their kids and tried to raise them the best way they knew how. They did a good job.

April finished speaking and I called Susie up. Susie had a grim expression on her face. She talked briefly with reminiscences of better times when she was young. Between April and Susie people got a good sense of who Lois was, though many there had known the Blackmans and had been to their home for various social events. Lois had been quite active in Women's League and Sisterhood. She and her select friends hung out at the country club and played Mah-Jongg on Sunday afternoons.

I chanted the El Mole, a prayer asking God to receive the soul of the deceased.

The body was lowered into the grave and people lined up to cover the coffin with dirt. The tradition was to use the backside of the shovel and put three small shovelfuls in, then reverse the shovel and use it regularly. When done, you put the shovel down and let the next person pick it up. The idea of the reverse shovelfuls is to show respect for the deceased and symbolize that we're not in a rush to say good-bye. April helped her dad with the shovel, then she and her sisters each did it. Irwin followed and then friends and congregants joined in. There were several shovels available.

Ten minutes later I did a reading and chanted the El Mole again. The service was concluded with Kaddish Yatom, a prayer that has nothing to do with death, but praises God. Afterwards I had the congregation form two lines and repeat after me the traditional words of comfort as the family walked between them.

"Ha-makom y'nechem etchem b'tok sha-ar ah-vel Ziyon v'yerushalayim." (May God Comfort you with all the Mourners of Zion and Jerusalem.)

As I followed the family several people shook my hand and wished me a Yashar Koach (sort of like congrats on doing a good job).

The family was sitting Shiva at the Blackman home. Deb and I followed the procession.

"You did a nice service," whispered Deb. "I was proud of you."

"You've seen me do funerals before, including for you."

"I know." She looked out the window at the passing trees. "But this is special for you. Part of it is because of April and her family, and part of it is because of this congregation and this place."

She turned and looked at me, then reached over and squeezed my hand. My wife could be very insightful and astute.

There were several cars in the driveway when we pulled up. I took the 'shiva kit' a small suitcase containing special prayer books and some kippot. We would do a short afternoon service so the family could say Kaddish again before having the Seudah Chavurah, the Meal of Consolation. Outside there was a small bowl of water and a roll of paper towels to wash hands with. We did so and entered. The spread was set up in the dining room: tuna salad, egg salad, cut vegetables, fruit trays, bagels, cream cheese, and some hard cheeses. Typically hard-boiled eggs, symbolizing the life cycle, are the first food the mourner's eat. The seven-day yahrzeit candle had already been lit and sat as a centerpiece on the table.

I unpacked the shiva kit and we did a short Mincha (Afternoon) service. At end of the service I did another El Mole prayer and led the Blackmans in Kaddish. I read slowly, not sure of their various Hebrew or Transliteration skills. Afterwards people came forward and offered them condolences.

As people filtered into the dining room to fill their plates and schmooze, April came up to me and gave me a hug and kiss on the cheek. "Thank you, Jeff. That was a beautiful service." She took a step back and looked at me. "You've changed. You've got a feeling of compassion and humility. You were quite brash the last time we saw each other."

"Life experience, it changes you. I've lost too many people I've cared about. Gotten some upandcommance too. At one time I use to think age produced automatic wisdom.

But that wasn't true. I had a boss once who said, 'You can learn something from anyone, even the bum on the street.' He was right."

"Well, we appreciate what you've done. I know you'll keep an eye on dad too once we leave."

"Yes, I will."

I went to get a cup of tea and Susie stopped me. "That was a nice service. Thank you. You know, I was really angry with you for a long time. You really hurt April. But you're not the ass you were."

"Thank you. And how are you doing?"

"Ok. Mom and I had a lot of issues, but what you said made me sorry we didn't say good-bye on better terms. Now I don't have the chance."

"Yes, but you can try and not make the same mistakes with others."

"How's Morrie? What's he up to?"

"Big time lawyer out in Los Angeles. He's got two kids. His son Sam is at law school at UCLA, and his daughter, Miriam is studying art history at Berkley."

"When I was little, I was sure I was going to marry him." She smiled wistfully, then laughed. "Kids live in a different world, don't they?"

Deb came over. She had a plate of vegetables and Tzazziki. "You going to get something?"

"I have tea."

"Uh huh. I meant maybe something to eat. It's been awhile since breakfast."

"Not really hungry right now, maybe later."

"Well, everyone thought it was a nice service. It's very interesting talking to people here. I'm getting quite a different perspective of you. You were a bit of a scoundrel and hell-raiser from some of the stories I've heard."

"You've been talking to Audrey again?"

"The Katzmans and the Fines have some interesting stories too," said Deb.

"Gossip is evil."

"Uh huh." She kissed me on the cheek. "I'm going to mingle a bit more. Who knows what else I'll dig up."

"You know Dad always said there were three sides to every story."

"And one of these days I'll hear yours." Deb grinned, gave a swing of hips and wandered off.

Jessica came over. She was shorter than her sisters' with dark black hair and warm brown eyes. "Rabbi Reimer?"

"Yes?"

"I just wanted to thank you for a beautiful service. Mom would've liked it." She looked around.

"I hear you just got back from Israel."

"Yes, my husband Alex and I are doing some volunteer work there. We're working with new immigrants. We're both Registered Nurses."

"I'm sure it's appreciated. The country has a lot of needs."

"You've been there?"

"Yes, I did my first year of Cantorial studies there and was there as part of a USY tour. I have some of my late father's family there, as well as some colleagues and friends. We've been there three or four times over the years. Our kids went on March of the Living."

"We're thinking about making aliyah, but with mom gone," Jessica hesitated a moment then continued, "well, we'd like to be here for Dad. It's going to take him a long time to adjust."

"Yes, it's quite the change."

"Well, I just wanted to say thank you."

We shook hands.

I finished my tea and worked the crowd as it goes, talking to various friends and family members. Julie Kalinsky and her parents came up to me.

"Well done Jeff. You have a very soft and spiritual tone. I found the service comforting," said Sharona Fine, Julie's mother. The Fines had been close friends of the Blackmans for years.

I looked at Izzy Fine. He had to be in his early 80's, but other than a bit of gray on the temples he looked ten to fifteen years younger. Izzy owned a couple of small convenience stores. He still put in a full week of work. He clasped my hand in a vice-like grip and in his gravelly voice said, "Good job. I'm glad the board hired you. You belong here. So, your Mom going to come up and visit sometime?"

I laughed. "Actually she'll be here for the High Holidays."

"Well tell her to save some time to spend with us."

"I will."

Deb came up to me. "Ready to leave?"

"Just about. So, you hear more lies about me and my wayward youth?" I asked.

"Were your ears burning?" She teased.

"You don't see the lobes are charred? Just want to say good-bye to April and Jake, then we'll go."

"Ok."

I wandered and weaved my way back into the kitchen, the last place I'd seen April. Irwin was there, pouring himself a glass of fifteen-year-old Glenlivet.

"Care for a drink?" he asked.

"Actually I'm going to leave. Just wanted to say good-bye to April and Jacob."

"They're in the main bedroom. Upstairs and first door on your left."

I turned to go. Irwin spoke. "Just wanted to say thank you. It was a nice service. I wish I'd had someone like you when my grandmother passes away."

"Thank you."

He took a sip of his drink and took a step towards me. "Look, I know you and April have some sort of history."

"It was a long time ago. We were kids."

"I know, but I still think down deep she still has feelings for you. Just wanted you to know. We are good together. I do love her."

"I know you do. Thank you. Next time you're in town, we'll have you over for a BBQ. I do some mean beef ribs."

"Now you're talking. And maybe I can introduce you to golf properly."

We laughed and shook hands. I went upstairs to find April and her dad.

I found them sitting on the bed looking at a family album. I tapped lightly on the door. They looked up.

"Just wanted to say good-bye. Deb and I are going. Jacob, if you need anything, I'm here for you. I'll be here to do the evening Shiva services this week. I'm leaving the kit downstairs in the living room."

"Thanks." He rose and came over and shook my hand. "Thanks for everything."

April came over and gave me a hug and we kissed briefly. "Welcome home, Jeff."

The End

About the Author:

David M. Mannes is a Cantor-Educator and member of the American Conference of Cantors. He has served several congregations in United States and Canada. He is also a former educational writer and film producer-director. His documentary, "Writing-on-Stone" was nominated in 1990 for best non-dramatic script by the Alberta Motion Picture Industry Association (A.M.P.I.A.) awards. Solstice Publishing published his latest novels *The Reptilian Encounter* and *Scarlet Justice* in 2015. He is also the author of: *Nahanni* , and *Creature Feature* among others. David's novella *A Walk on the Strange Side* and a short story, *Deadman on the Highway* are available on Kindle.

Social Media Sites:

Website: http://davidmannes.wix.com/david-mannes
Twitter: https://twitter.com/saint2000ca @saint2000ca
Facebook: https://www.facebook.com/David-M-Mannes-237951143013679/?fref=ts

If you like this novel by David M. Mannes, check out his other Solstice Publishing books!

Scarlet Justice

The Canadian—United States border is a dangerous place. Join Royal Northwest Mounted Police constable Alfred Kingsley and his alcoholic, gunslinging American scout Charlie Buck as they patrol along the Canadian-Montana border in the mid-1880s. Kingsley deals with a railroad rebellion in the Kootenai's, an Indian land swindle, and a band of murdering whiskey smugglers. Hold on to your hats, this is an action packed rough ride.

http://bookgoodies.com/a/B01849WQ82

The Reptilian Encounter

This fast, paced action-packed, harrowing adventure-sci-fi novel features Daiman Wynter, an agent for the clandestine black agency known as Majic-12. When a restricted site is breeched and a 4,000 year old flying saucer goes missing, it's up to Wynter, Michelle Martin and their extraction team to retrieve it. Crossing into a parallel earth where Reptilians evolved into a humanoid species, the team finds danger and death at every turn.

http://bookgoodies.com/a/B011VFG3BM

58423929R00149

Made in the USA
Lexington, KY
13 December 2016